Bliss It Was

Steve Cottrell

To Gaye and Matt, for their invaluable support and encouragement.

ISBN 978-1-7385829-0-7 Paperback
ISBN 978-1-7385829-1-4 e-book
ISBN 978-1-7385829-2-1 Audio Book

BSP *Publishing*
New Zealand

ONE

They parked at the gates of the property, at the end of the long metal drive down from the road. It sure was isolated. There was a sign over the entrance *BEATITUDINE,* whatever that meant. It was still a two or three-minute walk to the house. When they were twenty or thirty metres away, Shane was surprised that their feet crunching on the white pebble driveway had not alerted Bello. Stupid name for a dog he'd always thought. Perhaps he wasn't on the property, which would be good, although with the woman and the old man gone maybe he could pinch the dog for himself? He was momentarily excited, who'd look after him otherwise? Then the old pattern. Nah. Wouldn't work, dead giveaway, and besides there was a son who'd probably want him. He vaguely recalled the name, Carlos was it? Anyway, no sign of the dog yet, great old boy that he was.

They were all puffing after the meth and the slight uphill walk, and very much focussed on the work ahead. Had they been even slightly interested they might have been impressed with the manicured lawns, palm trees and pōhutukawa fringing the golden beach which looked across the sparkling sea to Rotoroa and the Coromandel. And exactly as Shane had told Bob, at the right-hand end of the beach, tucked under the promontory sheltering it was the jetty, with a beautiful traditional fifty-foot ketch moored alongside, its gleaming white hull and immaculate, varnished brightwork glinting in the early afternoon sun. To the left, just before and parallel to the main building, was a long row of what looked like garages, partly set into the low hill rising up alongside and behind the house. The car collection.

They had no time for all that though and were now at the front of the house. Not that there was a front door. There was an enclosed section at each end, but half of the wide frontage was one long, deep verandah the family called the loggia. In front of it was an infinity pool overlooking the beach. At intervals, there were sections of wall a couple of metres wide which were both structural, supporting the roof, but which also housed the glass doors which slid out to close the place up in bad onshore weather, or if the family were away.

Oh yes, there was money here.

* * * *

'Bliss it was in that dawn to be alive. But to be young was very heaven'

Jim had always loved that quote. True, it was a good bit past dawn, and he was a long way from being young, but it was a stunning morning and there was no doubt that he was feeling a certain... lightness of being today. He was here on his own this week, to do some odd jobs around their holiday house at Palm Beach on Waiheke Island, while his wife Sue was working in the city and staying in the apartment. He was enjoying the solitude, as he increasingly did as he got older.

On days like this he would sometimes pause whatever he was doing and reflect on his sixty-five years. It had been pretty good by and large. He loved his work, although semi-retired now, his wonderful wife of three decades, and his brilliant son, Tom. And really without trying he and Sue had done ok financially too. Both had had good careers and earned well, and with various moves over the years had benefitted hugely from endlessly increasing property prices. Nonetheless, and trying not to feel smug, he felt he hadn't done too badly for a boy from the mean streets of the East End of London.

There were also plenty of times when the clouds gathered and he felt he was just biding time... filling in time now, before the final curtain - either from old age, illness, or a bullet. But not today. Life was good and this was going to be an exciting year; Sue was retiring soon, and they had lots of plans once they both no longer worked. More and longer trips overseas particularly to their beloved Italy, and more of those they had become accustomed to and loved, around New Zealand.

This morning's paper was again full of bad news - what seemed like endless drownings, road deaths and violent crimes. One headline caught his eye. *Home Invasions Linked.* It was written by an Anahera Harris, a name he vaguely recognised. In recent months there had been four or five brutal home invasions, all in isolated rural or semi-rural locations and all involving deaths. The similarities between the attacks, and the types of wealthy properties targeted had led some media commentators to speculate that they were carried out by the same people. All were within an hour or two of Auckland.

"...and the head of the Police Northern Region confirmed to me today that police were now convinced that these were not random, unrelated, or even copycat crimes, but were planned and committed by the same offenders, who number three or four. Forensics had established the same weapons were used in the attacks and Superintendent William Smales said police believed they were burglaries gone wrong. He said a dedicated team was pursuing several promising leads, and he was confident arrests would soon be made..."

How terrifying that must be for the victims Jim thought. He always read *The Herald* over breakfast, did the crosswords and various word games, to check his brain was still more or less working, then browsed two or three news websites and his emails, before starting the day.

Next was the gym. He belonged to a gym in the city, and here at the bach he had a basic set up which meant he could maintain his programme, largely consisting of free weights, while away from the city. The only thing he missed was his weekly one-on-one boxing class. He was reasonably fit. Still smoked, and drank too much, but he saw it as a case of old dogs and new tricks. Plus, he'd never expected to live even as long as he already had. Every year since he had been in New Zealand felt like a bonus.

Like most people, he suspected, he had a love/hate relationship with exercise. Great while you're actually working out but hard to contemplate doing when you're not. This morning was no different. He tried to find a good reason to avoid it but failed, and finally dragged himself downstairs to the basement to do penance.

* * * *

Three days earlier, Superintendent Smales was addressing a meeting of six or so Northern Region senior officers, all but one of them men, at Police HQ in Auckland City.

"They use stolen vehicles for each job and torch them when they're finished. They choose their hits carefully and nobody's ever seen them. They kill and rape without compunction and leave no witnesses. So far, we have the murders of four males and the rape and murder of three females. Forensics have identified matching weapons at four of the crime scenes, and we've gone back through ballistic records and discovered they were also responsible for that raid on the P house in Te Atatu a year or so back. So that puts their body count right up there.

"There's one DNA match, a Robert Collins. His whereabouts are unknown, and he has no known associates. He's done time, but it's unlikely any of them are new chums. And this is awful, but the coroners think one of the rapes in each case might have been 'post-mortem'. I'm sure you can work out what that means.

"We don't know how many burglaries they might have committed where there were no people in residence. We suspect there are three or four of these guys, and they're vile, but they're not silly. We need to find and stop them. They're operating in our patch and with more and more interest from the media we'll get more and more heat, plus people will start to panic. I've had a call from the Commissioner, and *Stuff's* crime reporter Ana Harris is right across this. Enough said. We need to find these people, if we can call them that. Questions? Please ID yourselves."

A good-looking middle-aged Māori man stood in the middle of the room.

"Inspector Warren, Whangarei. What hardware are they using sir?" he asked.

"They don't feel the need to change weapons for each gig and so far, a .22 rifle, a .38 handgun of some sort, probably a revolver, and a 12-gauge shotgun. Most options covered there. Oh, and all three of the rape victims died from knife wounds. Not nice. Bloody. No semi-autos it seems, which is something. Talking of blood, they've started calling themselves 'The Wild Bunch.' It was scrawled on a mirror, using the blood of one of their victims."

Various reactions, mostly of disgust, drifted around the room.

"Davis, Auckland Central. Any sign of gangs or drugs involved?"

"Impossible to know about any gang connections, but interesting you ask, traces of meth were found at one crime scene and cocaine at another. They take their time it would seem. We don't know whether they're just users or dealers as well. Could be a possible lead."

"Hi. Paora, Manukau. So, these boys tool up, drug up and go wild. Have they made any mistakes yet sir?"

"Nope, and we've got no leads. What we do know is that their rate of offending is increasing. If you look at this chart, first offence of this type nine months ago, then a gap of three months, and now two in the last ten or so weeks. That might mean they're doing less research into their targets, maybe getting a bit careless, or they're just getting more and more of a taste for it, who knows. They might start to make mistakes, let's hope so. Their M.O seems set and I'm pretty sure we'll be hearing more from them. Oh, and they're reasonably sophisticated thieves, no big items; cash, jewellery, watches, phones, laptops, stuff that's easy to carry and cash up, and they obviously know a good fence."

"Hi, Stan Williams, sir, Waiheke. Any pattern geographically? Anything to suggest where they might be based?"

"Not really. Probably somewhere in Auckland, but the hits are all out of town, one as far north as Mangawhai. The only common feature at this stage is the type of target. All I can say is this is a number one priority. When the press gets the full picture there will be huge public interest. I mean we've not long put all the pieces together ourselves. So... talk to anyone you can think of, interview the victims' families again, see if we're missing any connections. Check in with me on a daily basis, even if you haven't got anything to report, and we'll have a zoom in a few days. Ok?" No more questions.

"Thanks all."

The meeting broke up, a pall hanging over the officers as they left.

* * * *

It wasn't a long workout. He just couldn't push himself today, and besides he had a slightly dodgy rotator cuff after attempting just a bit much weight on the bench press the day before. It was a real problem at this age, your muscles could handle more weight than your joints could cope with. He thought it would be ok if he took it easy for a couple of days. Ah well, only to be expected he supposed. He was very nearly an old man.

In many ways he quite liked getting, being, older. You softened, didn't get as angry over things. He'd always had a bit of an issue with his temper, a tendency to flare. He thought this was a result of having a father who was a bit of a doormat. He used to observe his dad with other men, and he was always trying to be funny. It never worked, and Jim didn't feel he ever commanded respect among his peers. He sometimes saw him in his work environment, and it was the same as socially. Funnily enough Jim's father would talk flat out to other people, but never much to him. Jim had made a point of being different with his own son.

These things had affected him quite profoundly for some reason. He grew up determined not to be weak nor anyone's fool. He had a self-image of a strong man, a proud man. London was a rough town in those days, and with this attitude he got into quite a few fights, and never backed down. He'd even got into one or two scraps here in New Zealand. It all felt a bit silly in retrospect, but it had a lot to do with the choices he made when he left, or more accurately, when he was kicked out of school. After a quick dip in the pool and a shower, Jim made himself an espresso, lit a cigarette, and settled down to look at the local *Gulf News* he had bought the day before. Another ritual, albeit a weekly one. He checked upcoming events, general Island news, alternative health treatments and 'wellness' services, which he always found amusing. Still a few hippies on the island, he smiled to himself. Then he perused the For Sale section as he always did. You never knew what there might be. He'd always been an inveterate, almost compulsive collector. It had been an ongoing conversation throughout their married life

"Do we really need another..." or "We can't spend that much money on..." Sue would say, and she was usually right. But she shared his love of collecting and, equally often, agreed. As a consequence, they both loved virtually all of their possessions.

They'd gone for some years collecting Georgian sterling silver, antique Persian rugs, a number of vintage wrist watches, many pieces of furniture by a particular Kiwi designer, as well as quite a few works by Kiwi painters and sculptors. He'd also always had a keen interest in cars, a vice he hadn't been able to indulge as much as he would've liked.

It was hardly surprising then, that one ad in particular piqued his interest. It was brief and to the point. *Cars, art, watches, and yacht. Ph. 0270 81955.* Wow. Interesting. All the glorious years of sailing briefly came to mind, although he was certainly not in the market for another boat, however large or small. He rang the number immediately.

"The number you have called is not currently active or is invalid, please...." the pre-recorded voice intoned.

Bummer. Jim tried to put it out of his mind and continued browsing the rag. Oh well. Just enjoy this lovely summer Sunday.

* * * *

Shane and Bob were lying, smoking a joint, under a beautiful pōhutukawa tree, the last of its crimson blossom drifting down around them in the soft breeze.

"Shit this is good weed..."

Shane was a balding, rather overweight forty-year-old, never married. Bob was a wiry hippy type, a bit older, with long unkempt hair and piercing blue eyes, somewhat dulled by the dope, but still with a slightly manic look and a tendency to blink more often than most. Shane's eyes were entirely different. He didn't blink much at all, and his gaze shifted only slowly from one object, or thought, to another. He also moved slowly, and this gave him a decidedly reptilian, lizard-like quality, even when he wasn't stoned. Bob was more like a bird of prey. No, much more accurately, a vulture.

Both long term Waiheke residents, they had few friends, probably because both engendered a sense of unease among those they knew and encountered, and neither had anything approaching social skills, nor much interest in other people.

Bob was abandoned by his mother soon after his birth and was raised by various foster parents, with some time in juvenile detention; he was in and out of trouble from a young age. There were suggestions of physical and possibly sexual abuse in his early years, and he'd never had anything approaching a close relationship in his life. He simply didn't, couldn't, connect emotionally, not that he realised it.

Shane was as close to a friend as he had ever had, and on some level this mattered to him. After a few stints in prison he was now mostly unemployed and unemployable. He did start training as an electrician during one of his longer spells inside, but never finished. He had however developed some skills over the years, particularly with disconnecting power supplies and disabling alarm and CCTV systems, which came in handy sometimes in his partnership with Shane. There's not too much more to say, or know, about Bob. He had simply missed out on anything much good in life.

They had some things in common, but Shane was different from Bob. He'd grown up in a relatively stable, strict Catholic family, with two brothers and a sister. Stable, in that despite all the problems in their relationship, his parents stayed together. His mother had simply given up and was just going through the motions, but had been as good to the kids as limited money and her frayed emotions allowed.

His father was an auto mechanic who drank too much and, when drunk, would hand out serious beatings to any family member, including his wife, who put a foot wrong - although it was often hard to know what had provoked him - particularly on Friday nights when he would arrive home around seven with a huge pile of fish and chips and a flagon of beer. He'd grown up with six o'clock closing and had never changed his drinking habits.

Apart from barking orders at him, Shane couldn't remember his father talking to him, ever.

* * * *

Anahera Harris had arrived an hour earlier hoping to get an interview with the Superintendent or someone else senior, about this recent wave of home invasions. Ana was a freelance journo, with a particular interest in crime reporting. She was a regular visitor here at Police HQ, often turning up without an appointment, following up some story or another, and often lucking in and getting to talk to someone. She was never pushy though, and her slightly cheeky, engaging, girl-next-door persona had a lot to do with her success in this regard.

Also, the senior guys at HQ were very PR savvy, knew the value of keeping on-side with the media and were aware of this young woman's growing mana. Superintendent Smales was particularly generous with his time even though he would often talk to her for ten minutes without actually answering her questions or telling her anything useful. At least he talked to her, and she liked him. He was a good old school cop, he'd seen it all, done the hard yards, and seemed very comfortable with himself and where he'd ended up. Smales's PA Sharlene, with whom Ana got on well, told her that the Super was about to go into a meeting and could be a while.

Ana had seen the top brass trooping into the building and decided it might be worth hanging about. She sat in the sun on the steps outside and waited.

She'd won an NPA award the previous year for Best Feature Writing – Crime and Justice, for a series of articles about what she believed was a miscarriage of justice in a particular police prosecution. This had led directly to an internal inquiry, an officer being stood down and the charges being withdrawn. It was a real coup for the twenty-seven-year-old. Of course, this success was at the police's expense and was a bit embarrassing for them, but it didn't seem to have had an adverse effect on her relationship with the force or make her any sort of persona non-grata. True, the Superintendent, for example, was a bit more careful with her, but he admired her tenacity and commitment; she'd have made a good cop he'd always thought. She was a nice kid and what's more, she reminded Bill a lot of one of his daughters.

* * * *

From when Shane was quite young he was the one who seemed to get under his father's skin the most, and so was the primary recipient of the violence. It seemed to his older brother Phil, that he almost intentionally provoked his father at times, and then was determined to show no pain or be cowed by the repeated blows to the body and heavy cuffing around the head. Phil had wondered since whether these had damaged Shane's brain. He was always a bit... different.

The three brothers were close and as they got older, they discovered they could, between them, physically restrain their father until he calmed down after flying into a rage. Often this was to protect their mother. As the years passed, each of them discovered they had inherited their father's propensity for irrational fury, and all had a history of bullying, overreacting, fighting and a lack of empathy with those around them. Perhaps as a way of dealing with this and to have a framework of discipline in their lives, both of Shane's brothers, Phil the older and Kevin the younger, joined the police force. This had always amused and disgusted Shane, in equal measure.

Phil and Kevin, at Auckland Central, were good cops with unblemished records. It's true that Phil had had numerous times when his anger threatened to get the better of him, but he would remember his training and, with great difficulty, not unleash the violence he sometimes badly wanted to dispense.

Their sister Mary, the youngest, had largely escaped the domestic terror they had all endured and stayed for her mother's sake. As soon as her mother died prematurely at fifty-five, she left, never to return and going as far away as possible, to Japan, where she now had a good job as a translator. She had an aptitude for languages, studying French, German and Japanese at school, with some success.

Shane never achieved at school. He was bright enough, just couldn't be bothered. When he left school at fifteen, he got a job with a dog grooming and walking company. He liked it. He liked dogs, well most dogs, just not the ridiculous little yappy ones; he was always sorely tempted to tread heavily on them. But medium sized to big dogs, yes, he liked them. He understood them somehow, and they related to him. It was the only time he felt something in himself approaching warmth and softness, when he was with dogs, largely because they made sense to him, with their primal, instinctual, predictable responses and their naïve trust and loyalty. Over the years he'd often been sorely tempted to get a dog of his own, but he knew he couldn't handle the responsibility, the constant worry, the unbearable grief if they got lost or died. He enjoyed looking after other people's dogs though, and the work took him all over the district, and to some expensive homes. Even at that age he would notice properties, possessions, access. He thought sometimes he must have been born a criminal.

Shane left home at seventeen and never returned. He moved out on a Friday night, after giving his father a premeditated and severe bashing with a baseball bat, which put him in hospital for ten days.

None of the children ever saw their father again once they left home. Only Kevin saw the death notice in the paper and was unmoved.

* * * *

He'd tried to forget it, but Jim kept being drawn back to that ad. He rang the number again; the phones sometimes did funny things on Waiheke. Same result. Then he looked more closely. What was it that drew his attention? After some time looking at it, he realised what it was - the number - 027 081 955. Apart from the last of the eight digits, it was the same as his birth date, 27.08.1956. Surely that wasn't the actual number and there was a typo on the last digit, the 'five' being repeated by mistake? That would be too weird, but just for fun he called the revised number, his birth date.

It rang! It actually rang! It rang several times before a soft, very mellow woman's voice answered "Pronto" then quickly, in a distinctly Italian accent. "Sorry... hello?"

This was too extraordinary to believe, but Jim gathered himself and replied. His Italian wasn't great, but he knew the basics.

"Buongiorno signora, I'm calling in response to your advertisement in the *Gulf News*."

"Ah si", she replied.

"I wondered if I might come and look at the things you have for sale."

"Certo, certainly. You are the first to ring." Hardly surprising Jim thought to himself. "I'm here all the time, when would you like?" Her manner was quite formal, and almost offhand.

"Today? In a couple of hours? After lunch, say 1.30?"

"Sure" the voice replied.

"Grazie mille" Jim said.

"Prego" she replied and hung up.

How amazing is that! Jim thought to himself. What sort of bizarre karma is at play here?! Then he realised that he had no idea where to go. His mobile rang. She had had the same realisation. They laughed a little and she told him the address, a bay down on the way to Man O' War Bay. A gravel road in and just a letterbox with the number on the road. Her tone softened in this second conversation, and she really did have a beautiful voice. Jim found himself looking forward to meeting her. She mentioned her husband had died and she was returning to Italy. He had resisted the impulse to ask for more detail about what was for sale.

Jim's imagination went into overdrive. What if there were a Patek Philippe at a good price? They were one of the few watches he had no examples of, they were just too expensive. Or a painting or two he could afford? Probably not.

But what an adventure and again, how very, very, strange.

* * * *

Shane had set up a small dog-based business on Waiheke when he moved there in his late twenties. He could have built the business into something significant, but he didn't want a regular routine, staff, early starts or schedules, preferring to potter around on his own, with just a few regular clients. It paid the bills, but only just.

Now, ten or so years on, brothers Shane and Phil both lived on Waiheke. Phil had wanted a quieter life than being stationed in South Auckland afforded him, but he also wanted to be closer to his younger brother to try to re-kindle some sort of relationship with him. He had applied for and got a posting as sergeant to the Waiheke station and moved there with his wife Helen. They had no children; they'd decided against it.

Sadly, Shane had shown little enthusiasm for contact. They'd spoken on the phone, but Phil hadn't seen him in the nine months he'd been on the island.

* * * *

Ana saw the Super coming down the steps. She bounced up to him.

"Morning Superintendant Smales. Lovely day."

"Anahera, kia ora!" he was surprised at how pleased he was to see her. His head was still full of these bloody home invasions, and this was like a breath of fresh air in his morning, a welcome respite.

"What can I do for you today?"

"Just wondering what the big meeting was about?" She greased.

"Oh, just the regular monthly catch-up..."

"Nothing to do with this spate of home invasions?" Cheeky Ana in action. A brief pause followed while Bill Smales made a decision. It really was time for a press release. He said

"Listen, I was on my way to get a coffee." He hadn't been. "Why don't you join me."

* * * *

How Shane and Bob met neither would remember. They had known each other for several years and had committed several burglaries together, invariably of properties when residents were out. They always carried weapons though, guns and knives, just in case. And they both had drug habits which needed funding.

About eighteen months ago they had very boldly raided a known meth house in West Auckland. The three inhabitants were supposed to be out at the time but were not, and they shot and killed all three of them. At the time, the police understandably assumed it was gang related and Shane and Bob got away, not only scot free, but with a great haul of drugs and cash. They found the whole experience hugely exhilarating and it signalled a shift in their approach, so much so that they started targeting properties where people would more than likely be at home.

They revelled in the adrenaline rush, the power, being in control for once, and the drugs gave the whole experience, from the planning to the execution, a surreal, almost cinematic quality. They had become addicted. Neither would acknowledge it, nor perhaps even be aware of it, but they undoubtedly had characters from the western, gangster, and cops-and-robbers movie genres they grew up with, swirling around somewhere in the back of their addled brains. Neither felt any remorse whatsoever for their victims, and there was something truly fascinating about all that blood.

That's where the name came from. Shane had always loved the movie 'The Wild Bunch', which he'd seen when he was quite young. It was the first film he'd seen where people didn't just get shot and fall over. Bits of them got blown off, blood spurted - just like in real life. He loved it. He and his brothers had also called themselves that name sometimes.

They'd never discussed it, it just sort of happened on their second such outing, but it quickly became crystal clear that Shane and Bob also had a shared interest in sexual violence.

"Whaddaya reckon Bob?"

"Nah mate, too close to home. We've always said -"

"Yeah, but it's not. Look, it's miles from nowhere, right down the bottom end. It'd be a Sunday, so the staff'd be off, and there's always someone shooting rabbits down there. It'd just be the bitch and her old minder who never leaves her side. Since her old man died she's never left the house, and it's full of goodies mate. There's a collection of sports cars and a bloody huge yacht tied up at the bottom of the garden, so there's sure to be plenty of bling and shit. And ya never know, she's no spring chicken but she might do us, eh? Beggars can't be choosers. Bit of fun. And no rush, no-one ever goes there apparently."

"How'd you find all this out?"

"Overheard the gardener blabbing at the RASA, and there was some stuff about them in the local rag a while back. Rich Eyties they reckon."

He wasn't sure why, but for some reason Shane neglected to mention that he had groomed the Italian family's dog a few times. Bello was a beautiful big black and tan German Shepherd, and they got on ok. He was looking forward to seeing him again and was really hoping he wouldn't have to be shot.

"Whaddaya say?"

After a long pause Bob replied, "Could be worth a go."

"I'll tell the others."

* * * *

Ana started writing her article. Her inner-city apartment was small, just a living/dining room, a bedroom, and a tiny kitchen. That didn't bother Ana, she didn't cook much. The flat did however have a nice outlook, across Myers Park. While not exactly spartan, it had only basic furnishings. There was a couch, an armchair, a coffee table and a dining table with two chairs, a framed original photograph of her great-grandfather Mohi - which she loved - on the wall above the couch, a neglected potted palm in the corner, a bookcase overflowing with all manner of titles, and more books and magazines piled on the floor. The table was covered in newspapers, court reports and magazines, her laptop barely accessible amongst them.

She pondered her interview with Bill Smales. Apart from having learned never to take anything at face value, Ana had a sixth sense when it came to people lying to her. Bill Smales was in fact a terrible liar. He didn't like not telling the truth, even when it was necessary, and in some barely perceptible way his eyes signalled this. Ana had spent enough time with him over the last couple of years to pick it.

She was grateful for what he had given her, but what wasn't he telling her? She wouldn't ever expect a cop to give her all the facts of an investigation, but this felt different. This case was really starting to get under her journo skin.

Ana hadn't always been this interested in crime and justice, not this sort of crime anyway. Her parents were small run-holders near Tolaga Bay. Her mother was Māori, her dad Māori with some Irish blood. Neither of them had been at all academic and were surprised when their daughter wanted to go to university; no-one in the family ever had. But they were very supportive and hugely proud of their wee angel. She was the only child they'd been able to have, and they doted on her. She flew through her degree with honours, was admitted to the bar, and scored a job with a small but solid Auckland law firm. She took several mostly minor cases to court, but on some basic level it never felt quite enough for her, and increasingly she felt like a break from the law. Journalism had always appealed, so despite it being a job with far less security and financial reward, at twenty-four she changed careers, much to her parents' dismay.

She was a committed feminist, and when first starting work as a reporter had focussed seriously on women's issues, particularly domestic violence, the treatment of rape victims by police and the courts, advocacy for women generally, and Māori women in particular. She was also a volunteer at a women's refuge. She worked long hours and it was hard, the constant exposure to that level of distress, injury and even death, as well as what seemed to her to be the lack of any real progress in so many areas. It all took a toll on her. She was sleeping and eating badly and realised one day that she was in danger of becoming quite seriously depressed. She sought advice, got some very helpful meds, and took six months off to recover. It was clear she needed to shift her focus a little, and when she returned to work her interests broadened, although she was still drawn to the wider justice system.

Where would this investigation lead? Ana felt strongly there was much more to it than Smales had let on, and a lot more of it yet to play out.

* * * *

In the sleepy 1970's and 80's there were just two officers stationed on Waiheke, now that number had grown to more than a dozen, but it was still a relatively small operation.

Burglaries and thefts of cars, mostly from vacant holiday homes, minor violence offences, damage to property, traffic violations, road accidents and the odd drug bust comprised most of station's caseload. It's fair to say Waiheke is not exactly a hot bed of crime, so it's no great surprise that Inspector Stan Williams opened the meeting with

"Morning all. Well, here we are at the end of another frantic week! Not a whole lot to report. I got to say I liked the way you handled that old bloke on the houseboat Phil, you seem to have put the fear of God into him. I think he'll settle down now, at least for a while, and I believe you had a hand in that Sally. You two seem to be working well together so you can stay a team for now. Good work. Talking of boats, I dunno what we can do about these lunatic protesters down at Kennedy Point. The new marina's definitely happening, penguins or no bloody penguins, but they won't give up. We're gonna have to clear them out, I just don't know the best way to handle that. Legal's having another look at it; we've just gotta try to make sure no-one gets hurt or killed in the meantime. There's a roster for regular patrols of the area, and if you get called down there, remember, it's a PR nightmare, so softly softly."

Present in the Waiheke Police Station meeting room were the station chief Stan Williams, secretary receptionist Alice Considine, Sergeant Phil Smith, Constable Sally Reynolds, Constable Andy Tyler, Sergeant Tim Adams, and three others of the station's full complement. Four were currently on leave.

"Also, Andy and Tim, you did a great job defusing that scrap at Charlie Farley's the other night, it could've got right out of hand, and it was a good call not making any arrests. Talking of which our clearance rates are still among the highest in the country, so well done all, keep up the good work. Oh, and before I forget, I had an interesting meeting at HQ yesterday about this gang that's been doing these home invasions. Nasty bastards. You get the broad picture in the media, but it's a lot worse than Joe Public knows. Up to now anyway. Won't bore you with all the gory details. Fortunately, they're most unlikely to visit our little island paradise, it's too hard to get in and out of unnoticed. Just thought I'd mention it. I'll keep you posted. Ok. Off to work, and like they used to say on the tele 'be careful out there'."

He fancied himself as a bit of a wag, our Stan, but he was a good solid cop, and an observant one. During the meeting Stan thought he noticed some interesting exchanges of looks between Sally and Phil. Decidedly interesting. Surely they're not... he thought. Big age difference, not to mention Phil's marriage.... Probably imagining things.

Sally was indeed a good bit younger that Phil, nearly twenty years in fact. She wasn't long out of Police College and this was only her second posting. She'd just finished her two years' probation and was proud to be a 'real' cop now. At forty-five Phil was still a good-looking guy but Sally was, in Stan's eyes at least, a stunner. Five-foot-seven with a mane of blonde hair; nicely proportioned, with pretty eyes and a great smile, she could have any young bloke she wanted.

Yep, just Stan's imagination running wild for sure, with maybe just a bit of wishful projection.

Stan wasn't imagining things.

* * * *

Shane and Bob and two others were sitting in a car on a layby just off Cowes Bay Road. The others were Kyle and Rawiri, Ra. Kyle was a big, blonde, surfy type in his twenties, while Ra was just a kid, seventeen at the most. He didn't really know how old he was himself. They were in the back seat of the innocuous RAV 4 Bob had stolen from a vacant holiday home the night before. All four were tooting on the meth pipe being passed around. They all got through a lot of coke too, and preferred it, but P was better for this sort of job.

Kyle and Ra were both locals. Kyle seemed easy-going, quick to laugh and with a carefree demeanour, but beneath that exterior was a hard-edged, nasty core. He was bi-polar, possibly schizophrenic, and had spent time in and out of psychiatric units, referred by the courts after convictions for armed robbery and very grievous bodily assaults. He'd not been long out of jail and his history suggested he'd be back there again soon. Bob had met him in prison and he was the only person, apart from Shane, to whom Bob felt any connection. Kyle was already a seasoned criminal, and while he could be seen as a liability, they all knew that he would never narc on them. He too was addicted to drugs and violence.

Ra on the other hand was just a lost child, a sad by-product of social inequity. He'd never had any love or affection and was yet another dead-eyed boy with no future, desperate to belong, to belong to... something, anything. He was determined to join a gang when and if he got off the island, and his association with these guys would certainly lend him some serious cred. He was also very drug dependent, and these jobs were for him the quickest and easiest way of getting some real money; Shane made sure everyone got a good whack of the proceeds. Apart from any concept of fair play, it kept them on side, and on tap.

Ra didn't like or relate to the killing and rapes, but he'd seen a lot in his short life and almost took such things for granted. They didn't really impinge on him at all. He looked up to Shane, and he too would never, ever betray these men he saw, quite erroneously, as his mates. Also, he'd always loved guns.

A motley crew, but for the job in hand a highly effective one. And now, a bit like a sheriff leading a posse about to descend on the baddies, or maybe a Chicago gang boss, Shane said

"Ok Wild Bunch, let's do this thing."

* * * *

Phil and Sally were on patrol, slowly cruising along the Onetangi beachfront.

"Christ this is boring." Phil said.

"Apart from the company, eh?" quipped Sally, and then, reaching over to Phil's lap "Unless you want to go somewhere quiet and...." Phil livened up.

"Now that's not at all a bad idea."

Sally was in love with Phil. She'd had a hard time with sexist yobbos at Police College and then two disastrous relationships with guys her own age, so went for a couple of years not dating at all. When she moved to the island and met Phil, everything changed.

It happened over only a few weeks. They spent a lot of time together as a unit at work and got on really well she thought. He seemed to fancy her, but was so cool and relaxed about it, she couldn't be sure. Even though she'd never even vaguely thought about being with an older man, she started to wonder what it might be like with Phil. Then quite suddenly one night after work, over a drink with him at an Oneroa bar overlooking the bay in the setting sun, she realised she wanted him.

Phil was just the same when they became lovers, unhurried, gentle, generous, and without any sort of pressure. It was as if he could read her mind as well as her body, and it was everything she'd ever dreamed sex could be. She put the fact that he was married as far back in her thoughts as she could.

* * * *

Francesca and her manager Giuseppe were seated across from each other at the table in the loggia, studying some accounts and sipping espressos, under one of the many slowly turning ceiling fans. Some metres to their left was a well-stocked bar, while a similar distance to the right sat a huge couch, several armchairs and a very large low table, complete with a vase of flowers, matching those on the dining table where they sat.

Giuseppe had been with the family since he was a teenager in Calabria, first with Pepe's father, his uncle, when they were all as poor as church mice. They now had properties and business interests across Italy, in South America and Europe, and lived mostly in Venice, in a wonderful palazzo that Giuseppe loved, on the Grand Canal.

Pepe, the Don, had done well. Then one day after a holiday in New Zealand he'd decided he wanted them to have a place there. "Good place to live and do business. Perfetto" he'd said, and they'd been here most of the time for over five years, with only two or three months a year back home. Giuseppe looked forward to those trips.

Pepe loved it here, and they now owned three vineyards on the island and one in Central Otago, as well as several other properties. He became more and more attached to the country. He had come to know and love much of the work produced by Kiwi artists, and believed there were more classic cars here than anywhere else in the world. Giuseppe on the other hand hated every minute they spent in this godforsaken antipodean dump, and in this steel, concrete and glass mausoleum. He liked some things about the house, but it was too hard-edged and... modern for him. Then out of the blue, a few weeks earlier, Pepe had a massive heart attack and died. Giuseppe was distraught. He loved him like a brother. He wasn't even that old, twenty years older than his wife but still only in his sixties, and some years younger than Giuseppe. The only comfort was that they were moving back home.

There was music playing, a selection of popular arias from Italian opera, not loudly but loud enough that neither Francesca nor Giuseppe had heard Shane and the others approaching. Normally Bello would have alerted them, but he was in the city with Carlo.

"Well, hello there" Shane crooned as they entered the loggia.

Francesca and Giuseppe turned, startled, and Giuseppe said

"The dog man? What are you doing here?"

Bob missed that reference, but he loved this stage of proceedings. Shane turned from his usual gruff, laconic self into this sideshow huckster, this... ringmaster. He just needed a top hat and cane.

"I'm here - we're here - to make your worst nightmares come true. So, roll up, roll up, for the show of your lives."

Francesca said "Get out of my house, all of you, or I'll call the police". Then she saw the guns that Bob, Kyle and Ra were carrying. Shane only had a knife in his belt. He didn't like guns much and on jobs like this three of them fully armed was more than enough.

"Oddio! what are you doing?" she said in a panicked voice.

Giuseppe too had noticed the hardware and stood up suddenly, reaching behind him for the Beretta he always carried out of habit, as much as thinking he might need to use it. Bob was much too fast for him.

He lifted his Colt and shot him in the belly before Giuseppe could even get the gun out of his belt. He sat down heavily in his chair and looked at his midriff, his face shocked and suddenly ashen.

Francesca screamed and moved quickly around the end of the table to tend to him, but Shane stopped her in her tracks with a backhander which lifted her off the ground and sent her sprawling across the table, knocking over the vase of flowers and sending the coffee cups crashing to the floor.

Bob moved towards Giuseppe, raising the pistol again to finish him off, before Shane stopped him.

"Nah, let him live with it for a while, but get the piece out the back of his pants. Hurts like a motherfucker I'm told, getting gut shot. That true old man?"

The pain on Giuseppe's face was answer enough. Shane laughed, a touch maniacally, and the others joined in, in a low key, uninterested way. Apart from Ra. He was looking around him. He'd been in some flash houses with these guys, but this place was something else. How did people ever get this much money together?

Giuseppe was indeed in severe pain but was surprised he wasn't bleeding more. He might survive this if he got help. He'd been shot before, back home, but never this badly and not without a gun in his hand shooting back. He was more concerned about Francesca. What would they do to her?

Then he made the connection. Is this the gang he'd read about? If so then they were done for. He should have taken security more seriously, the way the old man had, but he'd never thought they were at much risk here on Waiheke. He was pleased that Carlo wasn't here, although he'd have handled it better. A good soldier that boy. And if Bello had been here, he would've warned them. Yes, it was a conspiracy of circumstances, but the fact was he simply hadn't done his job.

He felt like a washed-up old failure. O Mio Bambino Caro, now playing, didn't help.

Francesca had been knocked unconscious by Shane's heavy hand and was bleeding from the mouth. She started to recover and lifted herself onto one elbow.

"Darling, you're back in the land of the living, how nice" Shane said, continuing with his exaggerated, quite camp showman persona.

"But for how long eh? That's the sixty-four-thousand-dollar question!" he giggled, then changed tone abruptly, turned, and announced in a steely cold voice to the others

"Ok, Bob and I are gonna have some fun. We'll turn the place over after that. Kyle, you keep watch out front, and Ra, you... do what you want. Maybe find out how to turn that fucking music off."

* * * *

Ana just could not get this case out of her head. As she did frequently, she'd walked up through the park to St. Kevin's arcade for breakfast and coffee. Nothing more in the Sunday papers. So far at least, she was up with the play. The big question was, would these guys strike again? Bill Smales had implied he thought it likely, and if so, when? And where?

Criminal investigations often struck her as being a bit like sporting events, games of cat and mouse, and who will get to the finish line first. Winners and losers. In fact, a very similar view was shared consciously or unconsciously by many cops, and crims. She had read somewhere that, at least in times gone by, cops and criminals had come from the same social class and shared a degree of mutual understanding and respect; there were norms and expectations which both sides adhered to. She'd have to ask Bill Smales what he thought of that analysis, in this day and age.

Ana had been researching home invasions. They weren't a recent phenomenon, there'd been a lot over the years and they did sometimes leave people dead, but most were gang and/or drug related - sometimes with the wrong houses targeted - or burglaries gone wrong. As far as she could tell there wasn't a history of repeat attacks of this sort, by the same offender or group of offenders.

It also struck her that this current series of such crimes, if connected as the police believed, really couldn't all be burglaries gone wrong, surely, unless they were incredibly incompetent villains and they clearly weren't. Did they not check whether property owners were at home? Did they not care either way, or were they deliberately targeting properties with residents in situ? That was a really disturbing possibility. This led Ana to wonder, did they want to kill, and enjoy killing?

Her thoughts segued to something else she had often wondered about. How did murderous couples like moors murderers Ian Brady and Myra Hindley, Paul Bernardo and Karla Homolka, Gerald and Charlene Gallego and others, discover this shared... passion? One thing was clear from her research was that such people became addicted to this behaviour and needed to commit more and more such crimes. All were caught when they became reckless in finding new victims.

Similarly, how would a group of three or four common crooks discover they had this shared, psychopathic taste for killing? If that were indeed the case. Was that the case here? It defied belief, but it had to be a possibility.

Ana could not have known how close she was to the truth.

* * * *

Shane turned back to Francesca. "Now rich bitch, it's your turn."

Without another word, Shane grabbed the neckline of her stylish print dress and ripped it down its full length, revealing Francesca's underwear which he also ripped off with somewhat more difficulty.

"Oh, very nice" Shane looked down at her, sneering. Still somewhat dazed and in pain, Francesca barely noticed this new assault.

"Now I'll tell you how it's gonna go. We're gonna tie you to this table - it's a good height actually - and then...

He leaned in and whispered in her ear, spelling out in graphic detail what was to befall her.

"And then Bob here will take his turn. Who knows, you might still be alive even, but I doubt it. He loves that. Don't you Bobby boy?"

"Sure do" the vulture wheezed. As Shane had been talking, Bob had taken some grubby nylon cords from his jacket pocket and tied Francesca's arms back to the table legs. The hand holding his boning knife trembled with anticipation and excitement.

A look of horror crossed Francesca's face, she gasped, then composed herself and spoke, clearly and with calm conviction

"You do not know who you are dealing with. My son will avenge me, he will hunt you down and I assure you, my suffering will be nothing compared with yours, all of you. Do your worst, pig!" she said and spat in his face.

"Shut it, bitch!" He snarled and hit her again, this time with a closed fist, but not so hard that she passed out - for long anyway.

The music - Nessun Dorma - stopped.

TWO

Driving down the dusty road into the property, Jim was running a bit late. It probably wouldn't matter but he did like to be punctual, to do things as he said he'd do them. He'd missed the letterbox up on the main road the first time and had to double back. Just a plain, old, tin letterbox, no fancy stone walls with pretentious gates, a refreshing change. Old Waiheke. He wondered what sort of house it might be; a rambling old villa perhaps, like the one or two you see when sailing around the bottom of the island.

The Outback was perfect on roads like this. It was a great car, four-wheel drive, lots of space, good for towing, could take tons on the roof racks, and it was a sensible size for the island's roads. He hated the huge SUV's which seemed to be all the rage. He'd even started seeing those absurd Ford Rangers - the same actual size as a Sherman tank. He thought them too dangerously big for the island, the majority weren't work vehicles and many of them had less capacity than the Subaru. Ah well....

He was still buzzing and still could not believe the events of the day so far. He was approaching the entrance to the property and could see the white pebble drive leading to a stunning modern structure a hundred or so metres away. On either side at the beginning of the drive was a simple galvanised steel box section post supporting a galv steel panel above, with *BEATITUDINE* laser cut out of it. He didn't know that exact Italian word, but it had to be something to do with...blessing? Or beauty maybe?

And how truly beautiful it all was. The lawns, trees, the beach. Was that a pool coming into view? And that yacht! My God! He and Sue were still thrilled with the house they had built on the island fifteen or so years earlier, it had a pool and it had won a design award, but this place was next level. And that endless row of garages cut into the hill like wine cellars?

Ah yes, the cars. Then he saw the loggia. What an amazing place. Vaguely Italianate, despite being so contemporary.

He'd heard overweight American tourists all around the world exclaiming 'It's like being in a m-o-o-v-i-e!' But this really was.

In fact, there was something about it that reminded him of a specific movie. Why would it be The Godfather?

* * * *

The squad car was a few metres below the grassy knoll where Phil and Sally lay, relaxing after their tryst on the travel rug Sally had thoughtfully 'popped in the boot'. They were just off the road to Orapiu, in the driveway of a house they knew to be vacant, and partly surrounded by regenerating bush.

Both were still semi-naked, enjoying the dappled sunlight, the breeze on their lower bodies and the view across the hills and valleys.

"That was wonderful Phil. I do love you."

"I know baby, I love you too." Phil said, although he really had no idea what he meant by that. He sure did like Sally a lot and she was undoubtedly the best lover he'd ever had, but he'd never been able to pin down or relate to this thing called 'love'. He would say he loved his brothers but that was different, that was blood. He thought Sally was great, he couldn't believe he was with her and he certainly cared for her at least as much as he did for Helen, but 'love'? Was he even capable of it in the way other people obviously were? The way Sally was? He'd asked himself that question many times. He suspected he wasn't.

He'd often wondered if there were something missing in his emotional makeup. Perhaps he should have had kids, would that have helped? Who knows. He knew Sally wanted kids. But Phil didn't like thinking about things too much. He put it out of his head.

* * * *

Jim pulled the Outback up at the left-hand end of the loggia. The first of the panels along the front obscured most of the interior space from this angle. He couldn't wait to see the rest. Thoughts of watches and art had gone completely from his mind, although he couldn't help noticing what looked like a large Trusttum on the back wall.

Jim was on the second of the three steps up to the loggia when Kyle stepped out from behind the panel, the somewhat sawn-off 12-gauge pointed straight at Jim's chest. This was a shock, to say the least.

"Whoa, whoa, take it easy mate." Jim spluttered.

"Yeah, I'm taking it easy, whadda you doin' here?"

Jim wasn't sure if Kyle's smiling eyes and affability should reassure him or not.

"I've come to look at the stuff advertised in the *Gulf News*. You... security?"

Jim couldn't think of anything else to say. His heart was pounding.

"Sort of." Kyle laughed. Then a voice called from inside

"Who the fuck is that?" It was Shane.

"Some old bloke answering a for sale ad." Kyle called back.

"Well just fucking shoot him." Jim couldn't believe this. What the hell was going on.

"O-o-o-kay" Kyle called back, then to Jim, still in his laid back, easy way

"Sorry mate, you heard the man" and pumped a shell into the gun's breech.

Something suddenly changed, and even in this mad moment Jim registered the cliché. His senses seemed to heighten, he felt calm and clear, and time slowed down. It really was slow motion, and it was familiar, he remembered this. He did a classic double-take towards the inside, as though someone had just joined them, saying to this non-existent person

"Look mate, you can't just...."

Kyle's eyes lazily followed Jim's, expecting to see one of the others, and before he realised it was a ruse, Jim had rushed him, pushing the barrel aside and smashing him across the nose with a heavy forearm blow. The shotgun went off, but Jim barely noticed the deafening blast, stepping back and dealing Kyle a flurry of lefts and rights to the head. Kyle hit the steps and rolled down them, along with the shotgun, unconscious.

"Is he dead?" Shane barked from inside. "Yep" Jim replied, trying to copy Kyle's light baritone.

Right, that was the fight, now the flight. His pulse rate was up again. He raced down the steps to the car. His hands hurt. It had been years since he'd hit anyone without gloves on and he suspected he'd cracked a knuckle or two, or three. He was opening the car door when from inside he heard

"Aiuto, aiutami, per favore, please help me, help me!!" It was that beautiful voice again, distinctively the same despite the terror. Fuck! Jim thought. He hesitated. No, he decided, not my problem. But he couldn't get in the car. Then it happened again, everything slowed down. He shut the car door, stood up straight, walked calmly back around the bonnet, picked up the shotgun, pumped it, and walked up the steps.

For some unknown reason, something he'd noticed on the way into the property came into his mind. The ground at the far end of the beach had been built up, a bit like a levee. Maybe that was where the heaviest waves came in during storms. The song *American Pie* came to him. Would this be the day that he died? Was this his fate? Every strange thing today, perhaps his entire life, had led to this moment, there was such a strong sense of inevitability about it.

In these few split seconds of flashing thoughts Jim decided he was ok with it, if it were to happen. He thought of Sue and Tom. They would miss him, but they'd survive. He couldn't dwell on that, this was the right thing to do. He wondered how many of them there might be inside, and how heavily armed they were. All those years of hiding, they would be over. The feeling of peace was almost intoxicating.

The light inside the loggia was relatively low, and it was as if he'd walked onto a Peter Greenaway film set. To the right was an older man sitting slumped in a chair, head down and sobbing quietly like a baby, his whole torso red with blood. To this man's right, in the centre of the tableau was a table with a woman's legs hanging off the end. Further up the side of the table was a skinny guy with long greasy hair, licking what must have been the woman's breasts and, standing between the woman's legs was a large man with his pants around his ankles, his flabby, very white bare arse facing Jim. Neither were in a position to have seen him enter. Reality kicked back in. Tom looked around. Two of them. Could be a lot worse.

"Hi fellas." Jim said, with a nonchalance that surprised him.

Then things sped up again, to super-fast. Shane wheeled around revealing an even uglier front view and Bob uncoiled like a cobra, picking up his .38 handgun from the table as he did so. He was so quick.

Amazingly, Jim had never been shot. He'd heard that it was like being punched. This was more like a sting. He felt the bullet hit him in the lower torso above his right hip and pass straight through. Then it hurt. Without thinking he almost simultaneously discharged the 12-gauge, hitting Bob full in the chest. He was dead before he hit the floor.

Everything froze for a moment, both Jim and Shane temporarily transfixed by Bob's inert body, his chest resembling a rather large beef patty.

"Pull your pants up, you fat fuck, you look ridiculous!" Jim shouted at Shane. He started to do so and Jim noticed the sheath knife in his belt.

The second bullet did feel like a punch. It hit him in the left side of the chest and it really hurt. He pumped the shotgun as he turned. It was Ra. Not wanting to see Shane and Bob's 'fun' he'd been admiring the rest of the house, rushing back to the loggia when he heard the gunshots. Now he stood there in front of the bar, rifle in hand. Jim stopped dead. This beautiful boy couldn't be more than sixteen surely. Someone's child. What was he doing here for God's sake?

"Son, son, put the gun down, please, don't make me shoot you." Jim begged.

He felt the blood seeping from his wounds and started to feel faint. That second shot must have been close to his heart. It had certainly hit a rib, maybe that had saved him.

"Shoot him Ra, shoot the fucker! He's killed Bob, shoot him again" Shane screamed, and Ra shot him again. Jim closed his eyes and pulled the trigger. Ra flew backwards, knocking over some bottles on the bar as he did so. Jim couldn't believe what he had done.

Ra's second bullet had hit Jim in the upper thigh. Possibly because he was so angry and upset, apart from the impact he hadn't felt it at all. He turned back to Shane.

"What the fuck are you doing bringing a boy on a gig like this!" Jim yelled at him "What sort of an arsehole are you? I should fucking shoot you where you stand!"

Shane said nothing but Jim noticed his eyes shift to something over his shoulder. Too late, as Jim started to turn, he felt an excruciating thump in his back. He turned, instinctively bobbing down as per his training, as Kyle, on his feet again, swung the knife a second time at where Jim's head and neck were a moment before. Jim shot him, unintentionally from this oblique angle, under the chin. It completely blew his good-looking face off, and most of his head. Jesus Christ! Jim thought to himself, feeling the vomit rise in his throat. What next?!

What next was Shane, launching himself at Jim. It was like being tackled by a front row forward. As he fell, Jim managed to twist his body around so at least he was facing Shane, who now had both hands on the shotgun, trying to force it down onto Jim's neck. Jim had his elbows locked on the floor and could just keep the gun up and away from him. But for how long?

"I'm really going to enjoy this, you bastard. You've killed my whole crew, you old cunt. You're gonna die slowly boy."

Shane was breathing heavily. They both were, and Shane's disgusting sweat was dripping onto Jim's face. Plus, he had really nasty halitosis. Jim knew he couldn't keep this up for long; his right wrist was struggling with the weight, and that bloody left rotator cuff wasn't liking it either. This could be it. The Don McLean song flashed through his mind again, then he suddenly remembered seeing the knife on Shane's belt. But was it on his left or right side?

His right wrist and arm gave way. The butt end of the shotgun crashed down to the floor, but Jim's other arm stayed in place and the barrel of the gun was still mercifully a few millimetres from his throat.

"Won't be long now fucker!" Shane was enjoying this arm wrestle, which he would soon win.

With his now free hand, Jim reached down to Shane's belt. Please let it be on this side. It was.

It seemed to take Shane a second or two to realise he was being stabbed repeatedly in the side of his neck. A shocked look crossed his face. Blood spurted from his carotid and started to gurgle from his mouth, again down onto Jim's face. His strength left him, his lizardy eyes rolled back in his head, and he slowly crumpled down onto Jim. They lay there as if in some ghastly embrace as the pool of blood grew around them. Silence at last.

It was over, it had to be over, surely it was over. He might yet survive this. Despite the damage, and the fact his body hurt almost everywhere, Jim didn't feel like he was dying. He'd known a guy who'd survived more wounds than this, but he had to get this dead weight off him. Christ, he was heavy. Maybe he'd just rest for a minute.

His ears were still ringing from the gunshots but after a time he became aware of a soft mewling sound coming from somewhere in the room. It sounded like a puppy missing its mother. It must be the woman. What had they done to her? Got to move. In nothing short of a herculean effort, he managed to push the great lump mostly off his body, then squirmed the rest of himself out from underneath. In the process, he rolled in what was now a large puddle of blood so that, from one source or another, the larger part of him was covered in it. He tried to stand but his legs wouldn't work, so he crawled slowly toward the table. As he neared it, the old man in the chair raised his head.

"Ciao vecchio" Jim said "Sono Jim, James... Giacomo".

"Giuseppe" the man said, his breathing shallow and rasping, then in very good English "and what's this 'vecchio' bullshit, you're not so young yourself."

They shared a painful chuckle.

"See to the signora, yes?" Giuseppe said, and Jim pulled himself up on the table.

Francesca's arms were still tethered, but she had pulled her legs right up to her chest. She just lay there whimpering softly. The right side of her face was puffy, and blood from her nose and mouth was drying on her olive skin. Bob's knife was still on the table beside her. Jim used it to cut her free. It was razor sharp. She slowly curled her arms around herself and was now in a full foetal position. He did the best he could to pull the tattered dress across her body.

"Signora? Signora?" Jim said softly. No response. "You're safe now, those men are all dead, no harm can come to you now." She stirred slightly. "I'm here for you, signora. Sono qui, you're safe. You're safe now."

She stopped the little sounds she had been making and opened her eyes. Then a look of panic. "Giuseppe?"

"He's still with us."

She sat up and seeing all the blood on Jim "You're hurt too!"

"I'll be ok" Jim said although he was becoming less and less sure about that; he was feeling very very ragged. He looked Francesca in the eyes and said

"Did he...?" He made some silly gesture that he hadn't planned.

"No, he did not, thanks to you. Your timing was perfect. Thank you so much."

Without intending to, Jim slid down the side of the table and slumped on the floor. Francesca leapt back to life. She jumped off the table with seemingly no thought to her attire, going first to Giuseppe and crouching down, her hands on his knees.

"Oh, caro, look at you, my poor dear man. Please be ok. Ti voglio bene. I love you so much."

"Perdonami signora, I let you down, I'm so sorry. Mi dispiace, mi dispiace."

"No, no, no... What can I do... call the police? And an ambulance. Yes." She turned to go.

"Not yet" Giuseppe said firmly, to Jim's surprise. Then after a pause "A grappa would be good."

"Si certo" she said and went towards the bar.

"Make that two, please" Jim called after her. Right then, that was just about exactly what he felt like, and...

"Don't suppose you smoke?" he asked. In his excitement Jim had left his cigarettes at home. Unlike him.

Giuseppe reached into his jacket and pulled out a slightly crumpled and sticky-with-blood packet of Marlborough. Not one of Jim's favourite brands, but any port in a storm...

So it was that these two aging men sat, bleeding, one on the floor and one on a dining chair, smoking and drinking grappa together.

"I can't believe it, all four of them" Giuseppe said "Bravo, bravo, e grazie, grazie mille. I could have used you over the years! But listen, there's some things you need to know before the signora returns".

Francesca had gone to put some fresh clothes on, no doubt after a shower. She hadn't wanted to leave them but Giuseppe insisted. This was an interesting relationship. He was her subordinate it seemed, yet clearly had status in the house, and some degree of authority over her.

Giuseppe started with "Never trust the police. Not here, not anywhere. Not ever." Then he changed tack, telling Jim that the old man, Pepe, whom Giuseppe referred to as 'The Don', had been paranoid about security so when he built the house in the bay, he had installed many well-hidden hi-definition security cameras, with audio. There were four covering the approaches to the house, two on the jetty, four in the loggia, and several others throughout the house, including the main bedroom. They were all linked, uploaded automatically to the cloud, and accessible via two web addresses with separate passwords for a period of four weeks after recording. It meant if there were any doubt about what had happened here today - which seemed to be of concern to Giuseppe - there was a comprehensive record of it.

"La polizia do two things, they protect their own, and people they like or who pay them, and crucify the rest." Giuseppe added. This seemed a rather broad generalisation to Jim. "Here on this island, it depends who you get."

Apparently, Francesca's son Carlo was, among many things, very computer savvy, had been involved in the installation of the cameras, and knew all the details of the setup. Jim commented that his son Tom was similarly skilled, their business having always included high end 3D graphics, and complex post-production FX. Basic editing of footage of any sort was child's play for them.

Giuseppe was wheezing. It was obvious that he was fading, but he was hanging on. Jim liked him a lot. He was wondering how long he could last himself. He had pretty much stopped bleeding, apart from the stab wound - he could feel the blood trickling down his back - but he was now in severe pain and feeling very unwell.

"We will call for help, but we need to do this first, for both our families." He took out his mobile, dialled in a number, and waited. "Answerphone" Giuseppe said. There was a pause, then

"Carlo, Giuseppe. We've had some trouble. Assassini. A man called Jim saved my life today, and la signora's, and he will always be my brother. You must help him however you can, and his son Tom. Fanno parte della nostra famiglia si? Tom's phone is..." and he repeated the number as Jim told it to him. "Give him the codes for the cameras and anything else he needs. I say again, they are family. And get home as soon as you can, your mother needs you. Ti amo, mio figlio caro, I hope I see you again."

What a good old boy Jim thought, took another mouthful of the very smooth grappa and asked

"Shall I call the cops now?"

"Si" said Giuseppe.

"I don't suppose I could bludge another..." Jim asked.

"Si" said Giuseppe.

* * * *

Jim's 111 call went straight to Auckland Central and was then immediately transferred to the Waiheke station. The call went straight through to Stan, who was rostered on this particular Sunday. He quite liked these odd Sunday duties; they were usually fairly quiet and he could catch up on paperwork. His desk phone rang. He picked up.

"Hi Inspector, Briggs here, Central. This could all be bullshit, but we've had a 111 from your neck of the woods. This guy Jim... Carruthers reckons he walked in on a home invasion, possibly by this gang that's been in the news. Sounds a bit unlikely, but he reckons there's four dead and three injured - two men and a woman - the two guys seriously, and in need of urgent medical attention."

"What?" Stan was a bit stunned. Surely not, not on Waiheke, surely?

"How long does the Westpac chopper take to mobilise?"

"Matter of minutes - if it's not on another job." Stan replied.

"Right, well let's get an ambulance and some feet on the ground first and see if we need it. Oh, and he reckons the shooters are all down, so you shouldn't need to do a lot of tooling up, even if it's true."

"Ok, good. I have officers in the field. Leave it with me." Stan said

"This is the address he gave us." Briggs reeled it off. "Report back to us when you know more. Good luck."

"Will do. Thanks mate." Cowes Bay Road, Stan pondered. Certainly out of the way, and plenty of money down there, but surely that gang wouldn't... probably some mad, drugged up locals. Right, who's on the road today? He checked the roster. Andy and Tim on traffic.... Pete and Dave down Kennedy Point.... Phil and Sally general patrol.

Right, call them, then the ambulance. Should he call an ambulance now, or wait until Sally and Phil assess the situation? No, call St. John first, then Phil and Sally. Whew! Not your average Sunday!

* * * *

"We should hit the road honey" Phil said, standing and pulling up his underwear and pants.

"Have you thought about when you might talk to Helen" Sally asked tentatively.

"Ah, no not yet, but I will, I will." Phil would consider leaving his wife, particularly for Sally. The whole thing with Helen had become pretty stodgy, but the thought of the mechanics of getting out of the relationship, the property, possessions, money... It was too tiring and another matter he'd prefer not to dwell on, although he knew he'd have to do something. It was that, or dumping Sally, which he badly didn't want to do, and which would almost certainly make life at work exceedingly difficult.

Just then the radio in the car crackled into life. "Hi guys, Stan here, where are you right now...?"

"Bugger" Phil said, heading back to the car and tucking in his shirt, as if Stan might notice and suspect something.

"Sorry boss, just away from the car briefly. We're on the road to Orapiu".

"That's good, you're close. Listen, there's been a 111 call about what sounds like a gun fight down off Cowes Bay Road, some dead and injured apparently. Could be someone playing silly buggers, but get down there and check it out will you, and report straight back. Two ambulances are on their way."

"Jesus. Sure Stan, right away."

"And take care. This guy reckons there's no danger now but take the Glocks in with you just in case."

"Will do."

New Zealand police cars now had lockboxes with two Glock 17 handguns and a Bushmaster semi-automatic military grade rifle in them.

"It's Cowes Bay Road, number...."

* * * *

While waiting for help to arrive, Jim called his wife Sue. She was in a meeting. Then his son Tom. He'd always loved being a parent and couldn't believe he was the father of a nearly thirty-year-old man. A man he'd seen grow from a tiny baby to a man, a big strong man, a man he admired and respected, and actually liked. A lot. They shared similar values, political views, tastes, and sense of humour. They could talk and laugh for hours. More than that though, he loved his son with all his heart.

"Hiya boy."

"Hey pops. Wassup?"

"I... um... ah... got into a bit of a scrap..."

"Not again. You're a bit old for all that, aren't you?"

"Whaddaya mean, it's years since – "

"You alright? You sound a bit wheezy."

"I'm not so good. Been shot and – "

"What?!! Jesus dad, shot?!! You alright? How bad is it?"

"Quite bad. But listen. There's a guy called Carlo who's going to ring you. His dad Giuseppe's here with me. He's badly hurt as well."

"Christ! What happened. Where are you, I'll be right there."

"No no, I'm on the Island. Help's on the way. Can't get hold of your mum."

"I'll tell her. Oh mate...."

"Yeah, it's a bugger... I'm, uh, running out of puff. If I don't make it, I love you son."

"You too dad. Heaps 'n heaps. Hang in there. Don't die. Please don't die."

Tom hung up. What the fuck?!!

* * * *

The big Skoda slowly approached the house, its tyres crunching on the pebble drive like a hearse in a cemetery. They heard it inside the house and as the car neared the loggia, Francesca appeared and came down the steps. They had clipped the Glocks to their belts. Phil's was holstered, Sally's was on her lap. When they saw Francesca, Phil said

"Shit, she looks a bit knocked around. Maybe something has gone down here".

Francesca had washed off most of the blood but her nose continued to run slowly and the whole side of her face had swollen. The bruising, particularly around her cheekbone was starting to colour up, blue and green.

"Put the gun away baby" Phil said, "she's upset enough already", as they parked behind Jim's Subaru and got out. Tears welled up in Francesca's eyes as she approached them.

"Thank God you're here, is the ambulance far?"

"On its way, madam." Sally said.

They followed her up the steps. Both had their hands on the gun on their belts. It was instinctive, it didn't look like they were going to need them.

It was like an abattoir, no, a splatter movie. They just about tripped over Kyle, on his back, his face entirely gone and what was left of his head looking like a mashed-up tamarillo. Sally retched but kept it down. Phil just managed to as well. There was no movement in the room, and it was deathly quiet.

Phil's eyes adjusted to the lower light in the loggia. He looked around. Another body a bit away to his left, a young Māori boy, with his guts... a bit further into the space a big guy face down in a huge pool of blood, then further back two older guys he realised were alive, one of them looking straight at him. They were both seated, one in a chair, the other a few feet away on the floor leaning against the end of a couch. Both were covered in blood, and smoking cigarettes and drinking, which struck Phil as bizarre. And was that another corpse against the wall behind them, with long hair and his chest blown open? He'd never seen shotgun wounds before. Nasty.

Christ almighty what a mess! He was standing between the two women, the Italian on his left, and Sally to his right.

"Sal, go and call this in, tell Stan it's all as reported, and tell him there's a big lawn out front if the rescue chopper's available."

Sally scurried outside, only too pleased to get away from the horrific scene. Apart from one very nasty car crash, she'd not seen anything like this in her short career, but then most cops never saw anything vaguely like this in all their years of service.

Phil was pretty shocked. He was trying hard to keep calm and be professional. He remembered the woman to his left.

"Are you ok madam?"

She didn't answer him as she moved back towards the two wounded men. Phil followed her. They didn't look good. As he neared them Jim said

"G'day mate, how you doin'?" with a silly little laugh. What a stupid thing to say he thought. Oh well, he told himself, I've been shot three times and stabbed as well, maybe I'll be forgiven. What for? Well, for sounding like a dick and... some other stuff he didn't like thinking about.

Phil crouched down. "More to the point" he said "how are you guys doing? Is it as bad as it looks? Tell me."

"He might live" Giuseppe rasped out. "Me? Mi, non credo..."

Phil had severe doubts about either of them making it. The wounds he could see looked serious, particularly the Italian's. He could try some first aid, but where would he start, and the ambulances shouldn't be too far away. He said

"Are either of you still bleeding much?" Both shook their heads.

"Good. Well, I guess we just have to sit and wait." Phil straightened up and moved to the couch.

* * * *

Bill Smales was enjoying his Sunday afternoon, sitting under a tree in his back garden, reading a novel. He loved fiction, particularly thrillers, Stieg Larsson sort of stuff.

It was a modest villa in a quiet Mt. Eden street that he and Edie had owned for nearly thirty years. It had seemed like a lot of money at the time, but what it was worth now was eye-watering. Since the kids had all left home it was much more than they needed, but they weren't interested in moving, they loved it here.

Ana Harris and his meeting with her had popped into his head and he was deep in thought. How can people take lives so casually, and rape, that was completely beyond his comprehension. Then his mobile had rung

"...you said to stay in close touch sir, so I thought I should call. Sorry if I - "

"Stan, Stan, you did the right thing." Superintendent Smales insisted.

"These might not be our guys of course, but if they are then our prayers have been answered. Tell me again what you know so far."

Stan ran through it again, trying not to show how hyped he was. If this was the gang, the kudos that would attach to the station - and to him - would be amazing. And great for Phil and Sally to be the first on the scene.

"Stan?"

"Oh sorry, sir."

"Ring me again when you know more detail..."

"Of course, sir."

"Wait. I've got a feeling about this... listen, book me some accommodation for tonight. I'm coming over."

* * * *

Sally came back in, still looking very pale, and said to the two wounded men

"Hi, I'm Sally, are you guys alright?" Giuseppe grunted, and Jim, trying to be his normal, in-control self

"Hi Sally, pleased to meet you. I'm Jim and this is my new friend Giuseppe." Careful James, don't get silly again.

"Oh yeah" Phil said from the couch "I'm Phil. Sergeant Phil Smith."

"And I'm Francesca."

Francesca was sitting on a chair behind Giuseppe, her arms around him and her head resting on his shoulder. It reminded Jim of a Renaissance painting he'd seen on some arts programme.

Sally joined Phil on the couch. They all just sat, staring ahead of them. They might have been watching TV.

"God this is awful" Sally said quietly to Phil.

They sat in silence. After a while Phil, who had been more affected by this experience than he realised, thought ...what should I be doing? I need to do something; this waiting is killing me. He tried to remember the training. Check for ID's, yes! But should he touch anything in the crime scene before SOCO go over it. Can't recall. Bugger. No, better not. How long does it take to get here from bloody Oneroa?!

He looked around him. The faceless man, the Māori boy, the skinny guy with the long hair, and the big guy in all the blood. Was this really the gang all the fuss was about? The Wild Bunch? Odd bunch more likely. He also made a mental note of their hardware, a shotgun, a rifle, a semi-auto handgun, a knife on the table and another on the floor by the fat guy. The fat guy had died from the neck wound for sure. Anyone would have, he'd been seriously sliced and diced.

He looked past them, to the pool, the lawn, the palms, the beach, what a spot. There was a simple bench seat on the edge of the lawn where it met the sand. Phil could see himself sitting there at the end of the day, drinking something nice with Sal... his Sally. Yes, he decided in that moment, yes, she was the one. He'd tell Helen.

Phil's eyes refocussed inside. The fat guy. There was something about him. Did Phil know him? Maybe he'd have a closer look. He got up and crossed the room to the lifeless body, face flat on the floor. He used his foot to roll the guy's head to one side. He hadn't seen Shane for many years, nor his weight gain and hair loss in that time, but it was him, without a shadow of a doubt.

"Jesus Christ, it's Shane!" he yelled. Startled, Sally asked

"Who's Shane?"

"My brother!"

Phil stood transfixed by the sight of his bloodied, beloved sibling with whom he'd suffered so much, about whom he'd worried so much, tried so hard to understand and care for. Images of them as kids cascaded through his mind - being hit, playing, walking to school, fighting in the playground, going to the movies, running through the paddocks of long grass behind their house down to the creek to catch eels. Good times and bad, and here he was, his little brother, his neck shredded, his always-strange eyes open wide in shock and disbelief.

Phil knelt in his brother's blood and stroked his cheek. "Shaney, Shaney, oh mate..." he said softly, as the tears streamed down his face. Sally's hand was on Phil's shoulder. Francesca had got up too and was watching from a little farther back.

Jim had been watching this scene unfold. What a weird, weird day, and getting weirder by the minute. Brothers? It was another cliché but maybe this was all a crazy dream and he'd wake up hugely relieved, and fully resolved never to buy another *Gulf News*. Surprisingly, he had started to feel a bit better. How could that be? His shoulder seemed to have stopped bleeding, and he wasn't in nearly as much pain. Could he make it through this nightmare? He looked across to Giuseppe and recalled his warning about cops. How would this Phil react to his brother's death? And he, Jim, had killed him.

God, Giuseppe looked dreadful. His face was ghostly white, he was sweating profusely and his whole body was shaking. Poor bugger. Jim heard a calm, measured voice to his left. It was Phil, holding Ra's .22.

"Who did this?" Jim turned to see Phil, no longer crying, standing straight and tall, his eyes blazing, barely a metre away. Giuseppe raised his head and, looking Phil straight in the eyes, said

"I did, and I'm glad I did. He was an anim - " Giuseppe knew he wouldn't finish the sentence. Phil raised the rifle and shot him between the eyes, at pretty much point-blank range. Giuseppe's head flew back, and he and the chair toppled to the ground.

Sally's scream was eclipsed by Francesca's, whose long-drawn-out, feral howl was something Jim would never forget. She rushed toward the prone Giuseppe but was stopped short. In an almost exact repeat of Shane's blow, Phil hit her with a backhander. The difference was that Phil's hand held nearly a kilo of Glock steel. Jim heard bones cracking. Francesca dropped like a stone.

So much for thinking I might get through this, Jim thought to himself. This cop has crossed the Rubicon, there's no way he's going to let me live. Poor Giuseppe, and poor sweet Francesca with the beautiful voice, they didn't deserve this. It was starting to annoy Jim the way quotes kept infiltrating his thoughts. Now another one.

'I am in blood stepp'd in so far that, were I to wade no more, returning were as tedious as go o'er" or something like that. Stop it!

Sally had run to Phil's side, clutching his arm.

"Baby, baby, what are you doing?! She wailed.

"What has to be done."

Phil pushed her gently but firmly aside. This is who he was, he finally knew, who he had always been underneath, who he had always tried not to be. Ice cold, no fear, no doubts, no compassion, all his father's fury, primal and pure, but completely under control. He felt ten feet tall, exhilarated and invincible. He'd forgotten about the job, the gang, the ambulances and no doubt other cops on their way. This was all that mattered. Utu. Someone had to pay.

"It was you wasn't it" he said, looking at Jim.

Jim dug deep in himself, searching for some of Giuseppe's courage. What about that guy, taking the rap, trying to save his new-found friend. Jim found what he was looking for.

"Yes, it was me. He was a thug, a nasty prick, and he was about to rape this lovely woman you've probably killed. And this man you just murdered was worth ten of you, you piece of shit. You're supposed to be an officer of the law for Chrissake! You're worse than your lunatic brother."

Jim was hugely surprised at himself, and a wee bit proud. He was also surprised that Phil had let him finish. He waited for the bullet. He was remarkably calm. Would this be penance enough?

"Get up."

"What?" Jim said.

"Stand up" Phil said, dropping the .22. "I'm not going to shoot you. I'm going to kill you with my bare hands."

Sally was in a state of shock, deeply disturbed and confused. Nothing could have prepared her for this. She couldn't cope, didn't want to see any more. She turned from Phil, walked distractedly to the front of the loggia, and looked out to sea.

"Stand up!" Phil shouted.

Jim didn't know if he could, he'd been sitting for what felt like hours. He tried, and creakily stood up, as straight as he could. The slo-mo thing was happening again.

Phil immediately let fly with a hard jab followed by a right hook and a left cross. They were big punches, but Phil was no boxer. He was slow and he telegraphed every one of them. Jim saw them coming and dodged all three. He kicked Phil between the legs, hit him with a right uppercut as he bent with the pain, then full on the side of his face with a short, clubbing left hook. His trainer, Jason, told him often that this was one of his best and most effective shots. He was right.

Jim's punches didn't have their usual power but were still well-timed and solid. More damage to his poor old hands. Phil staggered backwards dazed, tripped, and landed heavily on his bum on the floor. Jim was kind of amazed. How had he managed that? He felt a thump on the right side of his chest, and stabbing pain. Christ he'd been shot! Again! He felt dizzy, lost his balance and fell to the floor.

It must have been the woman cop. Phil was still sitting, a bit out of it, on the floor. Sally fired again, missing him. Phil was getting to his feet and pulling his Glock from its holster. Jim suddenly felt very weak. This new wound was bleeding profusely and hurting like hell. He was finding it hard to breathe, had she hit his lung? There wasn't much else in that vicinity as far as he knew. Get away from the bullets. He crawled behind the couch. Pointless. Just delaying the inevitable, pure survival instinct.

Then his hand landed on something hard and cold. Bob's revolver, safety off and ready to go, with only the bullet in Giuseppe's belly and the one that went through Jim's side missing from the cylinder. Maybe it's not all over yet, Jim thought.

"Come out, you old cunt, you know it's over." Phil called, before firing three shots into the couch.

"I'm now armed and will return your fire" Jim said shakily and continued crawling. He was aiming for the far end of the huge couch.

"Oh yeah?" mocked Phil, firing another round into the couch. "Come out or I'll come and drag you out".

Jim had made it to the end of the couch. He rose up on one knee above the padded arm of the couch.

"Lower your weapons. Put the guns down."

Phil and Sally froze momentarily, then both swung their Glocks towards him. The three handguns fired almost as one. Phil's shot hit the wall just above Jim's head, Sally's round took a chunk out of his left ear, and Jim's went straight through Phil's heart. His legs buckled, his head flopped forward, and he folded up like a marionette onto the floor.

Sally screamed "Phil!" and in a reflex action holstered her gun as she ran to him.

What are you doing? Jim thought. I could just shoot you. He wouldn't have, but she wasn't to know that. His ear was burning and bleeding a lot. He wouldn't have thought ears had so many blood vessels in them. Another bloody quote flicked through his brain.

'...who would have thought the old man to have had so much blood in him.'

Did Sally think she had done for Jim? Did she think he wouldn't shoot a woman? No, she wasn't thinking anything at all, she was totally focussed on her man, her very dead man. She knelt beside Phil in total silence, looking at him. Then, as though he were not properly dressed without it, she put Phil's Glock back in its holster, straightened his collar and started sobbing, keening, as the blood bubbled from her beloved's breast.

Jim was draped over the arm of the couch, exhausted, bleeding, and losing consciousness. Sally was draped over Phil, her cheek resting on his. Both were lost in their respective reveries. Neither had even noticed the sirens getting closer and closer, louder and louder. Stopping.

THREE

"G'day Sharlene, how are ya doll?"

"I'm great babe, you good?"

"Yep."

Ana had made a point of getting alongside the Super's PA. They'd have lunch or coffee every couple of weeks or so and got on well. She was a good old stick from down country.

"What can I do for you today baby cheeks?"

"Any chance of a word with the boss?" Ana had woken up this bright summer morning determined to find out more about these bloody home invasions.

" 'fraid not."

"In a meeting?"

"Nope, out of town. On business."

"Oh really? Where Sharl?"

"Now you know I couldn't possibly tell you that."

"No, of course..." A long pause ensued.

Sharlene couldn't really see the harm, and she did like Ana.

"I'm thinking of taking a few days off. Going somewhere not too far away like... I dunno... Waiheke? I've heard it's very nice. You been there?"

Good old Sharlene. What was Bill doing on Waiheke? Not somewhere he'd usually go 'on business' surely. Bit of team building perhaps? Waving the flag? Or what?

"Yeah, it's really nice. You should do that. Lunch next week?"

"You betcha. By-e-e." They hung up.

Mmmm. Where to from here... Ana Googled the Waiheke Police Station number and dialled it. It went straight to Auckland Central.

"Hi, I was wondering if you could put me through to the Waiheke Station."

"I can do that. What's it to do with please?"

"Well, it's Superintendent Smales's wife here. He's over on Waiheke. He's left his cell phone at home and I need to talk to him."

"Sure Mrs. Smales, I'll put you through. Have a nice day."

This wasn't Ana's usual style. She didn't like impersonating people, it could come back to bite you, but needs must when the devil drives as they say. It didn't take long.

"Hello Mrs. Smales. Alice speaking." Shit. They were so efficient these cops. Transferred with caller details.

"Hi. I was wondering if I could talk to my husband, please." Was Smales even there? In case he was, Ana was poised to hang up should she be put through.

"Sorry, he's in a meeting."

He was there! Ana noticed that Alice was decidedly snuffly. Either she had a bad cold, or she was tearful.

"You alright Alice?" she ventured.

"No not really. Your husband will tell you I'm sure, but we've lost one of our boys." Alice broke down. Pulling herself together "Sorry. Is it urgent? I can interrupt them if... "

"No, no. Oh, that's awful. I'm so sorry. Look after yourself. I'll call back later."

Ana was very curious. That's why Bill was there, must be. Maybe this cop had had an accident of some sort, or maybe.... Worth checking out? I reckon, nothing much else on. Waiheke here I come.

* * * *

Superintendent William Smales and Inspector Stanley Williams were sitting at the table in Waiheke Police Station Meeting Room One. They had already begun writing stuff on the whiteboard. Right now, neither was talking.

They were both deep in thought, and very tired. The SOCO team had arrived on the island from Auckland around 5 pm and they'd worked with them throughout the night, finally getting a few hours kip about 4 am. It was now 9.05. Stan broke the silence.

"I know I've said it before, but I've never seen anything like it. It'll haunt me for years I know it will."

"Yeah." Bill Smales said. "I was in Dunedin when the Aramoana massacre went down. Just a rookie. It still wakes me up some nights, less as the years go by. You know, the special force boys must have pumped a dozen rounds into that guy? He just kept coming at them firing his rifle like a zombie, shot after shot after shot. It was only when they blew the gun out of hands that he stopped and fell over. Took four guys to hold him down, and then he broke the heavy-duty cable tie cuffs they managed to get on him. It was extraordinary how long he kept going."

Why had he told Stan all that? It was still so vivid. Gray killed thirteen innocent people that day. He pulled himself together. God, this gang had killed almost as many.

"Jesus" Stan said. A pause.

"Very sorry about the sergeant Stan, I know how tight-knit small teams can be."

A long pause.

"Any chance of coffee?"

Stan got on the intercom to Alice. "On its way. Oh, and your wife rang."

"What, here? That's odd." Why would she do that? Bill reached for his cell phone.

"Hi honey. Did you call me? No? No, no, someone must have got their wires crossed that's all. Bye." Very odd, and fishy to say the least.

Alice arrived with coffee. Smallish cups with milk, hot water and sugar on the side. They'd all got very sick, first of instant coffee, then plungers, and then having to go up the road for real coffees, which were always half cold when they arrived back. So, they'd all clubbed in to buy a moderately expensive espresso machine and grinder. The coffee wasn't half bad. They were very pleased with themselves. They'd only had it a fortnight or so and it would be several more weeks before nobody remembered to fill the machine up with water and it burnt out.

"Mmm. Not bad coffee."

"Good, eh?" Stan said, with some pride.

"By the way Stan, I might stay on this for a while. It's your case, I just wouldn't mind keeping an eye on things. You ok with that?"

"I certainly am sir." Stan was in fact hugely relieved. He was feeling more than a bit out of his depth.

No matter how much blood Bill had seen spilt, he never got used to it. Hated it. He didn't know why but whenever he saw a body he thought of his children. Grip up, he told himself.

"Ok back to business. Let's get the others in."

* * * *

Since his father's call at around two-fifteen the previous afternoon Tom Carruthers had waited nervously for news of his dad. Jim had said help was on its way so it shouldn't be too long before he heard something.

After more than two hours he started making calls, trying to find out what had happened. The police couldn't or wouldn't tell him anything. None of the Auckland hospitals could help, but they did take his number. He'd even called *Stuff* and *The Herald* to see if they knew anything. At 5.30 Auckland City Hospital rang him to say his father had been admitted some time earlier and was in surgery. They could say no more than that, except that they would call when he was out of theatre.

Tom had a difficult evening, expecting the hospital to ring any minute. Surely Jim hadn't been in theatre this long. Maybe he had. Should he ring... no, no news is good news. The hospital had been very good on the phone. He trusted them to do as they'd said. Again, there was no point in putting his mother through this as well.

Tom was on his own, he had been for some months now. He and his long-time partner Sam, Samantha, had decided to have a break. Not separate, just have some time apart. They both hoped it wasn't terminal, but Tom suspected it would be. At ten o'clock the phone rang. Yes, the hospital! No.

"Ciao Tom. Carlo."

Carlo, Carlo, who was...? Tom remembered. The son of the guy with his dad on the island.

"Hi Carlo. Good to hear from you. How's... Giuseppe, do you know?" Silence.

"He is dead." Tom didn't know how Carlo could be so sure.

"I'm so sorry if that's true.

"It's true. Your father?"

"In hospital. Surgery."

"I hope it goes well. He made quite an impression on Giuseppe. But we have work to do, you and I."

Carlo had quite a light voice. Flat, crisp, business-like, not a lot of inflection and just the hint of an Italian accent in his perfect English. A very 'English' English, as though he'd been through English public schools. Despite that, warmth too. An interesting voice; an interesting person Tom felt sure.

"I don't like talking on the telephone. When can we meet?"

At 3.10 am the phone rang again.

"Mr. Carruthers? Rick Jamieson here, Auckland City Hospital. Your father is out of surgery."

* * * *

"Let me start by saying that I'd like to try and keep this under wraps for a bit longer." Bill Smales told the meeting. "We don't have a lot of time, but I'd really like to have a better line on this before we go public. So, as we said last night, keep this to yourselves. Don't talk to anyone about it, particularly not the press. Ok. Let's go over what we know. Stan?"

"Righto. Six deceased, one our colleague Phil, sadly. Two injured and fighting for their lives - the man who rang it in, James Carruthers, and the woman who owns the property, Francesca Giordano.

"Carruthers suffered five gunshot wounds and a stabbing. How he's still alive nobody knows, and he's sixty-five for God's sake. They operated on him half the night and he's now 'stable' apparently. The family's been advised. Hopefully he stays stable and we'll be able to talk to him before too long. The woman has a major head injury and is in a coma. The doctors rate her chances lower than his. Only time will tell."

Stan continued.

"The problem is we don't know anything about the relationships between these people, who shot who, in which order etcetera. The Super and I have worked through several possible scenarios but none of them makes total sense. We won't know for sure until we hear back from forensics, but it looks very likely that some of these guys are the gang that's been doing all the home invasions lately."

Bill picked up the story.

"This Carruthers guy looks like a bit of a hero. Apart from the fat guy and the Italian, three of them died from shotgun wounds. Carruthers was the only one without a shotgun wound so we think that he was the one wielding it. Also, it looks like he himself was shot with just about every other gun in the place. Again, ballistics will fill in at least some of the gaps.

"If this was a home invasion what was Carruthers doing there? We're assuming he was a friend of the family and fought like a demon to protect them. He was unconscious and in a bad way when you and Andy got there Tim, so we think it most likely that one of the others, dying, shot Sergeant Smith, Phil, as a last hurrah. If so, why didn't he shoot Sally? Had he killed Phil with his last breath? These are just some of the questions we don't have answers for yet. We simply don't know.

"Apart from Carruthers, the only other witness is Constable Sally Reynolds. How's she doing Stan?"

Sergeant Tim Adams interrupted.

"Excuse me sir. I've just come from seeing her. She's still pretty groggy. The doctor arrived just as I was leaving."

"Poor girl she's been through a lot" Stan said.

"Well let's hope she can talk to us soon, although that'll be limited too" Smales said, "remember she and Sergeant Smith arrived after most of the action had already happened.

"I suppose you all knew about her relationship with Sergeant Smith?" Constable Andy Tyler said "I would never have guessed in a million years."

"I actually suspected as much, but they were pretty discreet about it." Stan said.

"It's not very relevant, although it does explain the level of her distress." Bill added.

"Oh, something else. Am I right in thinking Phil has a brother in the force? Auckland Central, I think. He needs to be told. Will you make sure that happens Stan?"

"Yes of course sir."

"Where was I... yes, of the deceased, we knew about Robert Collins, and we've Identified a Kyle Doherty. He had bank cards and stuff on him. He's done time too. We don't have a line on either the man who died from throat wounds, or the Māori boy. Neither had any ID on them although, funnily enough, the boy had a dog-eared photo in his pocket, of him when he was younger with an older woman, I assume might be his mother. Sad, really.... but it might help us ID him.

"Tim and Andy, I'll get you to go back over what you saw when you arrived on the scene."

Bill Smales added, as if thinking aloud

"Let's just hope Carruthers pulls through. He's the only one who really knows what happened."

* * * *

Less than an hour after her phone calls, Ana was on a ferry. The ten o'clock via Devonport. She was just passing Motutapu Island when her phone rang. It was the *Stuff* office.

"Hi Ana." Harry, the office manager, said. He wasn't super bright and he annoyed the hell out of her sometimes, but he was sweet, very organised, and good to her.

"I've been checking the phone logs from yesterday, and there's a call from a guy asking if we knew anything about a shooting on Waiheke."

"Really?" Yes! I knew it! Ana thought to herself.

"Yeah, you're pretty much our go-to crime gal, so I thought I'd give you first suck at it. Might be nothing but... any chance you could get over there?"

"Mate, I'm half-way there. Thanks a lot Harry. I owe you one."

Ana could've kicked herself. Sloppy. She rang back.

"Harry? Did he leave a number?"

"Yeah, he did I think. It's... hold on... give me a minute..."

Ana couldn't believe her good fortune.

* * * *

At Stan's instruction, Tim and Andy had travelled with the ambulances to Cowes Bay Road. For the ambo guys' safety, Andy and Tim had preceded them into the house, Glocks drawn, instructing them to wait in their vehicles.

The scene had shocked them to the core. There were bodies everywhere, mangled and disfigured, and so much blood. The only person who seemed to be alive was Sal, lying on the floor with Phil, their dead mate Phil. They called the ambulance officers in. When they tried to lift her off him, Sally turned on them, snarling like a wild cat in a trap, and going for her Glock.

They had restrained her and taken her gun, but it wasn't until the sedative one of the paramedics injected her with started to take effect that she stopped fighting them. It was hard work.

The whole night was hard work. Messy, ugly, hard work.

* * * *

It was 5.45 on Sunday afternoon when the doorbell rang at the Carruthers apartment in downtown Auckland. Sue opened the door. It was a uniformed police officer.

"Mrs. Carruthers?"

"Yes" Sue answered.

"Susan Carruthers?

"Yes, what's this about please?"

"I'm Constable Johns from Auckland Central Police. I'm sorry to tell you that your husband Jim Carruthers has been injured and is in Auckland City Hospital.

"In hospital? My God! Is he alright? What happened? Is it serious?"

"It is pretty serious apparently, yes."

"Oh dear. I'd better get down there." Sue turned away from the door.

"He's in surgery at the moment Mrs. Carruthers. Of course, go to the hospital by all means, but it could be a while. We've given the hospital your number and they'll call you with any developments if you'd prefer to wait at home here. I'm very sorry to be the bearer of bad news. We've given Victim Support your number and they'll be in touch soon to see if you need anything. Is there anything I can do for you, right now? Any one we can contact to be with you?"

"No, no, thank you for letting me know." Sue was shocked and a bit stunned. Tom had rung her some time before to tell her that Jim had been hurt on the island. He didn't say how, or that it was serious, just that Jim had called and asked him to pass the message on to his mum.

Sue had tried ringing Jim but there was no answer. She was worried. What on earth could have happened? Jim had a bit of a history of mishaps with power tools of one sort or another, perhaps that was it. Or had he fallen off a ladder? He'd been talking about replacing some guttering.

She must ring Tom back to see if he knew any more.

* * * *

They were sitting in a tiny Italian café in the suburbs, one Tom didn't know existed. It was 10 a.m, exactly twelve hours since Carlo had called him. Carlo had ordered a walnut and honey cornetto pastry and a cappuccino. Jim followed suit. Both were excellent. The waiters were very attentive and deferential, and he suspected this was breakfast for Carlo.

They hadn't spoken a great deal yet. It was as if the food and coffee should be honoured in their own right, in silence. Carlo wiped his mouth with the linen napkin and sat back on his chair. They were the only patrons in the café. Perhaps that was why Carlo had chosen this place. It was quiet, and very Italian.

"I will tell you why we are here. Giuseppe, whom I love, told me your father had saved his life, and my mother's, that your father and you were therefore family, and I should do all in my power to help and protect you. That is what I will do, and that is why we are here."

Tom was tempted to ask what he might need help with, and what he or his father might need protecting from, but he refrained.

"That's... great, thank you" he finally said.

Carlo was so cool and... suave and... cultured? He was very Latin. Olive skin, thick glossy black hair, quite long, and an angular face with large brown eyes. Tom imagined women would find him very attractive. He was dressed casually but Tom thought his clothes and shoes looked expensive. He was certainly very stylish. On his way into the café, he'd noticed a gorgeous, gleaming red Ferrari, a Testarossa from about 1990 he thought, parked outside. It had to be Carlo's.

"It appears your father has survived his injuries, and he will need our help. He has killed a police officer, quite justifiably, but they will not let that go unpunished."

What! This is too silly for words, Tom thought. His father, killing a cop? As if reading his thoughts Carlo said

"Yes. He also killed all the members of the gang that has been raping and pillaging for the last several months. Quite a man your father. My mother is in a coma and may not survive. If she does it will be thanks to your father. Either way you are my brother. You will soon discover how I know all this."

Tom could think of absolutely nothing to say.

"First, I will tell you a little about my family. We are 'Ndrangheta from Calabria in Southern Italy."

"But that's... mafia, isn't it?" Tom blurted out.

"That is a term people sometimes use. We never do." Carlo replied.

Tom could not believe his ears. At the same time, he didn't doubt it for a moment.

"Three generations ago we were dirt poor, barely surviving. Now we are very wealthy, with business interests around the world. I studied at the LSE so I could manage these for my father. It came at the price of blood, as most wealth does one way or another and, one way or another, it always needs to be defended with blood. Much of our success has been thanks to my father, the Don, and his faithful lieutenant and consigliere Giuseppe, who spilt much blood for us over the years. I do so wish he had been allowed to grow old and die in his sleep. Alas, it was not to be."

Tom was simply speechless. The timbre of Carlo's voice hadn't changed, but Tom was sure that his dark, almond-shaped eyes glistened with moisture for a moment, then he said

"That is enough for today. Your father definitely, and you possibly, are in danger, believe me. I will be with you on your journey. Here..." he passed Tom a folded piece of paper.

"Go to this website. Download the footage. Tell no-one of its existence. You will see exactly what happened yesterday and what your father achieved. He is a hero, a true and brave foot-soldier, another Giuseppe. I am honoured to be of service to him. Call me any time of the day or night if you need to. A presto. Ciao"

He got up and walked out. Tom sat, dazed and disbelieving. Could this be real? He'd read somewhere that Italian mafia were active in Australia, but here in Auckland? He watched the Ferrari pull away from the curb, sedately but that exhaust note, wow. He was about to turn back when he noticed a second car pull out behind Carlo. He'd been focussed on the Ferrari on the way in, he hadn't seen this late model, black, five series BMW with two, large, swarthy men in it.

A waiter approached his table.

"You want anything else for you sir?" Tom had noticed Carlo hadn't stopped to pay on the way out.

"The bill?"

The waiter smiled gently.

"No bill. Famiglia."

* * * *

Ana got the bus from the ferry up to Oneroa and went straight to the offices of the *Gulf News*. She'd known the current editor for some years. Her friend was sitting behind a desk in the plain open-plan office.

"G'day gorgeous. How's it hangin'?" she said.

"Anahera Harris, kia ora! Good to see you girl, to what do we owe the honour?" He wasn't a bad bloke, Mike.

"Oh, just sniffin' around. No particular reason."

"Come on, you know I know you better than that. Spit it out!" Mike laughed.

"Ok. Did you get any reports about anything unusual, like gunfire, on the island on Sunday? Yesterday?"

"Funny you should ask, coupla people from the bottom end rang –"

"What on earth is 'the bottom end'?" Ana laughed.

"Of the island, the... southern... eastern coast I guess... talking about quite a lot of shots being fired. There's always someone shooting rabbits or feral cats or something, but they said it was unusual for some reason. I sent one of our guys down there, but he didn't discover much. There was police tape across a driveway on the main road. There wasn't much we could do. I'll tell you what though, there were a hell of a lot of sirens across the middle of the afternoon. That's all."

That's all? Jesus, that should've been a big red flag for a journalist, surely?

"Does that help Ana?"

"Yeah, It might. It very well might. Thanks Mike."

* * * *

After his bizarre meeting with Carlo, Tom sat down at his computer somewhat hesitantly. Did Carlo really have bodyguards following him around? Part of him was still very sceptical, but he followed the prompts on the sheet of paper Carlo had given him. It was complex and very secure, but Tom was soon faced with layer upon layer of video, obviously from multiple cameras.

This was not silly tech. He quickly saw how it worked, and 'cutting' between cameras to see in linear and real time what had happened was quite easy. They were all in sync. and still recording of course. So many cameras.

He went back to the previous day. Clearly there was nothing much happening on most of them, but it was easy to 'mute' these and line up those on the front of the building, and those inside the big verandah. Amazing place, even from these specific and individually limited angles.

Tom slowly pieced it together, the gang arriving, Giuseppe's shooting, the imminent rape of the Italian woman, his dad's arrival, the confrontation with the guy guarding the front, then Jim's clear decision to intervene whatever the cost. It was so physical, visceral and gritty. He hadn't realised how adept a fighter his father was. And his facility with guns, where did that come from? Between them, the cameras covered every square centimetre of the space. This was extraordinary, exciting and... truly awful.

It was jumbled at this stage, but he knew he could edit this up and it would be the most amazing visual record of the day. And there was audio. It was cacophonous at the moment, with all the different sound sources, but Tom knew that once he'd chosen the shots he wanted, and tweaked the sound levels, it would be very coherent, and already the low-level background operatic music in the earlier shots was giving it an even more strange, dramatic and surreal quality. What about his dad? Carlo was right, he was a fucking hero!

It was also seriously disturbing. The violence and carnage was hard to believe, and hard to watch. And the blood! Then the Māori boy, how sad was that. Jim had taken another bullet trying to save him. He really was a good man, and then those two old boys, both quite possibly dying, sitting, smoking and drinking together. An amazing image. He saw and heard them calling their respective sons, Jim calling the police. Fathers and sons. What a bond that was. Brothers too. The ties that bind.

And at the end, shot to pieces, still standing up to this bully cop, smacking him down on his arse. Tom went through and through the footage, over and over some of it. He would start editing it tomorrow. It was two in the morning.

His eyes filled with tears. He did so hope his father made it.

* * * *

'Always step forward as you throw a punch and swivel your body weight around behind it as you do. Bang. Wow, that's good Jim. Heavy.' *I don't like shooting when I can't see the target!* This grappa really is very good. Felsina, a good vineyard, he'd had some of their wines. Expensive. 'Now the right. Good, good! Now bob and step to the right.' *There could be women, children!* You are not forgiven. I don't suppose I could bludge another... Marlborough, oh well, beggars can't be choosers. *It's a trap!* 'And now the short, left hook. That's your best punch.' What hurt so much? What was wrong with his breathing? *Fall back! We're dropping like flies!* And what's stuck up his nose? 'Shit that's good for an old fella. Hard!' What was hurting so much? *A teenage boy.* You will never be forgiven. 'Move, move, weave, that's it, good. Now the right.' *They're coming for you Jim.* 'Tell you what, I'm glad it's the pad and not my moosh!' *Blood. There will be blood.* What the fuck was going on? 'Good on you bro. Take a break, eh?' *Thicker than water.* Where was he, and what was that fucking noise? Bang. His eyes opened.

"Mr. Carruthers, you're awake! How good is that?! I was just passing and I thought is that Mr. Carruthers actually moving around?! And it was! You've done amazingly well, you're the talk of the hospital! How are you feeling?"

Jim just groaned. He didn't know which was more painful, his body or this incessant, piercingly chirpy voice. Who was it? Would it never stop?

"Now let me show you this. I'm sure you're in a lot of pain. Here take this in your hand." He looked up at the source of this assaulting din. This girl was very pretty. He reached up...

"No silly, this" and she put this switch thing in his hand. "It's morphine. When the pain gets really bad just pump it, as often as you need, it'll help. I'll see if I can find a doctor. Use this buzzer if you need help while I'm gone."

Thank God, the voice had finally stopped.

Jim wasn't sure if the pain was 'really bad' or not. Could it get worse than this? He decided not to wait to find out and gave the gizmo a few pumps. W-o-o-o-o, yes, that'll do me! He wondered if they'd let him take one of these home, then promptly drifted back into the vale of Lethe.

* * * *

Bill and Stan had been in the meeting room since eight o'clock and it was now getting on for midday. Tim and Andy had gone back to work. The whiteboard was covered in handwriting, rough diagrams, names, and a lot of question marks.

"We're no further ahead. This is so bloody frustrating. When can we talk to Sally... and Carruthers I wonder?"

They knew Jim had regained consciousness briefly, but the doctors said it could be some time before he was able to be questioned. Sally had lapsed back into hysterical distress earlier in the morning and had to be sedated again. She was in one of the staff overnight rooms at the other end of the building. The new probationary constable was on watch with her. Alice called over the intercom.

"Superintendent? Sorry to interrupt, but there's an Anahera Harris at reception. She's hoping to talk to you."

Bloody Ana? How had she got onto this so fast? Should he see her? Probably.

"Thanks Alice, give us a couple of minutes then send her in." Then to Stan "Turn the whiteboard around would you, don't want her seeing that."

The receptionist Alice was more in control of herself than she had been on the phone but was red-eyed and still a bit clogged up. Ana had already decided not to pursue her 'we've lost one of our boys' comment.

"This Ana is a reporter. The bane of my life. No that's not fair, she's bloody good at her job and she's very handy sometimes." Bill told Stan.

How did she find out he was on Waiheke? She hadn't been following him surely? Ah yes, of course. The door opened, and there she was.

"Come in Ana" Bill said cordially "or is it Mrs. Smales?"

Ana was halfway into the room. She froze, like a deer in headlights.

"Actually, I'm quite sure we could find a way of making that fit a serious offence category. Stan, this is Anahera Harris, reporter extraordinaire. Ana, Inspector Stan Williams. Come and sit down."

"Morning Superintendent, pleased to meet you Inspector. Look I'm very sorry about that, it's not something I do, I hadn't planned it, it just popped out of my – "

"Forget it. It's good to see you, as always. But what are you doing here?" He asked disingenuously. Ana collected her thoughts.

"The local rag told me there'd been some sort of disturbance down the bottom end yesterday." Ana liked that expression and liked that she could show it off. "So, I thought I'd chase it up, just in case it was... y'know, important. That's all..." It was more-or-less true.

Of course, that was not all. She'd spoken to Tom Carruthers on the phone and already knew more than that. She had only called in to the Police Station to see if she could glean anything else, before getting the one o'clock ferry home, to meet Tom, and to write the breaking news story that would be on-line before the day was out.

How was Bill going to handle this? He suspected she knew more that she was letting on, but it couldn't be a whole lot more. He decided to lie.

"Ana. First of all, I'm over here because Stan has some interesting plans he wanted to discuss with me, and I took the opportunity to have a day away from the office. Second, yes there was an incident here yesterday, and I shouldn't be telling you this, it's a bit... sensitive. A quite nasty domestic involving some very high-profile people."

Bill did the funny thing with his eyes that he always did when he was lying, and that Ana always recognised. She would have known it was bullshit anyway, but it amused her.

"For the sake of the family we haven't made an announcement about it yet, and I'm asking you to hold off writing anything about it for a day or so. No teasers, no speculation. Will you do that for me?"

Bill had never asked anything like this of her before. Yes, this is big. This could also be the end of her cosy relationship with the Superintendent. What could she say?

"Of course, Superintendent. I'll write nothing about a high-profile domestic incident on Waiheke."

Silence. It was the way she said it. She knows more than she's letting on. Bugger.

"Very well. Thank you, Anahera. Let's leave it there, shall we?" Bill said, coolly.

* * * *

"Mr. Carruthers? Staff Nurse Emma Blunt from Auckland hospital here. Just calling to let you know your father's regained consciousness. I've rung Mrs. Susan Carruthers too. He's asleep right now but he was alert and lucid. It might well be possible to visit later today."

Thank God.

* * * *

Tom wasn't at all sure about talking to this reporter woman. He had said very little to her on the phone, just confirming that he had enquired if *Stuff* knew anything about a possible shooting on Waiheke and if they had any information as to his father's whereabouts. He'd only agreed to meet with her to see if she knew any more about the case than he did. She was also charming and persuasive on the phone. He would decide how much more to tell her when they met. He'd also checked her out on-line. She seemed to be a reputable and well-regarded professional. Tom's major concern was that his dad had killed a cop. The security footage had confirmed it. Carlo's view that he would have to be punished for that, however justified it might have been, played on his mind too.

The coffee here was mediocre at best. He was reminded of the espresso at Quattro Leoni where he had met Carlo earlier. How good it was, and how strange that meeting was. A mafioso? Here in Auckland?

It was 1.40. He'd agreed to meet Ana at a café near the downtown ferry terminal. It wasn't far from the studio, and he loved being near the water, so he'd agreed. She wanted to meet with him as soon she got off the ferry.

"Tom?"

The voice came from behind him. He'd been watching the front door. Of course, the side entrance was a more direct route from the ferry terminal. It meant however that Tom had to twist around and look up to see her, against the light as it transpired. He had planned, without realising that he had, to see her coming, stand up, and greet her from his confident 6'2" height. In the event he immediately felt at a disadvantage, on the back foot. He even bumped the table as he stood up, sloshing coffee from the cup into the saucer. He felt like a schoolboy on a first date.

Why should it matter? Why was he so nervous and apprehensive meeting this Anahera Harris? It must be the whole situation, he thought, and the lack of sleep. Her first line disarmed him even further.

"Have you heard from your father? Is he alright?"

Tom tried to pull himself together.

"Sorry, you are Tom Carruthers?" They had told each other what they would be wearing.

"Yes. Anahera? Hi." They shook hands. "Can I get you anything?"

"No thanks, I'm good." They sat. A moment's silence.

"My dad survived surgery. Looks like he's going to make it. Thanks for asking."

Tom looked at her properly for the first time. She was lovely.

"That must be a huge relief. Thanks for meeting me by the way."

"What do you know so far Ana?"

He might as well get straight to the point, but he was surprised at how easily and quickly she had put him at ease, how comfortable he already felt in her company.

"Well not a whole lot really. There was definitely quite a bit of gunfire down the bottom end of Waiheke, it seems like your father was a victim of that, and I'm pretty sure a local cop died as well. That's about it, except all my instincts tell me that the gang that's been doing all these home invasions is involved. The Regional Superintendent's all over it. He's there today, so it's definitely no minor event. Do you have any idea why your dad was even there?"

"No." This was entirely true. He had no idea. Perhaps Jim knew these people and it was a social visit, although for some reason that felt unlikely to Tom.

"I should tell you Tom that I'm planning to break this story tonight, full of holes though it is. Everything about it feels big, and I want to be the first cab off the rank with it. Anything you can tell me would be most appreciated."

What would he say? How much would he tell her? He didn't know yet, he was still adjusting to being with this vibrant, magnetic person with beautiful and, he thought, honest eyes.

He felt he could trust her.

* * * *

Sergeant Kevin Smith was at his desk at Auckland Central. He'd been assigned to investigate a ram raid on a pharmacy the previous night and was looking through security camera footage of the incident. He was making notes of his observations when Inspector Davis's secretary poked her head in the door.

"Hey Kev, the boss wants to see you."

The two other guys Kevin shared the office with leapt in

"O-o-o-h Kevvy, whatcha done now?!" "The headmaster's office!'

"Wow, six of the best, is it?" and so on.

Kevin made his way to the Inspector's office, wondering what this could be about. He'd never been called into Inspector Davis's office before, not once in the five years he been at Auckland Central. What had he done, or not done?

"Come in Kevin, have a seat."

"Thank you, sir."

"Mate, I've got some bad news I'm afraid... There's no other way to say it. Your brother Phil..."

"What about him?" Alarm and fear grew in Kevin's chest.

"...he's dead. I'm very sorry Kevin."

"Dead?! How for Chrissake?"

"In the line of duty. He got caught up in a shooting on Waiheke. Don't know all the details yet, but...."

'Who did it?" Kevin almost shouted.

"Don't know yet. I'm very sorry Kev."

* * * *

More than feeling he could trust her, Tom also had a strong sense that Ana could be a valuable ally.

"Ok, I'll tell you what I know" he said. Ana just nodded.

"In fact, we might be able to help each other. I say that because my father could well be in a lot of trouble and I might need his story to be told accurately. Also, because in return, I can give you what you need to write the story of the year. The decade maybe." Even as he said it Tom thought it a bit hyperbolic. Oh well.

"Ok" was all Ana could manage. Where was this heading? Among everything else filling her thoughts, Ana registered that she found this guy quite interesting.

"I won't tell you everything I know until I've spoken with my father, and an... advisor of mine, but from the outset there's a proviso. I sign off everything you write, before you publish. Only in terms of the content, I don't want to cramp your style."

It was an attempt at humour. Ana had the good grace to smile, slightly.

"I'm not used to – "

"That's the deal. All I'm interested in is that you get the facts right." Tom added.

A pause. Ana quite liked this guy. A bit gauche, but no airs and graces, and yeah... ok.

"Fair enough. Deal" she said.

"Good. The cops have no way of knowing what happened yesterday, not yet anyway. Don't ask me how I know, but whatever took Jim down there, he walked in on a home invasion, and you're right, it was that gang that's been in the news."

"Jesus." Ana said, almost to herself. She was right! What else did this man know, and how? He'd said no-one, including him, had spoken to his father yet, so it didn't come from him. Most unlikely he had a mole inside police HQ but if it was true, it really was a scoop.

"I won't tell you how the cop died. That's another story. There's a connection I don't think the cops will have worked out yet. When my old man walked in, they were about to rape and murder the woman who owned the place, an Italian. They'd already shot her companion."

"Christ! And you're sure about this?" Ana asked.

"Absolutely. It's hard to believe but my dad took them on and killed all four of them. He was shot several times in the process."

For the second time today, Ana was lost for words, unusual though that was for her. This was barely credible and again, how could he know all this?

"Wow!" was all she could come up with.

"Well, here endeth the lesson for today. You sure you don't want anything to eat or drink?"

"No, I'm good thanks." She couldn't go to print with this, amazing though it would be to do so. She'd have to check it out somehow. She needed something, anything, to corroborate Tom's story.

"What hospital's your dad in?" she asked, as innocently as she could. Tom felt a huge sense of relief that he'd shared this with someone. He hoped he hadn't made a dreadful mistake.

"Auckland City."

He wondered how his dad was doing.

* * * *

Superintendent Smales was about leave the station, finally. He'd decided to go back to the city. There was nothing more to do except wait for the results from forensics, the coroner's initial report, the dental records and any DNA matches for the two unidentified bodies.

Bill was exhausted. He'd had no proper sleep for the better part of forty-eight hours. He'd had a shower at the motel but badly wanted to change his clothes.

No, he didn't want lunch thanks, he'd get something on the boat, and he wouldn't wait for Sally to come right; Stan could pass on anything she had to say. The only thing she could tell them was who had shot Sergeant Smith. It would obviously be one of the gang, and it didn't really matter too much which one. No, he'd rather be in the city to interview this Carruthers man as soon as he was well enough.

Bill was hugely frustrated and very worried. More than anything else, he wanted to have a press conference before Ana bloody Harris or some other journo got their hands on enough material to go to print. He didn't think Ana was there yet, but who would know. It always amazed him how few actual facts reporters needed to write sensationalistic articles.

Stan was about to run him down to the three o'clock ferry and they were in reception saying goodbye to Tim, Andy and Alice. Suddenly the doors into the corridor flew open and there was Sally, looking wild-eyed and shockingly dishevelled.

"Stan, oh Stan" she cried and flung herself into the startled Inspector's arms.

Perhaps I'd better not leave just yet, Bill Smales thought to himself.

* * * *

"Oh hi. This is Detective Sergeant Wallace, Auckland CID. Sorry to bother you but we have a small problem you might be able to help with. Just a procedural thing, nothing major."

The Staff Nurse said "Sure, if I can."

"You have a James Carruthers on your ward. I'm looking at the field report, and there's a discrepancy around the number of times Mr. Carruthers was shot. Was it three or four?"

"Not a problem. Hold the line and I'll check the notes. Give me a minute..."

"Sure, thanks." This was becoming a habit Ana thought. Much as she disliked cheap tricks like this they were working very well today.

"Let's see... four, five if you count the minor wound to the ear. And as you know there was a rather nasty knife wound to his back as well. He's very lucky to be alive."

Tom's story about his dad's injuries was right. Could she assume the rest of what he told her was also true? Ana decided she could. Now she had enough!

Bloodbath on Waiheke
Local Man a Hero.

'Six people died and two were seriously injured in a shocking incident on Waiheke Island yesterday afternoon, in what seems to have been a home invasion or burglary gone wrong. Sadly, one of those killed was a police officer who attended the crime scene.

It is almost certain that four of the others were the Wild Bunch gang which has been targeting remote, wealthy properties in recent months, leaving a trail of dead bodies in their wake.

It appears that a local man in his sixties, who happened to be at the location, engaged the gang in a gunfight. Despite being shot several times in the process, he managed to despatch all four members of the gang before collapsing himself. In a welcome development today, he is reported to be out of danger after lengthy surgery overnight and is recovering in hospital.

An elderly male resident of the property also died, and a woman at the scene suffered serious head injuries. It is understood that she too is in hospital, in an induced coma.

The exact circumstances surrounding the police officer's death are still to be ascertained. The New Zealand Police declined our request for comment, saying only that there will be an official announcement in due course. This story will be updated as more information comes to hand.'

Anahera Harris

She had rung Tom to get his email address and sent the copy to him for sign off, as agreed.

"Can't argue with any of that. Good work. Go for it." Tom had said.

* * * *

"....and the barman says to the pirate 'You've got a steering wheel down your pants.' The pirate says 'Aaaaargh, it's driving me nuts!' "

Jim laughed uproariously, causing every suture in his body to scream with pain. "O-o-o-h fuck!" he exclaimed and pumped the morphine drip furiously.

"Jim, Jim, take it easy darling" Sue said.

Tom said something similar. He hadn't heard Jim tell that joke for years. He was clearly a bit out of it, euphoric with the drip, but he was alive, compos mentis, and unless something major went wrong, he was going to make it.

Tom had deliberately arrived a few minutes before Sue. He needed to talk to his dad about stuff neither of them would want to share with his mum, at least not yet. But Jim was in no shape for a serious conversation. Tomorrow maybe. Jim drifted off again.

"Tom... he looks awful. Every part of him seems to be bandaged. What on earth happened? Do you know?" Sue asked.

"Yeah, some of it... I've only just found out, but..." This wasn't quite true, but he was pleased to be the one telling his mum.

"...for some reason, I don't know why yet, he went to this house on Waiheke and walked in on these guys. They were armed to the teeth."

"What?!" This was the last thing Sue was expecting to hear. So much for falling off a ladder.

"Well, he managed to wrangle a shotgun off one of them and dealt to them."

"All of them?!"

"Yes. Unfortunately, he got shot a few times himself. But look, you can see for yourself he's going to be fine."

"Good grief. How could he do that?! 'A tough old rooster', as my dad used to say." Sue added

"He sure is." They sat there looking at Jim for some time before Tom said

"Something else you need to know mum. This whole thing is far from over. It's complicated and messy, and it'll be all over the news tonight. You won't be able to miss it. A cop was killed too, and... " Tom decided to leave it there.

"Oh my God" Sue whispered.

"All I'm saying is, this could go any number of ways. Just remember I'm only a phone call away, ring me any time, any time at all. We'll help each other get through this. Ok?"

* * * *

"Feeling any better Sal?" Stan asked. He'd been shocked when Sally had thrown herself at him, but he immediately put his arms around her as she sobbed and clutched him. He was equally startled by his reactions to this embrace.

He would never in his wildest dreams have thought he would be holding beautiful Sally in his arms, under any circumstances, her perfect lithe young body shaking, her hair in his face, her firm breasts against him, and she wasn't letting go. She smelt amazing too, of sweat, very faintly of perfume, and something else, an earthy almost sexual smell. It was the dried blood on her clothes. Stan felt himself getting an erection. God, how awful, inappropriate and... wonderful. He panicked. She was pressed so hard against him she would feel it surely.

It took some doing but he pushed her away from himself. With Bill's help they half carried her into the meeting room and sat her down, while Alice organised coffee. Sally sniffled and blew her nose on the tissues they'd fetched for her.

"Yes, I am feeling a bit better thank you sir. I'm so sorry for – "

"Not at all, not at all" Bill said, and Stan, still recovering from his own personal ordeal said

"You've been through a terrible time, my dear, it's perfectly understandable, here try some coffee."

"I just loved him so much..." she began to dissolve again but kept it together.

"Of course, of course" Stan commiserated.

Bill thought maybe Stan was being a bit overly solicitous. Anyway, this was clearly going nowhere in a big hurry. He'd missed the three o'clock ferry. Just then his phone went. Email from Ana Harris. What does she want now? He read the message

Dear Superintendent. As a courtesy and a heads up, I attach the copy for an article I'll be filing in approximately one hour. If I haven't heard back from you by then I will assume it's factually correct.
Regards, Ana

PS. Apologies again for my duplicity today.

Then he read the copy. Shit shit shit shit shit shit shit! How does that bloody woman do it? Bill Smales raged to himself. How could she possibly have found all that out?

"Everything alright Bill?" Stan asked. Nobody could have missed noticing Bill's face, red, suffused with anger.

"Yes, I'm fine."

He'd just have to put this out of his mind for the moment. He had to get back to the city. He looked at the clock on the wall. He'd be lucky to make the four o'clock at this rate. Christ, would he never get off this bloody island? Time for a different tack with this... Sally. Bill said firmly

"Constable Reynolds. Do you feel able to talk to us about what happened yesterday?"

Perhaps it was the shift to a degree of formality, or perhaps Sally was now ready for this.

"Yes Superintendent. I do."

"Tell us what happened when you and the Sergeant entered the property on Cowes Bay Road."

"When we arrived everything was quiet, a woman came out, and it looked like whatever had taken place was over."

Both Bill and Stan were surprised at how calm, collected and cogent Sally suddenly was.

"We both had our hands on our Glocks and we approached with caution, but there was no movement inside. There were bodies everywhere. We thought everyone was dead. Then we saw there were two old guys still alive."

There was a long pause.

"Then all of a sudden, with no warning, one of the old guys turned around and...." Sally was getting tearful again.

"Turned around and... what Sally?"

"Shot Phil in the chest!"

FOUR

Ana's story was immediately front-page news. *The Herald* and the other metropolitans picked it up and it was a breaking story on all the local radio and TV stations' six o'clock News. Even *The Guardian*, which had reported on the home invasions, carried it. And every one of them had, quite properly, attributed it to her.

There had obviously been a groundswell of interest in and concern about this Wild Bunch gang and she had opened the floodgates. She felt an enormous sense of satisfaction, and achievement.

* * * *

Well, that's a bit of a turn up for the books! Superintendent Bill Smales thought to himself. It was a phrase his father had often used. He'd never known the origins of the saying but had looked it up not long ago. It was from horse racing. *'The books'* were the bookies' books. Constable Sally Reynolds' bombshell about the Sergeant's death changed everything.

He had long since given up all hopes of getting home for dinner. He was starting to think he might never get back across 'the ditch'. No, no, he should be back some time this evening.

It was now a bit after 6. He and Stan were still in Meeting Room One, finishing some rather good fish and chips. Bill often missed lunch, as he had today. When he was focussed on something important, he ignored the hunger pangs across the middle of the day. I'll just get to the end this report, or, I'll get something after the one o'clock meeting. Then he would stop feeling hungry and simply forget about eating altogether. Sharlene's nagging about getting food in for him rarely impinged.

He often wouldn't feel at all hungry at the end of the day either but, like now, once he started eating, he'd realise he was ravenous. The fish and chips were just what he needed. Shit, he hadn't rung Edie to say he wouldn't be home for dinner.

They had just watched the headlines on TV One News. Ana bloody Harris...

"What a mess" he mused to Stan.

"You can say that again" Stan answered, his thoughts still full of Sally, the effects on him of her hug, and her revelation about Phil's death.

"I still can't believe it. So much for our 'local hero'" Bill added. He had much preferred that narrative.

"Is there any way Sally could have got it wrong?"

"She's dead certain it was Carruthers" Stan said. "Sure, she was distraught after Phil was shot, but there was nothing wrong with her before that. She wouldn't get it wrong."

"Ok, let's take it as read that Carruthers shot Phil. All we have to do is work out why.

"Let's look at possible scenarios. We need to get a line on this. There's no way I can make an announcement until we do. The Media Centre's hounding me, but I've told them they'll just have to wait."

Bill and Stan, the two old-school cops who thought they'd seen it all, struggled for the next three hours to come up with answers. Bill had started thinking it might have to be the last ferry home.

"Ok let's recap" Bill said, looking at the whiteboard 'Possible Scenarios'.

"One. Carruthers was disorientated, saw Phil as another villain and shot him before realising he was cop. Which is why he didn't attempt to shoot Reynolds...

"Two. It was the old Italian guy who shot Phil, and Sally's confused him with Carruthers. No, he'd already been shot in the forehead. What's his name...?"

Stan looked at one of the papers the table.

"Giuseppe."

"Three. Shooting Phil was intentional. If so, the only possible explanation was that he wanted to escape justice.

"Four. If that were the case, why didn't he shoot Sally? Maybe he passed out before he could.

"Five. The big one. Why would he want to escape the crime scene?"

What was bothering Bill?

"Hold on, didn't Sally say that both the old guys were alive when she and Phil walked in? When did Giuseppe get it between the eyes then?"

"Oh look, she probably just got that wrong. That was a hell of a crime scene for a young cop to be confronted with" Stan said.

A cop of any age, Bill thought. He looked at the crime scene photos blu-tacked to the whiteboard and knew this was another series of images that would forever haunt him.

"It can only be that he was trying to get away. It makes sense... more or less... but why?!"

Both men sat staring at the whiteboard. There was a long pause. Bill suddenly felt very tired.

"Stan, I'm stuffed, and my brain's stopped working. I might pack it in for tonight."

"Sure boss."

"And I can't face the ferry. I'll stay over again and we can pick this up in the morning. Look we're about the same size, can I borrow a clean shirt and some underwear?"

"Of course. Why don't you stay at my place, I've got a spare room." That sounded good to Bill. What a day. What a couple of days! The only consolation was that it looked like Ana bloody Harris would have to eat humble pie.

* * * *

"What a beautiful morning for a walk in a park" Carlo said.

"It certainly is" Tom agreed. Carlo had rung and they had met at a café on Ponsonby Road, again at ten, and again Carlo had a pastry and cappuccino. When Tom had enquired, he discovered that this was indeed colazione, breakfast, for Carlo.

What Tom had not expected was that Carlo would be accompanied by the most magnificent German Shepherd that he had ever seen. Tom had grown up with a Shepherd, and he loved the breed. Their Shepherd had been a handful, and very hard to train. This was one of the calmest, best-trained dogs of any sort he'd ever encountered. He wasn't on a leash. He sat bolt upright beside Carlo at the table he and Tom shared on the footpath, his head well above table height, watching every person who walked by and totally ignoring the odd passing canine. He was working.

Seated on stools at a bar leaner immediately outside the cafe were the two men from the BMW. They hadn't acknowledged Tom when he arrived.

They were working too.

* * * *

The ESR forensic reports were at the Waiheke station when Bill and Stan got there.

"Pretty much as expected." Bill said. "Three of the gang died from shotgun wounds, the big guy from the throat wounds, the Italian from a .38 bullet to the abdomen and a .22 shot to the head. Sergeant Smith was also shot by the .38 handgun. These guns all matched those used in earlier invasions. Two sets of DNA matches now, Robert Collins and Kyle Doherty."

"Still no info on the other two perps? The big guy and the boy?" Bill asked Stan.

"Nope, DNA and fingerprints turned up nothing, and it looks like neither of them had ever been to a dentist. I've been thinking Bill. You don't suppose...."

"What?"

They'd had a slightly slower start than they'd planned, enjoyed a very pleasant breakfast in Oneroa village, and had arrived at the office around 9.30.

"...well, what if this wasn't a home invasion at all. What if all of them, including Carruthers, were there for some other reason... I dunno, a meeting of some sort?"

"What? That then turned nasty?" Bill's mind was working overtime. He was sceptical about this new theory of Stan's. Bugger, it had all been pretty straightforward until Sally.... but maybe it warranted more thought.

Right from the start of this investigation there was something that had bothered Bill. Well, a number of things, but one in particular. How likely was it that a semi-retired sixty-five-year-old, with no apparent background in armed combat, could take on a bunch of heavily armed men, all much younger, and kill all four?

He hadn't stopped to think about it, it was just there in the back of his brain. Stan's idea was starting to make more sense. Maybe it was a meeting. If it was a meeting, then obviously they must all have known each other. And what would they be meeting for? It certainly wasn't Sunday afternoon drinks.

While Bill was mulling over this new possibility, Stan had been flicking through the various reports that had come through overnight. One from the coroner caught his eye.

"Look at this. This Giuseppe... de Luca, had multiple old gunshot scars. How would he have got those?"

"What do we know about him? In fact, what do we know about the Italian family in general?" Bill asked.

Stan consulted the file.

"Mr. and Mrs. Giordano emigrated here from Italy five years ago, along with their son Carlo, and Giuseppe de Luca. They also brought four essential staff members with them, all under the investment criteria. And they've invested truckloads. They own the Cowes Bay Road property... three, no, four vineyards.... a tower block in downtown Auckland, and a boutique hotel and restaurant in Queenstown. Well! ...and three months ago the father, Pepe, had a heart attack and died."

"Why on earth would they be hooked up with a gang of psychopaths?" Bill asked

"No idea." They sat thinking.

*   *   *   *

Ana's phone had rung almost non-stop the night before. Family and friends, and calls transferred from the office. She'd even had a job offer. She'd turned it off about 9 pm and still hadn't turned it back on. She needed to think.

She'd slept fitfully and woken early. She was still very excited to have got the scoop on the Waiheke shootings and was amazed how it had been picked up and spread like wildfire. She looked forward to reading *The Herald* over breakfast. It would no doubt be full of opinion pieces about it, from 'experts' of one sort of another – social commentators, criminologists, psychologists, ex-cops etc. etc., possibly even a politician or two. She could easily get it online along with all the other news outlets, but there was something very pleasing about sitting in a café with coffee and a real paper newspaper.

What amazing good luck finding Tom Carruthers. The big hole in her story was how the cop had died. That wasn't necessarily a problem in itself. If she could discover the details quickly, it would be the makings of a good follow-up story. Tom implied that he knew, but would he tell her? It still bothered her how he knew so much, and there was still a tiny voice somewhere asking *'what if he's lying?'*, but what he had told her all made sense, and why would he set her up?

She would call him later. Yes, she decided, he was alright. She liked him, maybe even... no, no time for that. Moving right along...

* * * *

"What say the Giordanos had something going on the side with the gang, nothing to do with home invasions... the gang was doing other stuff for them." Stan pondered. He was pleased with all these ideas he was coming up with. This case had energised him.

"Like?" Bill asked.

"Drugs maybe? Traces of coke and P were found at two of their earlier hits."

That's about the only thing that makes any sense, Bill thought, although he was still a bit dubious. If Stan was right, this was obviously a conflict between two groups – the bosses and the workers, the officers and the troops. If so, the bosses were definitely Carruthers, Francesca and Giuseppe.

He badly needed to get a statement from Carruthers. Yes, that was a top priority. If he were ever to get back to town that is. The intercom beeped. It was Alice.

"Excuse me, I have the Commissioner on the phone. For the Superintendent."

"Put him through." This was the last thing Bill needed.

"Bill" the voice on the other end said "you know why I'm calling. This Waiheke business. The media are going mad. They want to know what's going on and so do I, I must say. You have to get something out there and I don't much care what it is. Well, I do of course. What I mean is even if it's just an acknowledgment of last night's news story, confirming what's accurate about it, and an update. That would do, but it has to be today, and earlier rather than later today. Copy that Bill?"

"Yes Commissioner. I'm sorry. It's a complicated case."

"I thought it must be, you know I have a lot of faith in you Bill. I apologise for being so brisk just now but the Minister's really on my back on this one."

"Consider it done sir." They hung up. The intercom went again.

"Sorry to bother you sir, but I have another call, from a Dave Bretherton. Shall I put it through?"

Dave Bretherton, Bill hadn't thought about him in years. They'd done several courses together years back. Well, well, it sure was a small world, particularly in the police. What could he want? Probably a social call. Not now, get Alice to tell him he'd call back. No, wait, he'd always liked Dave. He could take a minute.

"Put him through thanks."

"'G'day Bill. Been a while!"

"It sure has. How are you?"

"I'm good thanks. Listen I bet you're snowed under, so I'll be quick. You probably don't know but I'm with the National Central Bureau now."

"The NCB? That's part of Interpol, isn't it?"

"Yep. I saw the news about this home invasion on Waiheke and that part of the island rang a bell. I made some calls, found out the address, saw you were on the case and thought I might be of some help. You'll know by now that the property is owned by the Giordano family."

"Yes, I do, but – "

"What you won't know is that - and this is sort of off the record but use it if you need to - they're very much part of the ongoing investigation we run into the international drug trade. They're Italian mafia, believe it or not. Giordano. Part of a notorious 'Ndrangetha crime family. They look totally legit here in New Zealand, but 'Ndrangetha interests control over 70% of the cocaine trade worldwide, including Australia and maybe here as well, so we keep an eye on them. Just thought you should know."

"Hey, thanks Dave. That could be a big help."

"No worries. Look after yourself. Ciao - as they say in Italy!"

Not very funny, Bill thought, in the circumstances.

* * * *

"Shall we walk?" Carlo said. They crossed the road to Western Park, the dog walking to Carlo's left, heeling perfectly.

"How's your mother Carlo, any news?" Tom asked.

"Sadly no. She survives, but no change."

"I'm sorry to hear that." Tom didn't know what else to say.

"This is the second oldest park in Auckland. Did you know that Tom? This is Bello by the way. My beautiful big boy."

At the mention of his name Bello looked up at Carlo. He really was a big, beautiful boy. Tom stopped; he couldn't resist the urge to touch this beast. Carlo and Bello stopped.

"Can I...?" and he slowly offered Bello the back of his hand. He couldn't read any expression on the dog's face.

"Un amico." Carlo said and Bello sniffed his hand. Tom slowly moved his hand, scratched him under his chin, then ruffled the soft, thick fur on his shoulder. Bello's eyes never left his.

"That is very good. You know dogs. He likes you." Carlo said. "His family and ours have been together for many generations. He is eight now and will soon sire his successors - we hope."

They walked in silence for a time.

"I was interested to see the news last night. You have obviously been talking to this Harris person. There's no other way she could have found out so much."

"Yes. She rang me. I have no idea how she got my number." Tom replied. He hadn't given it any thought until now. Of course. He had rung the *Stuff* office on Sunday to see if there were any leads as to his father's whereabouts, and left his number.

Carlo was walking at a leisurely pace. Despite that, Tom was not looking forward to the climb back up through the park. Unlike his father, he didn't work out, and was seriously unfit.

"No harm done. It is good to have the basic facts - as we know them truly to be - out in the public sphere. You didn't share with her the way the cop died? Or did she simply not include that in her article?"

"No, I thought it best not to."

"Very wise. That will be the real story. I shall be very interested to see how Bill Smales and his team twist the narrative to avoid the truth."

"Who's Bill Smales?"

"The Inspector in charge of the case. Fundamentally honest, but... you haven't shown Harris the security footage?"

"No."

"Good. Like cops, reporters are... what is the expression 'the curate's egg'? Good in parts."

Bello was interesting. Every now and then he would trot ahead, then return. It was the sort of thing dogs did, but it seemed odd behaviour for this dog. Then Tom clicked. It only happened when there was an obstruction, or a bend in the path beyond which the view was obscured. Wow. Scouting. Tom also noticed Bello carried a slight limp. Dysplasia was common among Shepherds.

"Does he have trouble with his hips?" Tom asked Carlo.

"No. It was back in Italia. We were in Puglia, the port of Taranto, on business. They came for my father. Bello was only two, but he warned us. He and Giuseppe were both shot. They survived. It was avenged." Then after a pause

"If only I hadn't brought him to the city this weekend. He would have warned Giuseppe and..."

Another world, Tom thought, still incredulous about the whole mafia thing. They were nearly at the bottom of the park. Tom was definitely not going to enjoy walking back. He'd never done this walk before, and most of it was quite steep. He'd lived in Auckland all his life and had passed the top of the park hundreds of times, but he had no idea it ran this far down into the gully.

He had noticed that only one of Carlo's minders had followed them on their walk. They were very alike, brothers perhaps, and he'd started thinking of them as very butch versions of the Thompson Twins from the Tintin books of his youth, minus the bowler hats and umbrellas of course. It felt odd to see them apart.

"Events are about to become unpleasant. I fully expect your father to be charged with murder within the next twenty-four hours. Again, call me at any time."

That can't be right. Surely? Carlo seemed very sure. "Ah, eccoci, we are here. I imagine you would prefer to be driven back to your car, rather than walk? Please, get in."

They had arrived at the black BMW waiting for them at the bottom of the park. The Thompson who had walked behind them joined his twin in the front.

Tom and Carlo sat in the back with Bello between them. It should have been weird Tom thought, but it felt... great.

* * * *

Yes, Bill mused. It all makes sense. What an extraordinary coincidence that Dave should have rung. Manna from heaven, just when he needed it. He had enough now to go to air. He should really see what Carruthers had to say, but what could he add, except lies. Then again when confronted with the truth he might tell all. Wouldn't that be good. Yes, he should interview him before making an announcement. He rang the hospital.

Mr. Carruthers had had a bad night, high temperature and an erratic pulse. He was stable now, but was sleeping. His wife was with him. The Inspector might be able to speak to him later in the day. First thing, get back to the city.

He boarded the one o'clock ferry. At last. How good. Edie's wonderful cooking and his own bed. There was some reasonable looking food in the cabinet as he passed it on the way to a seat, but he decided he wasn't hungry. He was just hoping that he could get a statement from Carruthers before he had to write the press release. How amazing that old Stan had come up with the answer. No, not really, Stan had always been a good cop. He'd never struck his colleagues as being very forward-thinking or particularly bright, and he'd never made Detective. Maybe he should have.

Bill was back in his office by two. He decided he would wait for as long as possible. He'd give it an hour or so, and he still had to write the release anyway. How would he phrase it? First things first. He didn't want Stan to be broadsided by what was going to be in the press release, so he rang him and told him about Bretherton's call, and the mafia and drugs connection. Stan took a wee while to get his head round it.

The night before, after images from Sunday's massacre - which is how he'd begun to think of it - had woken him, Bill realised that he was only eighteen months away from voluntary retirement should he wish to take it. He hadn't thought about it much before now but if this case went well, it wouldn't be a bad swan song. He'd been finding aspects of the job, particularly the stress, harder and harder to deal with lately. He wasn't his old self.

His cell phone beeped. A text from the Commissioner. Three question marks followed by three exclamation marks. Christ! It was 4.30 pm. How had it got so late?! He must've been distracted by the huge pile of paperwork on his desk. Bugger. Ok. Nothing else for it.

* * * *

'Commenting on the multiple homicides on Waiheke last Sunday, Superintendent William Smales has confirmed that four of those killed were members of the so-called Wild Bunch gang, responsible for multiple home invasions, murders and rapes, as first reported yesterday by Stuff crime reporter Anahera Harris.

In a major new development, Superintendent Smales says police do not believe the narrative in the press to date has been accurate. They believe the man lauded as a local hero is in fact an associate of the gang, quite probably one of its ringleaders, and that it was he who killed the police sergeant at the scene. Further, the deaths were not the result of a home invasion or burglary gone wrong, but arose from a dispute over a drug deal, quite possibly an international drug deal, in which all of those present were involved.

The Superintendent said the police family was mourning the loss of Sergeant Phillip Smith, a dedicated, long serving and brave officer.'

Had he done the right thing? Bill hoped so. Had he gone too far? He desperately hoped not. At least he could go home. He would interview Carruthers in the morning, not that it mattered much now.

* * * *

"What have you done, you bastard? I'll tell you what you've done, you've wrecked my career, that's what!"

She'd burst into the offline edit suite without any warning. Tom thought she was going to hit him. He'd been working on the security footage. He quickly switched off the monitor.

"Ana, let me – "

"What, feed me more lies? Have you seen the news?!!"

"I have, and I was about to call you. There is some stuff I haven't told you."

"Oh really?!" Ana laughed sarcastically. "Like your father killed a cop? Just a few minor details like that?"

She was so angry. There was no point in talking to her. He made a decision he hoped he wouldn't regret.

Tom turned the monitor back on. He dragged the cursor back to the beginning of the edited timeline and hit the spacebar.

"What the fuck is this?" Ana spat. It was the gang going up the steps to the loggia. She watched and quickly saw what it was.

"My God, is this... what is this, security footage?" Tom didn't answer. She slid down into the chair beside Tom's without taking her eyes off the screen.

She gasped out loud and jumped in her chair when Bob shot Giuseppe, and groaned loudly when Shane hit Francesca. She saw Bob tying her to the table, Shane ripping her dress and underwear off, pulling his pants down, the guns, and the knife in Bob's hand as he licked Francesca's breasts.

Tom let it run until Jim's car pulled up. He hit the space bar again, pausing the sequence. He turned to Ana. She was white and motionless, her eyes still riveted to the screen.

"That is dreadful... what ghastly people."

Tom suddenly realised he had become somewhat inured to a lot of this footage, he'd seen it so many times now. They sat in silence.

"It gets a lot worse I'm afraid. The rest is exactly as I've described it to you. And yes dad did kill a cop, but suspend judgment until -"

Ana turned from the screen, and to Tom's surprise put her hand on his.

"I'm so sorry Tom. I can see how hard this whole thing must have been for you. I can't imagine what it's been like editing this up. Thank you for confiding in me, and I'm really pleased you didn't lie to me. I thought I must be losing my touch." A wry little laugh.

Ana's eyes were no longer blazing, and her soft voice had returned. She's gorgeous, Tom thought.

"Trust me, my dad is a good man."

"I do trust you Tom." Ana said warmly, those beautiful tawny eyes looking into his.

"I should probably watch some more. Is that ok?"

If it meant she stayed a bit longer....

"Sure" Tom said.

She watched it all, wincing and at times squirming in her chair, once or twice turning away from the screen briefly. When Jim shot Kyle in the face she retched. She said 'Oh my God' several times throughout.

When they reached the point where Jim and Giuseppe were waiting for help to arrive, Ana asked if they could have a break. They went outside into the carpark at the front of the building. It was dark, to Tom's surprise. How long had he been buried in there?

"God that's a hard watch" Ana said, and surprised Tom by taking a cigarette packet out of her bag. Tom's heart gave a little leap. She smokes! He'd been struggling to give up for months.

"Could I...?

"Sure. So, what's left? The cops arrive and..."

"Yes, and more bloodshed I'm afraid, after it should have been all over." It's a terrible habit, Tom thought, but goddamn this cigarette's good.

"That's an amazing sequence, your dad and Giuseppe smoking and drinking and calling their boys. Quite moving." Ana said.

It had been a powerful moment for Tom too when he had first seen it. The whole experience of the phone call from Jim and then watching the footage had shifted him. His dad had been a great father to him, always attentive, caring, loving. Unlike some of his friends' fathers, he'd never once hit Tom. He'd spent endless hours helping him with homework, projects, teaching him how to use tools, build things, and simply talking to him. He'd been a great mentor, and friend, but he'd also always been his father, a generation apart and a distinctly... other person.

What this whole episode, including the footage, had done was to change his feelings for his father. No, that wasn't it. It hadn't changed his feelings, it had added a new dimension to them, and to his relationship with Jim, one Tom would not have known was missing. He was no longer nearly so 'other', and Tom had never felt this close to him, so much a part of him.

They went back inside and watched the rest, or at least up until Jim shot the sergeant.

"Brothers, my God" Ana moaned. "Your poor father. And you...."

She turned to Tom, shaking slightly and with tears in her eyes.

"Oh my, oh my oh my..." She very slowly and gently put her arms around him, sobbing into his shoulder. Tom felt his own tears rising. He started crying, really crying. He realised how badly he needed this release. They both wept like innocents for what felt like minutes. Then Ana eased back from him and said

"Would you stay with me tonight?"

* * * *

It was 9.30 am and Bill was finally interviewing Jim Carruthers. Jim had calmly told him in detail how he interrupted the gang, took the shotgun and confronted them, the gunshots, stabbing, Giuseppe having been shot before he arrived, calling 111. It all fitted the story Ana bloody Harris had told the world. So far just as expected. Hold on.... Bill felt a cold chill spread from his toes up to the top of his head. That was something that he and Stan had completely overlooked. They had gone over and over every detail, except.... If Carruthers was in with the gang, why would he call 111? It was him, it was on record, wasn't it?

"Excuse me for a moment please." Bill said, getting up as steadily as he could and walking out into the corridor.

"Stan. Have you got the details of the 111 call from the crime scene in front of you? Yeah, I'll wait... the transcript yes.... did the caller identify himself?"

"Yes. It was... Jim - bugger!" Stan said. He realised the implications instantly.

"Bugger is right. How did we miss that? Say nothing to anyone." He hung up. What have I done to deserve this? Bill asked himself, starting to panic. His heart was pounding.

He breathed deeply a few times and decided he should go back and hear what else Carruthers had to say. There must be some explanation he and Stan had missed.

"So... after you called 111...?

"Giuseppe and I sat and smoked and drank grappa while we waited. Strange in retrospect, but at the time... I think we were both expecting to die. I tried my wife on the phone but couldn't get through, then Giuseppe rang Francesca's son, and I rang my son Tom."

Ah, thought Bill, that's how Ana bloody Harris found out so much. She must have talked to the son. They'd obviously cooked this up between them.

"And then the two cops arrived." Jim said.

"Sergeant Phil Smith and Constable Sally Reynolds. And how was that? They were professional and... thorough would you say?"

"Yes indeed" Jim replied. "Smith told Sally to call for help. I thought it was all over and we'd finally get out of there."

"But it wasn't...?" This wasn't how it happened. He's lying. Bill was still rattled. He was coping, but only just.

"It was only when Smith discovered the guy face down on the floor was his brother, that things turned to custard."

It really was as if a bolt of lightning had hit the Inspector. Surely that can't be true.

"His brother?!"

"So he said - Shane - and one of the others called him Shane at some point as well I seem to recall. The big guy that is."

Bill was trying, but it was almost impossible to stay composed.

"Look I'm very sorry, but would you excuse me again for a moment." The corridor again.

"Stan. We need to know if Phil and Kevin Smith have a brother, possibly by the name of Shane. High priority, ring me back. "

Bill went back to his interview seriously disturbed by what he had heard so far. Jim told him what else had happened up until he lost consciousness, waking up here in hospital the following day.

"Well... thank you Mr. Carruthers. What an ordeal. I do hope you're up and about soon." He turned off the police issue smart phone he'd used to record the interview. Bill's phone rang as he was walking down the hospital steps.

"Hi Bill. Stan. It's true, there was a third brother, Shane."

"I don't believe it! How could... Who officially identified Phil...? Poor bugger, he's going to have to go through all that again." Both his brothers... God.

"And Stan? I want you to talk to Sally again. I think she might have lied to us." He hung up.

What on earth do I do now? Bill asked himself. Everything Carruthers had told him made perfect sense. He so wished he hadn't written that press release. He'd known there were too many loose ends.

He had never in his life felt so totally lost and alone.

* * * *

Constable Sally Reynolds had woken up feeling very pleased with herself. She had caught the news the night before. Good, her darling Phil had been praised as a hero. Quite rightly.

Sally wasn't a pathological liar, but in this instance she might as well have been. What started out as a bald-faced lie had now become the gospel truth for Sally. She had been determined that the man of her dreams would not have his reputation sullied. She had succeeded, look, it was all over the news. She might leave the police force now. Or she might not. She might stay and try to be as good a cop as Phil had been.

She wasn't particularly surprised, or worried, when Alice rang to say Stan wanted to see her, if she felt up to it. Of course she felt up to it, she was feeling almost back to normal. And she had Stan wrapped around her little finger. He would look after her.

Was that really his hard penis she felt against her belly yesterday, before he pushed her away?

* * * *

Tom woke up in Ana's bed. He woke as he had gone to sleep, holding Ana from behind.

They hadn't moved all night. There was no hint of anything sexual, that wasn't what the night was about, and both had slept in their underwear. Nonetheless Ana's body felt perfect in his arms. Ana stirred, then turned around to face him.

"Morning handsome" she said, opening her eyes. "I think that's the best sleep I've had for years."

"Hi." That was probably true for him as well. They lay there looking at each other.

She really was lovely, her glossy black hair and perfect olive skin on the white pillow. Tom felt he could lie there forever, gazing into those liquid eyes. Ana suddenly gave him a quick peck on the end of his nose and said

"Right, c'mon, it's late. We've got work to do" and leapt out of bed. "You use the bathroom first. I'll be in the lounge checking my emails."

* * * *

"I'm sorry to have to put you through this again Sally, but are you absolutely sure that's what happened?"

"Yes of course. Why would I lie?" Sally's face started to crumple.

"Nobody's saying you lied Sal, but it was a really traumatic time for you. Maybe you got a bit mixed up. You did get it wrong about the Italian guy being alive when you got there..."

Sally's eyes filled with tears.

"Sorry Sal, sorry." Stan couldn't stand this. He got up and turned away from her. He just needed a minute. He turned back just as Sally threw her arms around him. Again.

"I understand, oh it's all so awful... oh Stan"

Stan hesitated and then put his arms around her. She smelt entirely different this time, fresh and clean, that same perfume but a little stronger, her taut body and perky breasts against him, and... God no! It was happening. Again. He made a half-hearted attempt to push her away. She tightened her embrace. It grew, and grew. She didn't pull away.

"Christ, no-o-o!" thought Stan. It was so exciting. It had been so long. He couldn't stop it happening.

Sally stayed perfectly still for some time, then slowly disengaged from him, looked up into his eyes, and said softly

"Oh Stan" and gave him the smallest, sweetest, sexiest smile.

* * * *

It was now after ten, the breakfast rush at St. Kevin's was over, and the place was quiet. As Ana expected, T*he Herald* was full of it, from the editorial about responsible journalism, to several letters to the editor and everything in between. She was being pilloried.

"Oh God" she shook her head and sighed.

"It's not as bad as it seems" Tom ventured "remember we have the ultimate rebuttal. The video files." 'Rebuttal.' She hadn't heard that word since she left the law.

"True" she agreed. "But where has all this come from? It's ridiculous! Compared with the truth anyway."

"They're lying, well someone's lying."

"Yeah, but Bill Smales is running this. He's always been as straight as a die. There must be something else going on. Mmm, they do good coffee here." She was on her second cup.

"Ok. Let's look at it. Unlike us, they really have no idea what went on there." Tom said.

"No, but I sent Smales the copy and he never got back to me to say I'd got it wrong, which he would normally do. Something's happened between then and now."

"Who was the only witness to any of it? Apart from dad. God, I must go to the hospital."

"The other cop, Reynolds?"

"Yes. Now they were clearly an item. Remember her reaction when dad shot Smith? And when the cops and ambulances arrived? Absolutely, hysterically distraught. What if she's telling a different story, maybe to protect his memory?"

"That's possible I suppose. Good thinking. It's either that or Smales isn't who I thought he was. And what's all this about international drug deals?"

Tom had thought about this. What would he tell her? Would he tell her about Carlo?

"Well..." Tom debated with himself about how much he would tell her.

"Come on. I've got a great nose for when people are lying, or about to lie. Tell me." Ana demanded, gently but firmly. I might as well, Tom thought.

"The cops have obviously got on to the fact that the Giordanos are a mafia family, and they've cooked up this story about drugs." Ana just looked at him.

"You - are - kidding me?"

"A-a-a-h, no." Tom went on to tell Ana about Carlo contacting him and giving him the links to the security footage, their meetings, Bello, the Ferrari, the BMW and the Thompson Twins.

"This is fucking in-sane!" Ana exclaimed, loudly. The other two people in the café turned and looked.

"Sure is, and I know what you're thinking" Tom said "what a great story this would all make. Just remember our agreement, when it comes to this case, I approve everything you write."

"Yes," Ana said distractedly "yes, of course".

"Ok. I've got to go and see dad. Call you later?"

"Please do."

Tom hadn't planned to, but he leant down and kissed her on the forehead. She smiled up at him.

* * * *

Kevin looked down at his brother. He barely recognised him. It had been many years since he'd seen him. He'd aged so much, put on so much weight, and... changed so much. Kevin couldn't have voiced it but there was a hard, wild look about him. It wasn't a result of rigor mortis or early decomposition, these changes were deeply etched into his face. What had happened to him in those years?

Poor Shane, he'd never had a chance. Their father's brutality had affected him more than the others, both physically and mentally. He had retreated within himself from an early age and when he left it was clear he wanted to sever all links with the family.

Shane's savage beating of his father hadn't surprised Kevin at the time, he had seen the hatred growing in him for years prior. It was as if he was just waiting until he was big enough and strong enough to do it. Kevin was surprised that his father had survived. Had Shane intended to kill him? Maybe he thought he had. Kevin had given up trying to maintain contact with Shane years ago. Phil had kept trying, without any success, even though they'd both been on Waiheke for some time.

As when Phil looked down at Shane in the loggia, images of them as boys flooded into Kevin's thoughts. It was a dreadful childhood for all of them, but they were close and there were good times. And here he was. Dead and deathly pale. It wasn't fair really. He lifted the cloth covering Shane's neck. Jesus Christ, what a mess. Who could have done that? He knew now that Shane was part of this Wild Bunch gang, but what had really gone on at that house on Waiheke, and did his bro really deserve to be butchered like this? Bled out like a stuck pig? Both gone. Phil and Shane. Phil's funeral was on Thursday. He wanted Shane buried, cremated, at the same time, alongside his brother.

He was the last of the Smith boys, the terrible trio, the wild bunch they'd once called themselves. Ha. That's how the gang got its name, I bet, thought Kevin. Ironic. He felt there was something he should do. Needed to do.

He needed to find out exactly what had happened to them both. And who was responsible.

* * * *

Super Bill Smales went back to his office. Sharlene immediately noticed he looked very pale and drawn. He didn't even acknowledge her on the way past her desk. Most unusual. By the time she got to the door into his office he was slumped in his desk chair. He looked dreadful.

"Are you ok Bill?" She'd never once called him Bill. Neither of them even noticed. Bill looked up at her as if he didn't recognise her.

"Mmmm?" he mumbled.

"How long since you've had anything to eat sir?" He shook his head and looked at her.

"Sharlene, I... was deep in thought, sorry."

"You don't look well Super. It's been a big couple of days. I think you should go home and rest" she said, slightly assertively.

"Yes, I don't feel a hundred percent. Perhaps I'll do that."

She called for a staff car and then rang Edie. She was at home.

Sharlene checked on the Super. He was sitting, staring in front of him, oblivious to anything and everything around him.

* * * *

Kevin had no authority nor any reason, officially, to request the file on the Waiheke case. Who did he know over there? Of course. Tim Adams. He and Tim had shared a flat briefly when they were probationers in Christchurch, what would it have been... 12, 15 years ago? They'd had some times! Best not think about it. They'd got up to some dodgy shit, but they were young.

Once in particular Kevin had seriously overstepped the mark in a drugs and prostitution investigation. Tim had somehow managed to keep it under wraps. Kev would have been drummed out of the force. Yes, he'd ring Tim.

"Kev! G'day mate! You ok? No need to tell you how bad we're all feeling about Phil. He was a good man. So sorry Kev."

Tim didn't yet know about Shane. Nobody did, apart from Bill, Stan, and Kevin of course.

"Thanks mate, yeah, it's a bugger alright. But listen, what's really hard is not knowing what happened."

"Well... he was shot."

"Yeah, but – "

"In the heart. Would've been real quick apparently, if that's what you're asking." Tim said

"That's good to know, thanks for that. But who actually did it Tim? The Smales press release said it was the local fella. Is that right? I need to know."

"Sure Kev. I understand." Tim paused. Yes? No? Yes, Kev was family.

"Yeah, it was. Jim Carruthers."

Kevin didn't know whether Tim had let the name slip or he'd told him intentionally, but that was what he wanted. A name.

"And he took out all the others too yeah?"

"Sure looks like it. Yep." Tim said.

* * * *

Bill arrived home. Sharlene had said she was worried, so Edie was watching out for the car, went down the drive to meet it, and helped Bill inside. He seemed a bit unsteady.

"Bill, darling, you look awful! Are you alright?"

"Yes, I'm fine Edie, just need to take it easy for a bit" and Bill walked past her and out into the garden, to his favourite chair under the tree he and Edie had planted nearly thirty years earlier. He felt better already.

There was a gentle breeze and the flickering golden light through the leaves was lovely. Just a brief respite from work, then he'd get back into it. The Waiheke case was a total shambles, but he'd sort it out, the way he always did. And Stan Williams was a bit of a worry, but yeah, he'd sort it out. Ah yes, that's much better. He loved this garden, this tree.

"I might get myself a cup of tea. Yes, that's what I feel like" Bill thought to himself and went to stand up.

There was something funny going on with one of his legs.

"And what's wrong with my face? It feels numb. And my arm. It doesn't want... to... work...."

FIVE

Tom got to the hospital around 9.30, the time the ward nurse had suggested. Breakfast, meds and ablutions would all be over, then it was just the doctors' rounds, which could be at any time.

He wasn't expecting this bombshell. Why on earth would his father not want them to use the security footage?

"But they're going to charge you with murder dad, sure as eggs."

"I know that Tom, but I want to be very clear about this, I do not want that footage made public. It'd be on every media outlet around the world in minutes and I can't have that. I know it'd be a simple way out of this, but it can't happen. I'd rather take my chances in court."

"Can you at least tell me why?"

"No Tom, I'm afraid I can't. Some day I might."

* * * *

"The good news is we're making real progress. I thought the Super's press release last night summed it up pretty well. You've both seen it? Good. The bad news is that late this morning the Super had a stroke. Not a bad one, and he'll be ok, but he's off work for a while that's for sure. Maybe for good."

"Poor old bugger" Andy commented.

"Yes, so it's just us now, and that may be no bad thing. It's our patch after all."

Stan was talking to Tim and Andy in Meeting Room One at the Police Station on Waiheke Island.

"Right, the first thing is to put a round-the-clock watch on Carruthers. I wouldn't put anything past that bastard. Get him out of the ward and into a private room. I don't care what it costs. You see to that Tim?"

"Sure boss."

"And once that's set up the only visitors are family and legal counsel. No reporters! I'll get a warrant for his arrest and serve him with it today. In person. I'm heading over this morning, soon. One other thing, I'm going to spend a few days in Auckland. I might commute or I might stay over there, haven't decided yet. But you guys'll be fine either way. I'll leave you in charge of the station Tim. You know how everything runs."

"Excuse me sir. What's this about drugs, and international drug deals?" Andy asked.

Stan passed on what Bill had told him. He decided not to share the news about Shane just yet.

"Jesus" Tim said.

* * * *

"What's up Sharlene, are you alright hon?"

Ana was calling to see if she could talk to Bill Smales. Sharlene sounded very upset on the other end of the phone.

"Yeah, I'm fine. It was just hearing your voice, I lost it a bit. Been on top of it 'til now."

"What is it? What's happened?" Ana asked.

"Can't tell you, there'll be an official announcement about it soon."

What could it be? ...an 'announcement,' then it's not personal to Sharlene.

"Is it Bill?"

"Y-e-e-s-s." Sharlene said. "But you mustn't say anything. Not before it's announced."

"I won't Sharl, I promise, now tell me."

"The Super's had a stroke! He arrived back from Waiheke yesterday looking awfully tired. Then after he came back from interviewing that Carruthers man this morning, he looked just shocking. I persuaded him to go home. He was in the garden..."

"Oh, I'm so sorry. How bad is it?"

"Well, it's not a severe stroke apparently, but it'll still take him ages to get over it, and he might never come fully right."

Ana realised in that moment how fond she was of Bill. He'd been part of her life for a quite a while now and she had a lot of time for him. It had struck her more than once how much he reminded her of her father.

* * * *

"Hey Andy. Got a minute?"

"Sure Tim."

"Felt like a bit of a walk. Wanna join me?"

This was shorthand for 'I want to have a private yarn with you away from the office'. Tim and Andy got on well. They were about the same age, both single, had the same sense of humour, liked the same beers and had great times getting pissed watching the rugby and shoot 'em up movies. They regularly went out together, to bars and clubs, chatting up sheilas, and later recounting their adventures on the odd occasions when one or both of them 'got lucky'. They also liked sharing a joint and, all too rarely, a line or two of coke. Yeah, they were mates.

"'Sup bro?" Andy asked as they walked down the hill towards the village.

"It's this bloody case. I mean I think we're on the right track but... like... this drugs thing, we can't charge Carruthers or the Italian woman on the basis of a fucking phone call from Interpol, it'd never fly. It's hearsay, circumstantial at best."

"Yeah, I guess so..." Tim was a good bit brighter than Andy. This was a lot for Andy to take in. They had by-passed the village and were soon down on Oneroa beach, sitting on a bench seat under one of the many pōhutukawa trees.

"It'd be different if we'd found a decent stash of something... there hasn't been a proper search of the property has there?" Tim wondered.

"No, we weren't looking for anything outside of the crime scene..."

"The crime scene just got a whole lot bigger mate." Tim said. "What say we..." He dialled a number on his mobile.

"Kev mate how are ya? I was a bit worried about you after your call. You ok? That's good, that's good. Pleased to hear it. Look, I'll get right to the point. We really wanna nail these bastards that killed Phil, but we need some help. You see the Super's stuff on the news? Right, well I'll get straight to the point Kev, it'd be great if we could find some... ah... y'now..." Tim sniffed loudly a couple of times into the phone "on the property." A pause, while Kevin answered.

"I thought you might..." Tim gave a small laugh. "As much as you can lay your hands on mate, the more the better, but anything you can manage..." Another pause. "Yeah, call me back. Thanks Kev, you're a champ."

Tim hung up. He had meant to ask when Phil's funeral was but forgot.

"Jeez Tim" Andy said. "Are we really gonna – "

"Relax Andy, it's all good. Don't you worry your pretty little head about it!" Tim ruffled Andy's hair and laughed.

* * * *

Superintendent Smales heard someone clearing their throat. He opened his eyes.

"Ana... ...Harrish. So...rry... I have.. nothing to... shay... to you."

"It's ok Super, you don't need to say anything, I'm not on the clock, I just wanted to see you. See if you're ok."

Poor Bill, he looked awful. The whole left side of his face had sagged. He was dribbling and couldn't talk properly. He had a drip in his arm. He looked so... diminished. He said

"Sh..n.. ishe." Ana thought this was 'That's nice.'

"I'm told it could have been a lot worse" she said.

"Act.. sh.. ly Ana, ish a... re...lief-f-f."

"All getting a bit much eh?" Bill nodded and Ana thought he was a bit teary. Ana waited to see if Bill would try to say any more. He didn't.

"Bill, I just wanted you to know that I think you're a great cop, and a good man. Please get better soon." She got up to go.

"A... na... hera...."

"Yes Superintendent?"

Bill was getting drowsy. He lifted his right forearm off the bed and tried to say something. It sounded to Ana a bit like

'You were right' and he dozed off again.

* * * *

Kevin sat, brooding, at this desk. He hated being obligated, indebted. Fucking Tim, always on the make one way or another. Yeah, he'd owed him, big time, but they'd sure as hell be all square after this, he thought to himself.

Kevin had a very strong sense of right and wrong, fair and unfair, justice and punishment. He wouldn't have identified it this way, but it was a very Old Testament view, acquired through his Roman Catholic education and upbringing, school 'divinity studies', Sunday school 'devotions', and indeed his home life.... you gotta pay for your sins, boy.

It was all hell and damnation, fire and brimstone, and an eye for an eye under an omniscient, vengeful God. Love, mercy and forgiveness? Not so much. Or maybe he'd missed those bits. And the burden of guilt, deliberately inculcated by the teachers and priests, was oppressive.

As a child, he would desperately try to think of things he might've done wrong, so he had something to tell one or other of the priests, those living embodiments of God on earth.

One of his brothers, he couldn't remember which, told him once that he was feeling guilty because he wasn't feeling guilty about anything.

Whatever the reason, Kevin felt a resolve hardening within him, a righteous, almost religious zeal to make the evildoer pay. In this particular instance that evildoer, that almost... satanic figure, was the man who had killed and mutilated his brothers.

Of course, these were not conscious thought processes for Kevin, and he might well have disputed some of these observations. Nonetheless these influences and experiences, as a whole, provided the framework for his motivations and preoccupations. And there is no doubt that he had become almost totally preoccupied, obsessed even, with achieving justice for his brothers, and making this Jim Carruthers pay his debt to the family.

He clicked back to the issue at hand. Cocaine. Right, now who do I know...?

* * * *

"And my story's so much more credible than theirs. How absurd. Me, the ringleader of the gang? And where did this international drug deal bullshit come from?"

Tom had a fair idea but did wonder how the police had discovered the Giordano mafia connection.

"Ok dad, well I suppose we'd better start thinking about getting you a lawyer."

"I've already rung Bob Withers." Jim said.

"Old Bob? I thought he just did conveyancing. He's not even a barrister is he?"

"No, no, I don't want him to represent me in court. I just wanted him or one of the partners on standby to apply for name suppression - if and when I'm charged."

"Good."

"Actually, I'm thinking of representing myself, if it comes to court." Jim said.

"What? But dad, you've got no -"

The curtain to Jim's cubicle was pulled back. The staff nurse said

"Excuse me, we'll have to finish the visit. We've been told to transfer this patient to a private room. Immediately."

* * * *

"Can you get on the next ferry? I've just checked, there's a 1 o'clock. Good. I'll be by the seats near the ticket office."

Tim got off the 1 o'clock and walked towards the old ferry building. There was Kev, sitting on one of the bench seats to the left. Didn't look like he had a package of any sort. Oh well, even a small amount'd be better than nothing. Then Tim saw the bag under the bench.

As soon as Tim emerged round the side of the building, Kevin got up and casually walked away. Twenty minutes later Tim was on the same boat back to Waiheke. He gave Andy a quick call.

"Got it. Not sure, could be quite a bit. You'll pick me up? Use your own car. See ya soon."

What Tim had on the seat beside him was a medium-sized... sports bag he thought, but it was a bit hard to tell, it was covered in layer upon layer of plastic wrap. When he'd first retrieved the bag from under the seat it had felt quite heavy, a few kilos he thought.

Can't all be coke surely?

* * * *

Well, this is a lot more pleasant. My own bathroom, easy chair.... Jim thought to himself, although he knew the move wasn't designed to make life more comfortable for him. It's so they can guard me more effectively, he thought.

Jim was improving. After the scare with what seemed to have been an infection, or a touch of pneumonia, he was healing reasonably well. His smashed rib was still very painful, would be for weeks. The bullet wounds to his chest were clean. The surgeons had been forced to remove part of his lung but had assured him he wouldn't miss it. The stab wound in his back had done a lot more damage than they thought; another operation would be needed on that, but they were most worried about the Māori boy's second shot, to his thigh. There was a lot of muscle and nerve damage, and he was unlikely to ever regain the full use of that leg. The bullet had hit the femur and fragments of lead and bone were sprayed over a wide area. They thought during the operation that he might have to lose the leg, but they had managed to save it, so far at least. Again, they might have another go at that, when he was under the general anaesthetic for the additional work on the knife wound. One thing was clear. Jim wasn't going home any time soon.

He liked the lead surgeon. Rick Jamieson was a real bloke and talked about his work in down-to-earth terms, rather like a carpenter or blocklayer discussing a job, and he was always cheerful and breezy. Could have been a chippie Jim thought, he was tall, raw-boned and muscular, with big tradesman's hands. Hard to imagine them doing the delicate, intricate work that was so much part of his job. Yes, he was a good bloke. Unlike the nurses there'd also been no apparent change in his attitude to Jim since the latest news from the front. It was hero to zero for most of the staff, but not Mr. Jamieson. Maybe he'd missed the news. Jim doubted it. He was just very professional, Jim decided.

Shame about the leg, but it might come right. What Jim knew for sure was that one way or another, it would forever remind him of the Māori boy, whose loss he greatly mourned, and the Māori boy would always remind him of Colombia. He needed to name him. Shane had called him Ra. What was that short for? Rawiri? He liked that. Until he heard otherwise, Jim would think of him as Rawiri.

* * * *

On a side-road not far from the Matiatia ferry terminal, Tim and Andy were sitting in Andy's car, surrounded by metres of loose plastic wrap. It was indeed a small sports bag, and it was open between them on the centre console.

"Is it snowing on Waiheke or what?!" Tim exclaimed.

"Jesus fucking Christ!" Andy said, "Where'd he get this much blow?" There were ten, what felt like one kilo bricks of what Kev suspected was very probably 90% plus pure, uncut cocaine. Must be worth millions on the streets, he thought. Also, on top of the bricks, a piece of paper with something scrawled on it. ***QUITS***. Tim didn't even notice it.

"Can only have come from the evidence lock-up surely." Tim said.

"How did he swing that? Must have a mate somewhere in there. Who knows. Who cares?"

"Andy m'man? We are in business. All systems are go!"

"Do you reckon we could... sort of... skim a bit?" Andy asked hopefully.

Tim just smiled.

* * * *

Stan was walking past Sharlene's desk when Tim's call came through.

"Call for you - Inspector" she said, barely able to hide her contempt.

"Thanks, Sharlene."

She hated this. What was this lowly Inspector from bloody Waiheke doing, commandeering Bill's office? It was so... disrespectful, and... rude! She put the call through to him.

"Hey boss. How's life in the big smoke?"

"Good Tim. The Island?" Stan asked.

"Flat out, you know how it is!" They shared a bit of a laugh.

"We've been thinking Sir, Andy and me..."

Tim always included Andy. He would always give him the credit, or share the credit with him, for ideas that were usually solely his. It was what mates did.

"...there's never been a proper search down Cowes Bay, I mean of the whole house. You never know what we might find. With all this talk of drugs..."

"You're right! That's a bloody good idea!" Stan said

"Y'know, sniffer dogs, the lot..."

"I'll get right onto it. Should be possible tomorrow. Thanks a lot Tim!" He hung up and left his office, excited at the possibilities.

"Have to go out. Be about an hour" he told Sharlene.

Good bloody riddance! Sharlene almost said it out loud.

* * * *

"This is the official record of an interview of one James Carruthers, by Inspector Stanley Williams of the Waiheke Police. The date and time is as per this recording.

"Mr Carruthers, you are not obliged to say anything, but anything you do say may be used as evidence in a court of law. Is that clear? Do you understand."

"It is. I do." Jim replied.

"This is a copy of your arrest warrant. That's for you. I'll now read out the list of charges against you. Oh, and of course, you are entitled to legal representation. Should you wish, the court can assign you a solicitor under the -"

"That won't be necessary." Jim said. Stan read out the charges.

"James Carruthers, you are charged that on Sunday January...." Five charges of culpable homicide, including that of Sergeant Phillip Smith of the Waiheke Police.

"Is there anything you wish to say?" Stan asked.

"Not right now thanks. No."

I enjoyed that, Stan thought to himself as he left the hospital. He looked at this watch. Nearly 5 o'clock. Well, doesn't time fly when you're having fun. I might pack it in. Not a bad way to finish the day. Not bad at all.

* * * *

"He wouldn't say why, he's just adamant that the footage never sees the light of day. He said he'd rather take his chances in court."

"That's all very well but the way the police are spinning this, I don't fancy his chances one little bit." Ana said. "Why though?"

"I guess it must be something in his past, back in England. He was a journalist before he came here. Not exactly the sort of job... maybe there was some sort of scandal..."

"That's a coincidence, Jim being a journalist too. Talking of which, I rang *Stuff* today. Decidedly cool reception. It would seem I'm persona non-grata there as well. I was relying on the footage to 'clear my name' as it were."

"Mmmm. I can't see Jim changing his mind in a hurry, we might just have to find another way of challenging the police account of what happened." Tom said.

"Easier said than done I suspect. I think perhaps I'll just lie low for a while and see where this thing goes next. Tell you what though, I'm looking forward to this lunch tomorrow. Meeting a real-life mafia Don. Not something you do every day."

"Indeed. I'll be interested to see what you make of him."

"What day is tomorrow?" Ana asked.

"Thursday, I think... yes, Thursday. God, it feels like weeks since the killings, so bloody much has happened."

"Yeah. Talk about a crazy week..."

* * * *

It was a private, family service. That meant there was virtually nobody there in the small cemetery chapel, just the priest, Phil's wife Helen, Kevin, and his two dead brothers, Phil and Shane. Kevin didn't know the priest. He'd been business-like and brisk with Kevin when he arrived, and apart from some 'sorry for your loss' stuff, it was clearly just another day at the office for Father Gregory, Kevin thought.

Here they were, the three Smith boys. They hadn't been together for many years, not since the day Shane left home in fact. The coffins were closed, but they were there, Kev could see them; not as they'd been when he identified them at the morgue, but as they'd been as kids. The Smith boys. The terrible trio. The talk of the town.

They were gone now. He bade them farewell. He wouldn't wait for the committal, the coffins on the conveyor belt taking them to the fire, the cleansing, annealing fire, or the fire of eternal torment? Kevin didn't much care which it was, he'd lost interest in all that stuff.

"Let us pray" the priest droned "God, we thank you for the life that you give us. It is full..."

Kevin was reminded of another funeral, many years before. He was the only one of the three of them to have sung in a choir, the Catholic Cathedral choir no less. One spring day all the junior choristers were bundled into a bus and driven some distance out of the city to a beautiful, tiny, country church. They had no idea why they were there, what the occasion was. He remembered the daffodils massed in the long grass around the entrance porch.

The boys filed into the choir stalls. There was just enough room for them all, and there between the stalls was a coffin, an open coffin, with a white, mask-like, wizened old face barely a metre away, and there was a strange smell. The old priest must have had some standing in the church community to have warranted their presence, but at eight years old Kevin was horrified, traumatised as, most probably, were all of the boys. No-one had told them, warned them, and he'd had to sit there for the whole, long requiem mass and sing the requisite hymns. It had haunted Kevin for years. Still did, some nights.

"....to remember, and celebrate the lives of Phillip and Sean Smith, who were - "

Kevin jumped to his feet.

"It's Shane, you useless cunt!" Kevin snarled, and stormed out of the chapel, deliberately knocking over a tall, gilt candlestick by the entrance.

* * * *

"Ana, piacere. How very nice to meet you. Sono Carlo" Carlo said.

"You too" replied Ana.

"You didn't tell me she was so beautiful Tom, nor tangata whenua. Of course - Anahera - lovely name and unless I'm mistaken, a transliteration of Angel. You know with your dark hair and skin you could almost be from Southern Italy, which of course has the most beautiful women in the world!"

"Thank you, Carlo" Ana said.

"Prego. And this is Bello."

"Well, hello! Aren't you the handsomest dog in the world?" Ana said, crouching down and stroking both sides of Bello's huge head. Her face was inches from his.

That's taking a hell of a risk, Tom thought to himself, but Bello rolled his head in her hands and wagged his tail. What?! He hadn't ever seen the dog wag his tail, nor show any glimmer of 'emotion'. Until now. He even made a little gurgling noise in his throat.

"He really likes you Ana. That is rare, and good. Brava!" Carlo said. Tom felt a bit... miffed.

They sat down at the table on the grass a metre or so from the sands of Takapuna beach. It was just a standard picnic table, but it had been laid perfectly. On the crisp white linen tablecloth was a simple but delicious-looking repast - cheeses, prosciutto, ciabatta, olives, pickles, side plates, knives, napkins, a bottle of pinot grigio from Puglia, and three very elegant glasses. It was a sparkling day. There was a light breeze but it was from a westerly quarter, so it was calm and still where they were.

"What better than a picnic lunch on such a lovely day" Carlo said, pouring the wine.

"Indeed. It all looks fabulous" Ana said "thanks so much."

Tom looked around. He'd seen the Ferrari in the car park by the playground, but no sign of the BMW or the twins.

"Tom trusts you implicitly, he tells me, so you are now one of us Ana. This saga is far from over and I'm sure you will be of great assistance in getting us through to the end of it."

"I'll do what I can" Ana said. This guy sure was interesting. Tom's descriptions of him were bang on. Suave, sophisticated, very stylish and yes... sexy. She found his slightly pedantic, not quite perfect English and slight accent quite beguiling. Not to mention his wonderful dog!

"How's your mother Carlo?" Tom asked.

"She is showing signs of improvement Tom. Still unconscious but the doctors are cautiously optimistic. Thank you for asking."

"That's great." Ana said. Then, as if it were time to get back to business, Carlo said

"The police are, how you say, 'gearing up'. Have you looked at the cameras lately Tom?"

"Ah, no. I thought we'd pretty much finished with them."

"I flick through them most days, for a variety of reasons. There is more going on than only your troubles. Oh, that sounded awful. Mi dispiace."

"No, no, I'm sure that's true" Tom said.

"Last night two of our band of brothers in blue paid a little visit to the Cowes Bay Road property. It's all locked up, but they have keys of course. They also wandered down to la Bellissima. I wouldn't bother looking at the footage by the way, it's not worth wasting your time on."

Ana was trying to imagine what was coming next.

"What's la Bellissima?" she asked.

"The family yacht. Then this morning what should happen? A full-scale search, complete with drug dogs. Traitors eh Bello!"

"And...?" Tom asked, as intrigued as Ana.

"What did they find? Lo and behold, a bag full of cocaine. In a bedroom cupboard for fuck sake! Oh, forgive me Ana. And traces on the deck of the yacht. As if we are so stupid!"

"God" Ana said.

"They didn't even look inside the bag when they 'found' it. Why? Because they knew what it contained. How? Because of course they had put it there the night before. But they have a surprise coming to them, oh yes" and Carlo gave a strange, hard chuckle.

For the first time Tim sensed that under Carlo's smooth, benign exterior there was a deep vein of potential for... what? Anger? More than that, a potential for white hot, pitiless fury.

What would this man not be capable of? Tom shuddered to think.

* * * *

Sitting at Bill's desk, Stan was on his fourth draft of the news release. How does this sound...

'Police today revealed that a large amount of cocaine had been discovered at the Waiheke property where several people died last weekend. It is understood up to ten kilograms of the drug could be involved. Inspector Stanley Williams said this lent considerable weight to the police belief that the deaths that day resulted from a dispute over a drug deal. He said that

the investigation is ongoing, and more announcements should be expected in the coming days.'

Yes, that'll do nicely. Right. I'll just get that off to the Media Centre for release. Not bad timing. It would catch the drivetime and early evening news. Stan was feeling very pleased with himself.

* * * *

"Hey listen to this." Ana read from her laptop.

'At approximately 1.30 this afternoon, two men were shot and killed in a downtown Auckland car parking building, in what police say bore all the hallmarks of a gangland execution. The two men were Russians on expired tourist visas. The car park's security cameras were temporarily out of service for maintenance, and police have no leads as to the identity or motives of the killer or killers.'

Good God, Tom thought. That was when we were having lunch. The Thompson Twins weren't there. Coincidental? I can only hope so. I can hardly ask Carlo. But he was sorely tempted.

"What is it?" Ana asked. It would not have occurred to her to connect Carlo to the killings.

"Oh nothing, nothing. What's the world coming to, eh?" He'd never used that expression before in his life, but it was something his father had said often over the years. God.

Things were good with Ana. Very good. They were so comfortable and at ease with each other. Always tons to talk about, apart from the case. And they laughed a lot. Tom had been very careful not to assume anything about Ana, or how she might want the relationship to go. If there even was a 'relationship'. They were quite affectionate with each other, but it was more on the level of friends, at times he thought more like a brother and sister, than anything sexual.

He had stayed over three nights now, although he didn't really know how that had come about. It had been the same each time. Clothed and chaste, but cuddling, 'spooning', all night. Then this morning Ana had woken up, turned to him and said

"Do you think it's time we..."

"I do." Tom said.

They did, and it was pure bliss.

* * * *

The man walked straight up to Jim's door. His hand was on the door handle when Constable Matt Burrows said

"Hang on a minute mate. Are you authorised to be here?"

"I am the man's doctor. Of course I'm authorised."

'You're not the same one who was here earlier on." Matt said, trying to do his job well.

"No, we work shifts, just like you officer."

He certainly looked kosher. White coat, stethoscope, clip board, proper mask, even surgical gloves. Name tag, Dr. Paul Draper. He wasn't a Kiwi though, sounded more like a Pom.

"Good God man, will you let me do my job?!"

"Yeah, ok, way you go Doc" and Matt made a note of the visit in his log.

Inside the room Jim was dozing, with just the bedside lamp on. The door opening and closing roused him. Another bloody doctor? Why? Rick Jamieson only left a couple of - then the doctor took something out of his pocket. A handgun. This is it Jim thought. They've finally found me. Then the doctor pulled his mask down to his chin, smiled, and said

"Ciao Jim. I'm Carlo." Jim breathed a huge sigh of relief. So, this is the Carlo Tom has talked so much about. Giuseppe's... son?

"Carlo, good to meet you. But what are you doing here?"

"Piacere Jim. This is just a little something I have brought for you." Carlo put the gun on the bed. It was a Beretta M9, like Giuseppe's.

"You will have a visitor tonight. He will come here to kill you. If you can, you should wait for him there, just inside the bathroom door. Can you do this?"

The drips had been taken out of his arm and Jim had already taken a few steps from his bed and back today, his leg killing him.

"I can" he said.

"Bene. Pile up all the pillows in the bed like a body and turn off the lights. He will most probably shoot what he thinks is you asleep. When the time is right, turn the lights on. See, you can reach the switch from there."

"How can you be so sure about this?" Jim asked

"We have eyes and ears, friends and family, everywhere." Carlo smiled. "And now before I go..."

Jim wondered what on earth he was doing. Carlo very purposefully picked up the bedside chair and took it to the far corner of the room. He stood on the chair, took something out of his pocket and pushed whatever it was up into the corner. He got down, put the chair back, took out a cell phone and pointed it at whatever he'd stuck up in the corner. As if reading Jim's thoughts Carlo said

"It is a tiny camera. You would never know would you not? A little insurance policy. I am just setting and checking it... there, 'good to go' as you Kiwis say.

"Now, I will take my leave. You will be fine tonight, I am sure. All you need to do is stay awake and then... what you do so well. Buona notte my friend. We will meet again."

And he was gone. Jim heard him say

"Thank you, Constable. Enjoy the rest of the evening" as he shut the door behind him.

* * * *

Ana and Tom had just finished some rather good takeaways that Tom had gone out to get, and both had returned to their laptops, with the last glass each from the bottle Tom had brought back with the food.

It was an Obsidian Syrah, four years old. He'd seen it in the bottle store and thought it fitting, a Waiheke vintage. It was far more than he would normally spend, but they both agreed it was worth every cent.

"Hey, check out *The Herald*." Tom said. He was looking at Stan's release on the drug find. "Do we know anything about this Stan Williams?"

"Not really. I met him with Bill Smales on the island. Seemed alright. 50's. Average sort of bloke."

"Do you think he was behind planting the cocaine? Or at least knew about it?" Tom asked.

"Dunno. I'd be surprised, I'm not sure why."

"Well, if he didn't know he's sure fallen for it hook line and sinker. Don't suppose it matters, except it means more strife for dad." Tom said.

"Mmmm. Is there any way we could use the footage without identifying Jim?"

"No, he's in virtually every shot. Well, not every shot, but the vast majority. Wouldn't make any sense without him. Apart from the footage of the drugs being planted." Tom added.

"That's probably worth keeping in mind."

"We could fuzz out his face, but I doubt that dad would go for it. Quite apart from the footage, he does seem to want his day in court. By the way, what did you think of Carlo?"

"Dangerous. Interesting, and charming, but definitely dangerous." Ana said.

"And sexy?" Tom asked, fishing.

"Sure, very, but if it were a choice between him and Bello, I'd take Bello any day."

* * * *

Constable Matt Burrows was sitting, reading a book outside Jim's hospital room. He was on the graveyard shift and he'd be there for several hours yet. What's the time? 8.00. He didn't mind, he loved working nights.

"Hi Matt."

Matt, engrossed in his crime thriller, hadn't noticed Kevin approaching.

"Kev! G'day mate, what brings you here?"

Matt and Kevin had been through police college at the same time and knew each other well. Also, Matt had recently transferred to Central, so they saw quite a bit of each other.

"A friend of mine's just had a baby. I'm visiting them. How's Michelle, and the kids?"

"We're all good thanks Kev. " It would never have occurred to Matt to wonder about the location of maternity services in the hospital, relative to where he was. They were in fact several floors above them.

"Hey, terrible news about Phil, I'm very sorry mate."

"Yeah... bit hard.... can I get you anything? Coffee?" He knew Matt never said no to coffee.

"Coffee'd be bloody good actually. Thanks Kev. Milk and two. Help keep me awake!"

Kevin smiled grimly to himself. Not this one it won't.

* * * *

"Well apart from all the bad news, that was another very pleasant evening, thank you."

"You're most welcome. Thanks for the company - and the food and wine." Ana said.

Tom was deep in thought. What had his father done that his identity had to be kept private, and what if he didn't get name suppression? His picture would be everywhere anyway.

"Did I tell you, dad's got a lawyer seeking name suppression?"

"No, but I've been meaning to ask you about that. That's good. It'll be such a high-profile case, it should be granted. Listen, there will be a way through this. We know Jim's innocent, we just have to prove it somehow, in or out of court, recordings or no recordings."

"I guess so. Y'know, I really do appreciate your support with this." Tom said.

"Again, you are most welcome."

Tom yawned. "Don't think I'll be long out of bed tonight."

"Well, you'd better get going then. It's quite a walk back to your place."

He turned to look at Ana. She smiled.

"Just kidding."

* * * *

Constable Matt Burrows was sound asleep and snoring loudly in his chair outside Jim Carruthers' hospital room. His book was on the floor nearby, along with his overturned coffee cup, the last of its contents soaking into the carpet beside it.

Kevin looked down at him, snorted, took the handgun from his pocket, screwed on the silencer, and quietly entered the room. It was dark but he could make out the shape in the bed well enough.

Jim was in the bathroom with just his head, shoulder and the Beretta exposed. It was happening almost exactly as Carlo had predicted.

"Payback time motherfucker!" Kevin hissed and fired five quick rounds into the bed. Despite the 'silencer', the noise of the shots was still very audible, and Jim half expected it to wake the cop outside the door. It did not. Kevin was moving towards the head of the bed when Jim turned on the main, overhead light. Kevin said

"What the fuck?" at almost exactly the same time Jim said

"Drop it."

For a moment, they were both frozen in time and space. Then, at almost exactly the same time Kevin raised his gun towards him, Jim pumped four closely grouped 9mm bullets into his chest.

SIX

The sound of Jim's gunfire woke Constable Matt Burrows from his deep sleep. He jumped up and fell heavily against the wall, knocking the chair over in the process. What was that! Gunshots? W-o-o-o... my head! Christ what's wrong with me?

He crashed through Jim's door, nearly falling over, staggered into the room and again fell against a wall. He was confronted by a large man in a hospital gown holding a still-smoking handgun. Fear gripped him and grew by the second.

Jim raised the weapon towards him. Oh no! he thought. Michelle! The kids!

"It's ok mate, relax" Jim said as he flipped the gun around, presenting Matt with the butt.

"You'd better take this. He tried to kill me" Jim said, gesturing to the body half hidden behind the bed. Matt took the Beretta from Jim.

"What's going on?!" It was a voice at the door. A nurse and a hospital security guard were standing in the open door.

"Everything's under control. This is now a crime scene, so no entry please." Matt shut the door. He was starting to feel better, much better now his hands were on the Beretta, and Jim had sat on the bedside chair.

"Who tried to kill you?" he said moving, unsteadily, around the end of the bed. "Jesus Christ!"

It was Kev Smith, and he was very dead, having been shot several times in the upper torso. Matt had to get off his feet. He took the few steps back around the bed and sat down heavily on it. He looked around. The bed was shot to pieces too. Then he saw the gun and silencer where it had fallen from Kevin's hand onto the pillows piled up under the bedspread. What are you supposed to do in this sort of situation, Matt asked himself, what?!

"I'm Jim ." Jim said. Matt hadn't laid eyes on Jim until now.

"Matt." Matt said without thinking.

"You're my guardian angel I take it. Nice work, I could hear you snoring from here."

Matt ignored him. He was trying to decide what to do, who to call. He picked up Kevin's gun, went out into the corridor and shut the door, a gun in each hand. Bugger, he shouldn't be handling key pieces of evidence. Too late.

He was still feeling groggy as hell. He turned the chair upright and sat down. He never fell asleep on the job. It was as if he'd been... the coffee. Would Kevin have...? Well, maybe, if he was planning to kill Carruthers. With him asleep, and the silencer, he'd be in and out of there without a trace. And where did Carruthers get his gun from? It was all too much for Matt Burrows from Lower Hutt.

Who should he call? Who's in charge of this case? Inspector Williams. Yes. There was a phone number at the top of the log sheet.

What a fucking mess.

* * * *

Inspector Stanley Williams was thinking about having an early night. He was pleased with how the Waiheke case was going. He'd had a couple of restless nights worrying about aspects of it, particularly the business about the 111 call, but he'd find a way around that. No, there was nothing that would keep him awake tonight. Then his phone rang.

Stan was speechless. He couldn't believe what he was hearing. Recovering somewhat, he asked

"Does anyone else know about this Constable? Good. Let's keep it that way for the moment, say nothing to anyone. Stay put. I'll be there as soon as I can."

Stan decided he would take a couple of minutes to think this over. Poor Kevin. Poor stupid Kevin, why couldn't he just let justice take its course? Then again, if Carruthers hadn't had a gun, and prior warning by the sound of it, Kev might well have gotten clean away with it, and that, actually, would have made everyone's life a whole lot easier. Where and how did Carruthers get that bloody gun? And who warned him? He wouldn't have put the pillows in the bed like that unless he knew what was coming.

How would this look? A cop setting out to kill the prime suspect and getting killed himself instead. It was clearly self-defence, but such a bad look - for him, his case, and the force. And bloody Carruthers might get some sympathy in the process. A really bad look all round...

How could he spin this?

An idea began to form in Stan's mind. Apart from the odd exception, he'd always played by the book. In recent years anyway. Was this another 'odd exception'? Stan thought maybe it was. A big one too. It would all depend on Matt Burrows. Stan opened his laptop. Where's that email he'd got from Facilities. He found it. It was advising senior staff about a new crime scene clean-up company. Totally reliable and totally discreet, unlike the previous lot the police had been using. Fancy putting photos of murder scenes, suicides and rapes on social media. Disgusting.

He looked them up. A 24hr emergency service too, that's good. But no, too risky, much too risky, they'd file reports for sure; what was he thinking! Bugger. No, he'd ring a couple of guys he knew. They owed him, and with what he had on them, they were sure to be 'discreet'.

He'd better get to the hospital.

* * * *

Stan Williams and Matt Burrows stood a few feet along the corridor from Jim's room at the hospital.

"Thanks for calling me first Constable. You alright? Must have been a terrible shock."

"It sure was Inspector. Poor old Kev. I thought Carruthers was gonna shoot me too. I'm still a bit shaky, and that coffee didn't help."

"Yeah."

"Should we call this in sir?"

"Call me Stan. We will, we will, but I've been thinking about this Matt. Kevin was a good man. You knew him, eh?"

"Yeah, quite well. It's a shocking thing..."

"Yeah. Poor bugger. You know Carruthers killed both his brothers?"

"No! I knew he'd killed Phil but... I didn't even know there was a third brother. Jesus."

"Keep that to yourself, but you can sort of understand how that might've sent Kev a bit... well... crazy."

"I can, I can."

"I think it'd be a real shame if tonight's what he's remembered for. Spotless career otherwise."

"I reckon" Matt said.

"Right, I've told the staff to sort out another room for Carruthers; it's that one there on the right, with the door open. You take him there now and set yourself up outside. I'll wait downstairs. A clean-up crew will be here soon, and they'll put this room to rights. They'll have to work around Kev, but they'll cope.

"So, let's say you dozed off - which is true - and next thing you hear gunshots. Ok? It won't look great on your record, but it's not a major."

"Ok." Matt didn't like this much at all, but he agreed about Kev, and it wouldn't be down to him if anything went wrong. He was just following orders.

"Then I'll call it in. Oh, and give me the weapon Kev used. Thanks."

Matt did as he'd been told. He took a bemused and suspicious Carruthers to his new room, put the Beretta back in the crime scene, and settled down outside Jim's new room. He'd said goodbye to Kev, but he couldn't bring himself to look at him again.

He saw the two clean-up guys arrive in their dark blue overalls and push a large laundry trolley into the room. Then he heard a vacuum cleaner. That'll be for the kapok from the bedding that Kev's shots kicked up, he supposed. After a few minutes they came out again. Matt thought they'd finished, but they went into another room, came out with a complete set of bedding, took it into Carruthers' original room and left with the trolley a short time later. They'd obviously had very clear, and simple, instructions. Remove all evidence of there ever having been a second weapon in that room. They'd never once looked at or acknowledged him. What a horrible job, Matt thought.

God, it was still only 10.30.

* * * *

"Nothing here as pretty as La Bellissima." Carlo said.

It was another glorious morning in the city of sails, and he and Tom were having coffee at the Viaduct Basin, at a counter on the boardwalk, looking out across the berths full of expensive pleasure craft. It wasn't far from Carlo's downtown office apparently. The Thompson Twins were a little further along and Bello was alongside Carlo, as always.

"I'm looking forward to seeing her at some point" Tom said.

"Yes, I'll take you and Ana for a sail one day."

Tom felt he should tell Carlo about his father's attitude to the use of the recordings. It was frustrating not being able to just call and tell him over the phone, but that was not something Carlo would even contemplate.

"I must say I'm surprised and, like you, I wonder why. Don't misunderstand me Tom, but is your father... himself, his normal self, would you say?"

"I've wondered that too Carlo. Yes, he seems to be, well apart from his injuries. He's still on a lot of medication, and painkillers, but he seems clear-headed to me."

"Mmmm. He obviously doesn't want his name - or his face - to be seen. I wonder why?"

"He's always been a very private person" Tom suggested, rather limply, he thought.

"I suppose it is his decision. I have nothing to gain either way, although I would not wish Jim to spend the rest of his life in prison.

"There is also my mother to consider..." Carlo added, very seriously.

Tom couldn't think of much else to say. He suddenly realised he had never seen Carlo laugh. He wondered if he ever did. Not long ago he'd read an interesting book on Silvio Berlusconi.

Tom thought he would test the relationship a little and told Carlo what was reported in the book to be Berlusconi's favourite joke, about an Italian truck driver shipwrecked on a desert island with Claudia Schiffer.

Carlo laughed out loud and kept laughing. Old Silvio obviously knew a good joke when he heard one.

"That is very funny my friend. I haven't laughed so much in many a year. Berlusconi, you say? I had not thought him to have such a good sense of humour." A pause, and then Carlo said quietly

"I don't laugh very much these days. Which is sad."

Tom thought he would capitalise on the moment. He couldn't resist asking, trying to sound matter of fact.

"Hey Carlo. Those guys in the downtown carpark the other day... I noticed the Thom - your boys weren't around when we were having lunch."

Carlo looked at Tom. It was a different look from any Tom had seen before. Suddenly icy and as hard as crystal. Tom immediately regretted having raised it. Then Carlo's eyes softened.

"You are not so silly are you, my friend Tom" and he smiled, then looked down at his hands. "I am in a very competitive business. There is always some player or another trying to displace us or steal from us. Sniffing around, as they say." He looked up.

"It was just... sending a message."

That icy look had returned to Carlo's eyes, boring into Tom's like gimlets. A message indeed. Message received.

* * * *

The crime scene operations unit had arrived at the hospital within thirty minutes of Stan's call the night before, and he was there to meet them. It had all gone smoothly. Matt had played his part well and was calm and collected as he gave them his statement.

In discussion with the officer in charge, Stan had surmised that Sergeant Kevin Smith had gone to talk to Carruthers, no doubt about his brother's death. Perhaps he was seeking some resolution, reconciliation, or even just some understanding of Carruthers' motives. One thing was clear, it didn't look like he he'd had any malicious intent. It wasn't as if he'd been armed. Yes, he agreed, it was a shame Constable Burrows had nodded off. No, Stan had no idea where Carruthers' weapon could have come from, nor indeed how Kevin Smith had discovered his identity or whereabouts.

The officer in charge was happy for Stan to interview Carruthers, it was his case after all. He would do that in the morning, at the same time he served him with the warrant on the drugs charges.

Another moment to be savoured.

* * * *

Carlo was back to his usual charming, affable self.

"Oh, dear me. I had temporarily forgotten. I have some news for you too Tom."

He spoke as if he was about to tell Tom something of no great significance, like a new cafe or bar he'd discovered.

"You might want to visit your father this morning. I do not think he will be greatly upset by it, but he killed another cop last night."

"What?!" Needless to say, Tom was aghast. He nearly fell off his stool. How could he, he was in hospital, and under 24-hour watch.

"Yes, the last of the three Smith brothers. I knew he was coming so I called in and gave Jim a weapon so he could defend himself."

Tom was dumbstruck. He didn't even know there was another brother. How had Carlo managed to 'call in' to his father's room and give him a gun? What was the cop guarding him doing? And how did Carlo know the attack was imminent? Yes, he must go and see Jim.

"I also installed a camera while I was there. You might want to see what happened. Here is the link." He pushed a piece of paper along the counter to Tom.

"And now, I must go."

Without another word Carlo got up and left.

* * * *

Sitting in his office and feeling tired and stressed, Stan was seriously out of sorts.

This bloody coffee wasn't helping either, not nearly as good as theirs on the island. Fancy having to deal with this on top of everything else. At least it cemented in Carruthers as a major villain.

Poor old Kevin. Stan had been serious when he suggested that the death of his two brothers might have made him a bit crazy, mad for revenge. But it was good that he'd managed to fudge the reality of what happened in Carruthers' room. It wouldn't have been good for Kev's legacy, or the reputation of the force.

He'd decided against doing any sort of announcement about Kevin's death. Yet another murder charge for Carruthers to face, but he'd leave the details to come out in court. He was clearly guilty of the other charges, so Stan didn't feel too bad about setting him up for Kevin's death as well.

Obviously, there would be nothing broadcast about Kevin's and Phil's relationship to Shane either, that would no doubt be revealed in court too, unless the press got onto it first. The brothers didn't appear to have any living relatives, so apart from Phil's wife, there was no family to advise.

He'd disposed of the gun and silencer. Where had Kevin got those? Can only have been from some crim he knew... or the evidence lock-up maybe, lots of gear like that there, but how would he have got access to it? And who could have smuggled that Beretta into Carruthers? He must have someone helping him, but who? And when could that have happened? He'd only been moved to the private room earlier the same day - God was that only yesterday - and he can't have had the gun when he'd been moved, so it must've been some time after that.

The visitor log. The guys on duty at the hospital were keeping a record of all Carruthers' visitors. That might tell him something. He called Sharlene into his office.

* * * *

Sergeant Tim Adams was feeling good. His scam with the drugs had gone perfectly, and he and Andy had had a great time the previous evening with the small amount of cocaine that had somehow made its way into their possession. Shit it was powerful. Just as well they'd taken it carefully. And there was still plenty left. They'd drunk heaps as well, so he was feeling a bit hung over, but apart from that, and the inevitable runny nose... yes, life was ok, and it was bloody nice not having Stan around, silly old fool. What did he feel like? Yes. Coffee. That'll help.

He walked into the cafeteria. Sally Reynolds was there, bent over the coffee machine. He hadn't really noticed her bum before. It was cute. Fancy her and Phil...

"Hi Tim, just having coffee, can I get you one?" she said.

"Yeah, thanks Sal, that'd be great."

They sat opposite each other in the comfortable armchairs in the corner of the cafeteria, a low coffee table between them, sunlight drifting through the sun-filter curtains.

"So how are you, Sal? Coming right? It's been a rough time for you."

"I'm ok thanks Tim. Yeah, it's been rough." Sally replied.

Tim looked at Sally. She really was quite pretty, and she looked positively angelic, backlit and haloed as she was by the filtered sunlight. She lifted the coffee cup to her lips and Tim noticed her wrists were badly bruised.

"Hey Sal! What happened to your wrists?"

"That was you silly, when you dragged me off Phil. I took a bit of handling, eh?"

"Shit, sorry Sal. Yeah, you were a bit of a wild thing alright!"

"Yeah..." Sally said, her thoughts drifting back to that day. She shifted in her chair, uncrossed her legs and crossed them the other way. In the process her skirt rode up. She made no attempt to rearrange it, and Tim had a rather good view of her long shapely legs, to well up her thighs. Yeah, she was hot, Tim decided.

"Did Stan sort you out with some counselling Sal? I hope he at least offered it as an option."

Counselling was standard for officers these days, after potentially traumatic events and experiences.

"Yeah, but I didn't want to talk about all that stuff with a stranger." Sally replied.

There was a pause while Tim wondered what to say to keep the conversation going.

"You could... talk to me, if you think that'd help."

"Gee thanks Tim. That'd be good actually."

She looked at him. Not a bad-looking guy she supposed. Much younger than Phil, but... you can't have too many friends, and allies, Sally thought to herself.

"Not here at work though. Do you want to chat over a drink later?" Tim said.

* * * *

"Lunch delivered 12.10, Staff Nurse Taylor 1.30, Staff Nurse Taylor again at 3.15, Mr. Rick Jamieson 5.40, and Dr. Paul Draper 7.05. That's it for yesterday." Sharlene reported.

"7.05? That's late for a doctor's visit, isn't it? Maybe not... but less than two hours after the previous one? Listen, check the bona fides of both those doctors, would you?" Stan asked.

"Sure Inspector."

"And while you're at it, I've been thinking Sharlene, there's a hell of a lot that doesn't add up about this Carruthers character. He's not your average Joe Bloggs that's for sure, but I mean, what do we actually know about him? Bugger all. Would you dig up everything you can on him? Birth certificate, where he went to school, medical records, any military service, anything you can find."

"Of course, Inspector."

* * * *

Once again Tom was watching his father kill a man. Like the footage from Waiheke, there was an element of unreality about it. One step removed somehow, like watching a violent scene in a movie. But this was real. This was his father, and this new footage was no less disturbing than all of that which he'd seen so many times from the Cowes Bay Road cameras.

He was witnessing a life being taken, snuffed out in seconds by the man who had never once raised his voice to Tom, let alone a hand.

For the first time Tom was beginning to wonder how Jim could be capable of this, not just physically, but also emotionally. His father had always been so adept with his hands, building, everything from balsa wood planes to garages to decks and additions to houses, fixing things, showing Tom how everything from electricity to engines worked, that he hadn't stopped to ask himself where his obvious skill with weapons had come from. There'd never been so much as a water pistol in the house. Had he had military training when he was young perhaps? He'd never mentioned it.

Also, in none of his visits since last Sunday had Jim shown any reaction at all, let alone remorse, about the fact that he'd killed five people. Now it was six. How would he react to his latest taking of a life, a human life? Homicide. He suspected Carlo was right, he wouldn't be unduly upset. There was no doubt that Jim's actions were reactive and justified, nonetheless... What did he really know about his father? How well did he even know him?

"That's dreadful" Ana said. "Poor man, what more does he have to go through."

She had insisted on watching with Tom - in order to support him, not from any prurient interest in seeing more death and destruction - and the questions on Tom's mind were furthest from her thoughts. She just saw an aging man, yet again fighting for his life.

"I'd better get to the hospital" Tom said.

"Can I come?" Ana asked.

"Yeah, why not, if you want. Good idea." Apart from anything else Tom realised he'd like his dad to meet her.

* * * *

"First of all, Mr. Richard Jamieson is a Fellow of the Royal Australasian College of Surgeons and works five tenths at the hospital, but get this, Dr. Paul Draper doesn't exist. The hospital has never heard of him and no-one of that name is a registered medical practitioner of any sort."

"Damn. So that's how he got the gun. Who is he I wonder... can't be the son, he'd be recognised by the guys on the door. So, who's helping Carruthers? What else have you got?"

"On Carruthers? There's not much to tell... " Sharlene said "UK birth certificate and passport. Emigrated here in 1984, aged 28..."

"He's a Pom? I wouldn't have picked it." Stan said.

"Gained citizenship in 1989, married Sue Grant the same year. Still together. One child, a son Tom, born 1993." Sharlene continued

"No criminal record. Several speeding tickets over the years. Small but successful communications / media business. Still going. He and son Tom are Directors. Tom mostly running the business now, Jim pretty much retired. I managed to get a copy of his original visa application too... "

"Great. What does that tell us?" Stan asked.

"Again, not much I'm afraid. Occupation 'Journalist'. Previous employers 'Freelance, various'. Huh. Countries visited... lots."

"Doesn't tell us much at all... listen, what was the name of that guy from the NCB who rang Bill the other day?"

"Sorry Inspector, not sure what you're talking about." Sharlene said.

"No of course, stupid of me, that was on the island. Thanks for all that Sharlene. Good work."

Sharlene wasn't quite as dirty on Stan as she had been initially. He was treating her well, certainly keeping her busy, and seemed... ok. Nothing like Bill, but ok. Once she'd left his office, Stan rang Waiheke.

"Dave Bretherton, that's right, flick me his number? Thanks a lot Alice, see you soon. Oh, just a mo. How's Sally doing? ...that's good, that's good."

Stan's thoughts strayed for a moment.

* * * *

"Hello, is that Mr. Carlo Giordano?"

"It is."

"It's staff nurse Jane Coombs from the Critical Care Unit at Auckland City Hospital."

"Is there some news?" Carlo asked.

"Yes, and it's good news. Your mother is awake Mr. Giordano."

* * * *

I wonder how this will all go. Who was that guy last night? The cop minding me, Matt, knew him, that's certain... and he'd clearly been drugged the way he staggered into the room, plus he'd heard him snoring his head off. So, he wasn't in on it.

The move was well-planned and if Carlo hadn't warned me, and armed me, it would have gone off without a hitch. Who set it up? Did it come from someone on the case, Williams himself even, or someone lower down who knew their case was full of holes, and thought it'd be much easier without me around? Who else could it have been? What motive would they have? The guy did say 'Payback time...' which could imply it was personal, but why? And payback for what? Surely not.... Of course, Jim had no idea that Kevin was the brother of Shane and Phil Smith. His thoughts of possible revenge were for something much earlier in his life than this latest debacle.

No, it wouldn't happen like this, and why now after all these years? His cover had worked for nearly thirty-five years, and if he got through this without his identity becoming known it should continue to work. That security footage must never see the light of day though. Damn it! He should've walked away from that bloody house when he had the chance. No, he shouldn't have, couldn't have. In fact, since that day he had been feeling a hint of something he never expected to feel, ever. It was a sense of something like... redemption, and it felt good, calming, soothing him on some deep level. His 'soul' maybe? Maybe he still had one after all.

But he was tired, so tired, so sick of it all. It had been so lonely, and such hard work, every day, all these years. All the secrecy, all the lies, the guilt. And more guilt now for Rawiri, another child to add to the toll... Then Jim did something he had no recollection of doing since... when? Since his parents died. He cried.

* * * *

"Hello my dear man. You are looking so much better today!" Edie gave Bill a kiss on the forehead. She did so love him, her big strong policeman. It was very sad seeing him like this. He wasn't young anymore, but he wasn't that old either, and here he was incapacitated, weak and looking much more than his fifty-eight years. At least he was still with her, and he was improving already.

Bill was having therapy of various sorts, several times a day. The physio was intense, but he was making progress and was more or less mobile, at this point with the help of a walking frame. And the speech therapy was having quite startling results. His speech was still slurred and halting but was already at the stage where he could easily be understood.

"Hi ... E..die. Fee...ling mush bet..ter. You lo..ok nishe to...day."

The neurologists agreed Bill's cognitive skills didn't appear to have been damaged to any observable degree, and the team was pleased that Bill was quite quickly getting back on top of ADL - the Activities of Daily Living - the main focus in the days immediately following a stroke.

"They th..ink I might... come ho...me nex wee...k"

"That's fantastic darling. I've told them at work that I'll be taking extended leave, so I'll be there for you, full time. Won't it be nice, just the two of us? Like being on holiday!"

"Ye..sh, it... will. E..die, b..ring.. my lap..top nex t..ime you c..ome? And cell...phone and ch..ar..gers. P..lea..se."

"Sure Bill, but there's no rush to get back to work. Just take it easy, eh?"

* * * *

"Hey dad, how's it - " Tom stopped, halfway into the room. Tears were streaming down Jim's face.

"What's up dad? What on earth's happened? Are you ok?" Tom realised he'd never before seen his father cry.

"Yes, yes. I'm fine, everything's ok, it's just... sometimes the pain gets a bit much, that's all." Jim dried his eyes with a tissue from the bedside cabinet.

"Shall I call for a nurse?" Ana asked.

"Hello. No, no, I'm good now. Thanks. So, introduce us Tom." Jim said, now back in control.

Tom was still recovering from seeing his father in tears. He didn't buy the pain explanation for one minute. Jim had been in severe pain on at least a couple of his earlier visits, and it hadn't elicited a hint of a tear. So much for his father being incapable of emotion.

"Oh yes, sorry. Dad this is Anahera Harris. Ana, my dad Jim."

"Hi Mr. Carruthers, pleased to meet you."

"Jim, please. Love your work by the way Anahera."

"Thanks Jim."

"So, dad, what happened last night? I've seen the footage but who was that guy? And how'd you get the gun? Did Carlo - "

"Yes, Carlo came in, dressed as a doctor. He got past the cop at the door, gave me a Beretta, warned me someone was coming, put a tiny camera up in the corner of the room, and you've seen the rest. Afterwards they moved me to another room and that's all I know." Jim said.

"Well, we kept watching. Some guys came in, cleaned the place up and changed the bedding, all before the crime scene guys arrived. Sorry to tell you dad, but it looks like they're setting you up again. Wouldn't you say Ana?"

"Very much so."

"Damn." Jim said.

Ana looked at him. Big man, about the same size as Tom she thought. Same broad frame, strong face, Jim's more lined and weather-beaten, but clearly father and son. Same big hands, she liked men with big hands. Back on the East Coast all her Māori boyfriends had had big hands. Different eyes though. Jim's were sharper, edgier that Tom's, with a hardness just not there in Tom's lovely soft, gentle, grey-green eyes.

She knew Jim had been through a lot lately, but it struck her that it was more than that, she had a strong sense that those eyes had, in fact, seen a great deal over the years.

"As you know dad, Ana is right up to speed with the case. She's seen all the recordings, including last night's and - "

"She knows they can't be used? You do know that Ana?" Jim almost snapped at her.

"Yes, yes" Tom and Ana chorused.

"Sorry, I... it's just really important."

"I know it is dad, and we'll respect your wishes of course. I just wish you could tell us why."

Jim was sorely tempted to give them something. He could trust Tom. What about Ana Harris? He had the strong feeling there was something between these two. He might as well ask.

"I get the feeling... sorry to be so blunt, but... are you guys an item?" Jim asked.

That was a most unexpected question. Tom and Ana looked at each other, neither knowing what to say, neither really knowing what they had together.

"I... we've known each other barely a week dad..." I'll be honest Tom thought

"...but I'd certainly like us to be" he blurted out and turned to look at Ana. What would she say?

"Me too" she said, without the slightest hesitation, and gave Tom the loveliest smile. Wow, thought Tom. Wow!

"The reason I ask - I think that's great by the way - the reason I ask is that I would like to share something with you. I feel I can trust you... both."

"You can" they chorused again.

" There's a price - "

"What the fuck is this?!" a voice boomed from the doorway. It was Inspector Williams.

"What are you doing here Harris. Reporters are banned from visiting this man. Who did you pretend to be this time? Get out!"

Very calmly, Ana said

"I'm not here as a reporter Inspector. I'm here as a lawyer. This man's lawyer."

Both Tom and Jim were more than surprised to hear this. 'Flabbergasted' would not be an overstatement.

"Oh yeah, pull the other one. Go on, get out!"

Ana quietly opened her handbag and took out a card. It was the newly issued Law Society ID card, designed to give barristers easier and quicker access to court buildings.

"Of course, you can check this out, but I assure you it's real, and valid." She gave it to Williams. He studied the card and looked genuinely perplexed.

"I will check it out, and if you're lying..." for once Stan was lost for words.

"Please do. In the meantime, I'd like to resume the discussion I was having with my client. What, may I ask, is the reason for your visit? Anything that might concern me?"

"You might say so." Stan said as sarcastically as he could. "Another arrest warrant. He knows his rights by now." Stan very brusquely handed the document and the ID card to Ana and positively flounced out of the room.

There was a long pause.

* * * *

"Ciao mamma. Come va?"

"Carlo, bambino, che bello vederti."

Carlo and his mother continued their conversation in Italian, Francesca speaking with some difficulty given her facial injuries.

"Wonderful to see you too mama. You made it!"

Carlo could see very little of his mother's face, just her right eye and her mouth, around which there was still some nasty bruising. Fortunately, she didn't appear to have lost any teeth, not at the front anyway. The bandages completely covered the rest of her face.

The doctors had told Carlo that Francesca's cheek bone had been shattered, her jaw dislocated and fractured. Her skull had also been split and she had had major swelling on the brain. They were delighted and amazed that she was recovering, and with no apparent brain damage. It was nothing short of a miracle one of the nurses told Carlo on the way in to see his mother.

"Yes, what a terrible day that was. Giuseppe? Is he...?"

"He's gone mama, don't you remember? He was - "

"Oh yes. How awful, I never thought it would end for him like that. I will miss him so much. What about the man who saved me?"

"Jim. He's still in hospital, but he too is doing well."

"What a good, brave man. Are you looking after him?"

"As much as I can mama. The police are playing dirty tricks, as they do."

"And the policeman who killed Giuseppe and hit me with the gun?"

"Jim killed him too."

What a shame it was that Jim had been the one to kill Sergeant Smith. I wish it had fallen to me, Carlo thought. Killing Giuseppe and striking my beautiful mother. His death would not have been so... easy.

"Good. Good." Francesca said.

"Listen mama, you might as well hear it from me. Jim has been charged with murder and with drug dealing. Now that you are clearly going to survive, they will charge you with drug offences too."

"That's ridiculous! How could they possibly - "

"They planted cocaine in the house."

His mother slumped in the hospital bed.

"I want to go home. Italia." she moaned.

* * * *

Ana bloody Harris... A fucking lawyer too! Stan was fuming, drumming his fingers on Bill's desk, waiting for his call to be answered.

"Dave Bretherton."

"Hi Dave, Inspector Stan Williams here. We haven't met, but I've been working with Bill Smales on this Waiheke case. You rang him a couple of days ago."

"Yeah, yeah. Hi Stan, how's it all going?"

"Pretty well thanks Dave. Gotta say, your info gave us a bit of a breakthrough."

"Glad I could help. How's Bill?" Stan told him about the stroke.

"I'm really sorry to hear that. He's a good old boy, Bill. Give him my best regards next time you see him."

Stan told Dave about the drug discovery.

"Well, that's a stroke of luck. Unusually sloppy of them though I must say, the Giordanos. Getting careless obviously." It sounded highly unlikely to Dave.

"What I was ringing about Dave, is this Carruthers bloke, who took everyone out including a couple of ours, we know very little about him, and nothing at all before he emigrated from the UK. Wondered if you could run a check on him for us?"

"Sure Stan, it's what we're here for."

"His full name is - "

"Sorry to interrupt Stan, but if he's dodgy, the name he's using won't be of much use. Do you have his DNA on file?" Dave asked.

"Sure to have. He left a lot of blood at the crime scene."

"Ok, get your guys to flick the analysis to us, and if there's a match with one of our profiles, we'll know pretty much straightaway."

"Really?"

"Yep."

"If you've got anything, it'd be the thick end of thirty-five years old." Stan thought to mention.

"O-o-o-h, that's pushing it. But that's about when they started seriously collecting samples I think, so here's hoping. Ok?"

"Yeah, thanks Dave. I'll get onto it."

"Good man. Don't forget to pass on my best wishes to Bill."

Stan was amazed. He did a Google search.

'Interpol DNA Gateway...' database sharing tool.... over 250,000 profiles.... 84 member countries.... 5 to 7 minutes to find a match...

Well, what about that! Stan thought to himself.

* * * *

Here they were, Tim Adams and Sally Reynolds, sitting in a bar in Oneroa, Waiheke Island, overlooking the bay bathed in the last of the day's golden light. It was the same table where she had sat with Phil, months ago now, the night she decided she would invite him to her bed. She so missed that, and him.

She and Tim had talked for what seemed like hours. She was remarkably open with him, and he had proved to be a good listener. Perhaps it was the training in interviewing techniques, but he had asked just the right questions at the right time, to make her relax enough to let her thoughts and feelings just... flow, tumble out. And not just about that dreadful day, but all sorts of stuff about her childhood, family, police college, the job and not least, her feelings for Phil, what he had meant to her, and him as a lover. Not in any detail, but how he had let her express herself, made her feel....

Perhaps she had needed counselling. It felt very therapeutic just... talking to someone. And with the martinis too, Sally was feeling more herself, more alive, than she had for what felt like ages. It had been barely a week, but such a long, long week.

Had anyone been passing Sally's bedroom later that evening, they might well have heard a small voice say

"Oh Tim..."

* * * *

"Bingo." Dave Bretherton crowed.

"Really? Great!"

"There's some holes, but we've found your man. Jim Carruthers is none other than one James Sykes, born, same date as you have, at Royal London Hospital. Which means the birth certificate and passport he used to get into New Zealand were forgeries, obviously."

"Amazing!" Stan said.

"Only child. Middle-class, reasonably well-off parents. Went to middling good public schools, what we call private schools. I'll put all this in a report to you, but I thought you'd like to hear the guts of it straight away."

"Yeah. Thanks a lot." Stan said, trying not to sound too excited.

"When he was 15, parents killed in a car crash. Started getting into trouble.... o-o-o-h, bad boy... expelled from school at 16, then nothing after that..."

"Oh no." Stan said.

"...until he turns up in the army aged 18. Accepted into the SAS at 20. Did rather well there... at 23 was made Captain of a troop... 16 members in a

CRW Squadron, that's Counter Revolutionary Warfare. Sykes's specialties... Signals, intelligence gathering, and CQB - Close Quarter Battle."

"Wow!" Stan's mind was working overtime. That sure did explain his facility with weapons.

"Posted all round the world, just about every hot spot there was at that time. Then after three years he left. Resigned."

"Jesus" Stan said.

"At that point, the trail runs cold. A couple of years later he moves here. Unfortunately, those two years are a blank."

"Bugger."

"But I've got an idea I want to chase up, so give me a few hours and I'll see what I can come up with." Dave said.

"Well even that much is pretty amazing. Explains a lot. Thanks Dave, you're a beaut."

"You're welcome mate. As I say there might be more to come. I'll be in touch. Ciao."

Immigration fraud to add to the list, Stan thought to himself. This guy just keeps on racking up the jail time.

* * * *

"Are you really a lawyer?" Tom asked.

"Yes. Did all the bar exams, got admitted and took a few cases to court but after nearly eight years, including uni, I needed a break, and journalism had always appealed."

"Never tempted to go back to it?" JIm asked.

"No. I really like what I'm doing now. I renew my practising licence every year though, fifteen hundred bucks, and I always wonder why I do. Maybe there was a reason." And Ana smiled.

"Dad had thought to defend himself in court." Tom ventured.

"Yes, you said. But I could help if you want Jim, either as co-counsel, or an amicus curiae maybe."

"Friend of the court" said Jim "I've seen references to that but what is it that he or she does, in reality."

"It's a pretty flexible role. I could be there just to give you advice, or I could examine or cross examine some witnesses, or address the court for you. Obviously, I know a bit more about the law than you do. I haven't done a lot of court cases, but I know everything there is to know about procedure and protocols."

"Could be very handy dad."

"It could indeed. Thanks so much for the offer Ana, we'll talk more about that. I'd want to pay you of course."

"We can talk more about that too." Ana smiled. "I'm not exactly snowed under with writing work at the moment."

"So, what's this new warrant for?" Tom asked.

"It's for... 'The possession of a Class A narcotic, for sale or supply.' As expected. Did you know Jim, that there's a recording of one of the Waiheke cops planting the cocaine?" Ana asked.

"No, I hadn't got around to mentioning that" Tom said.

"Carlo and his cameras, eh?" Jim laughed. "Yes, making those recordings public would solve all my problems. All but one, that is..."

Tom and Ana waited. Would Jim return to what he had started to tell them before Stan barged in? He did, after a long pause.

"When I left school, or soon after I left school, I joined the British army. After a couple of years I enrolled in the SAS, and after a few more years I left the army and went... freelance."

Tom said "Freelance? What, as a soldier? Were you a mer - "

" 'Soldier of Fortune' I would once have been called. More latterly, yes Tom, a mercenary, a PMC - Private Military Contractor. I wasn't a hired gun as such, I had a lot of skills in intelligence gathering, reconnaissance, signals and the like. But counter terrorism broadly was my specialty, so at times there were... engagements. They weren't always successful, most ops were, but one in particular went terribly wrong. In Colombia. Bad intel from the useless bloody CIA...."

Jim paused. This was obviously difficult for him to talk about. He was pausing often.

"Several civilians were killed, including a young... person... we didn't see them...."

Tom was listening intently. What an extraordinary story. And had he really never shared this with anyone in thirty years? He saw what looked like a mixture of pain, and relief, on his father's face.

"They were from a very important local... family... cartel. All of my squad were killed too, except me, I managed to escape. Do you know, in all those years I was never once shot? 'Lucky' Jim they used to call me. Now look at me." Jim gave an ironic snort.

"I never touched another gun after that day and moved here to New Zealand soon after. Anyway, as a result of that episode, there's a price on my head. A very large price, and there's 'honour' involved, which is important to them."

Both Tom and Ana simply stared at him. Of the myriad thoughts and questions in Tom's head, one jumped out.

"But dad that was, what, over thirty years ago. Surely - "

"These people never forget Tom, or forgive, believe me. Never, ever."

SEVEN

"Hi Stan, Dave Bretherton here. Got some more intel for you."

"Great."

"As you know I had a sneaky idea about those two years Sykes spent between leaving the army and moving to New Zealand. Well. There's always been a percentage of soldiers leaving countries' armed forces and signing up with companies or agencies that supply what they call Private Military Contractors. Mercenaries in other words. There weren't that many in Sykes's time, now it's a huge international business of course. Anyway, that's what Sykes did. For those two years he worked on contract in different countries around the world. He had a lot of valuable skills and, apparently, he was also a good leader of men, so he was in high demand. The last location we have for him is South America, either Peru or more probably Colombia we think.

"It's always been a messy place, but the big drug cartels were starting to form around that time, FARQ was gaining traction on the left, and there were a number of private armies on the right, politically speaking. Both the CIA and MI6 were in there, and they used mercenaries for a lot of the more clandestine, dirtier stuff, as they tend to do.

"It had been assumed that Sykes was MIA, dead, but he obviously survived, and something must have happened down there that led him to pack it all in. Really interesting that he's turned up here, eh? Thirty odd years later."

"Sure is" Stan said.

"Dunno if that's any use to you..."

"It could be. It could very well be. Thanks a lot Dave."

"No worries mate. Ciao."

Stan wasn't sure just how he would use this information, but he knew he would use it, and he knew it could be a trump card at some point, probably in court. God, there was a lot going on. I could use a hand, someone I can trust... Stan thought, and picked up the phone.

"Tim? Stan here. Got much on? Good. Listen mate, how would you feel about spending a bit of time in the city. There's some things I need a hand with and I don't really know any of the troops here. Yeah, you can commute, sure. Tell Roger he's in charge for a while."

Tim's new relationship with Sally was going so well, the nights particularly, that he wasn't keen to miss any right now.

"Ok, great, see you in a couple of hours then." Stan said.

* * * *

"Hi Superintendent." Ana said.

Bill Smales looked up from his laptop. He was sitting in the armchair alongside his bed.

"Anahera, kia ora my dear, how are you? Call me Bill please."

Ana was a little surprised by the warmth of his welcome, but also by the quality of his speech. It was a little slower than it used to be, but there was virtually no slurring and the left side of his face, while not entirely back to normal, was very much better.

"You're looking and sounding so much better Bill. What an amazing recovery. Well done!"

"Yes, everyone's very pleased with my progress. Still need a walking-stick, but I'm going home tomorrow." Bill said.

"That's great!" Ana said.

"I must say, Ana, I really appreciated your visit the day after the stroke, and this one today. It restores my faith in... people." He smiled. "I'm flattered you take the time."

"As I said the other day Bill, I like and respect you a lot, and it's so good you're on the mend. When do you think you'll be back at work?"

"I'm not sure... I've been thinking of taking early retirement. To be frank Ana I'm not sure my judgment is what it once was. Over the hill maybe. This Waiheke case..."

"You really don't need to comment on that Bill, I know that you - "

"No, but I'd like to say a couple of things, off the record..."

"Of course." Ana was quick to agree. Bill continued

"I've always admired your work, your commitment to digging out the truth, and your boundless energy. Very much between you and me, I don't like how the Waiheke case is going, and I'm not sure I want to be part of it anymore. This stroke has given me the opportunity to bow out, and I think I'll take it."

"I'm sorry to hear that Bill, you've always been such a straight shooter." Ana said. "Yeah, it's getting pretty messy alright."

"I won't say any more than this, but I deeply regret that press release. I'm sorry for the strife it must have caused you, because... I think you were right."

"Thanks Bill. I appreciate it. You've heard about the drug charges?" Ana asked.

'Yes, another worry.... and no comment."

"Fair enough. Oh, one thing you should know is that before getting into journalism, I trained as a lawyer, and I'll be representing Jim Carruthers in court."

Bill Smales laughed out loud in amazement.

"Ana - bloody - Harris! You never fail to surprise me. All I can say is, I wish you the very best of luck. I'll be watching with great interest!"

* * * *

In another part of the hospital Sue was visiting Jim, as she had done every day, at least once, since he'd been admitted.

"Yes, so as I told you was likely, they've charged me with all that. I expect it to be announced any time now."

"Oh dear, how do think it will go?"

"Well, one way or another I intend to get off. Oh, and you haven't met her yet, but our Tom has a new girlfriend. She's lovely and rather special in my view."

"I look forward to meeting her, but how does that - "

"She's Ana Harris." Jim said.

"The reporter? Really?"

"Yes, but she's not only an excellent journalist, she's also a lawyer. I was thinking I'd represent myself in court, but I've decided that she should."

"That's amazing Jim. Is she any good - as a lawyer? These are serious charges, are you sure she's up to it?"

"She's not super experienced, but I'd rather have her than any QC."

"Well up to you I suppose, I just hope your faith in her is justified. And she and Tom are...?"

"Yes, and I have a feeling it'll last. But..."

"What?"

"There's some other stuff I need to tell you." Jim said.

"What is it Jim, you look very serious."

"First, I love you and I've loved you from the very first moment I saw you. I've loved our life together, having a child with you. I've never been unfaithful to you, and I could not have wished for more in a partner..."

"That's lovely Jim and I feel exactly the same, but you're scaring me, what on earth is it?"

"It has to do with my life before I met you, before I came to New Zealand. Tom knows my history now, and it's time you did too."

Jim told Sue much the same story he had told Tom and Ana, including that he was a marked man.

"Oh my God" Sue said when he had finished.

"It's selfish of me, but I feel a huge sense of relief having told you." Jim said.

"I'm sure you do" Sue said quietly. She was deeply shocked. And confused. How could he have kept these things from her all these years? A mercenary? A professional killer? Who was he, really? Did she know him at all?

* * * *

"I want to know where Carruthers got that gun, who that bogus doctor was. He had a mask on of course, but Matt Burrows describes him as medium height, slim, olive skin and medium length black hair. Also said he sounded English, 'posh' English according to Matt. Who do we know who fits that description?"

"No-one I can think of boss." Tim replied.

"Ok, let me ask you this. What was the gun he took in for Carruthers?" Tim looked up the notes. "...a Beretta, yeah, Beretta 9mm."

"And where have we seen another one of those recently?"

"Ah... not sure boss."

What's wrong with Tim today, Stan thought to himself. Looks half asleep. What's he been getting up to in his spare time I wonder.

"Come on Tim, wake up. Cowes Bay Road, yes?"

"Sorry Stan, yes, yes of course."

"And where are Berettas made?"

"Italy!" Got one right finally, Tim thought to himself.

"And so as not to overtax your tiny brain, I'll tell you what I'm thinking. I think that there's someone we haven't considered in all this, and that's the Giordano son, Carlo. If Matt's not describing him I'll eat my hat. With the mask it'd never stand up in court, but I want to meet this Carlo Giordano.

"Get a number for him and ask him, politely, to come in, would you?"

"Will do Inspector."

Stan's unusually motivated, Tim thought, positively on a roll. A few minutes later he reported back.

"Mr. Giordano says, and I quote, he'd '...be delighted to meet and have a chat, but why not over a coffee somewhere... nice.' He suggested a place in the Viaduct, in an hour if we can make it."

"Cheeky prick" Stan said. "Well why not I suppose? Yeah, confirm that. Thanks Tim."

* * * *

Often over the years Jim had considered sharing his history with Sue and, now that he finally had, bits of it started coming back, details he hadn't thought about for years and had all but forgotten, like how he came to leave the army and go over to 'the dark side...'

"G'day Lucky, how's it goin'?"

"Two-Toes! How are you? Long time no see!"

Most of the guys had nicknames. Jim was 'Lucky' because he'd never been shot, and Brendon Tuki was 'Two-Toes' because part of his foot had been blown off by an IED in the Sudan. He walked with a slight limp but was otherwise fully functional.

" 'Two-Toes' Tuki, well fuck me. You disappeared mate. One day you were in barracks, the next you were gone. What happened?"

It was 1981 in a bar south of the river in London, frequented, among other disreputable types, by regular British soldiers and SAS men. Part of the reason for its popularity was the fact it wasn't too far from the barracks, had good beer, some of the best strippers in London, and good DJs. Right now, they were playing The Specials' *'You're Wondering Now'*. It had been released a year or so earlier but was still one of Jim's favourite songs. He'd recently met a couple of the band members in this very bar.

'You're wondering now, what to do, now you know this is the end...'

Plus, you were always guaranteed a good game of pool and, every now and then, a chance to check out how your martial arts training was holding up. Jim was part of a group having an end of day drink.

"Shit it's noisy, come out the back. Bring your beer. 'Scuse me lads." Jim said.

Out the back was a scungy low-lit outdoor area with a makeshift tarpaulin roof and a few bar leaners and stools, where people went for a bit of smoke-free air, for a quick snort or knee-trembler or, as in this case, a relatively quiet chat.

"Yeah well, I got called up at very short notice mate."

"Whaddaya mean 'called up', you were already in the army."

"By KMS, a private military supplier. They contract soldiers to the CIA, MI6, Mossad, anyone with the money, for black ops, counter insurgencies, whatever governments don't want to be seen to be doing."

Jim had always liked Two-Toes, this big, strong Māori guy. He was irrepressibly cheerful and good natured, hard as nails but gentle as well, always happy to talk, and you knew you could rely on him to have your back, whether in a bar fight or in the field. He was always talking about 'back home' in New Zealand.

He made it sound like paradise and it was somewhere Jim had decided he would visit one day.

* * * *

"Inspector Williams, piacere. That's Italian for 'pleased to meet you'. Much nicer, to my ear. And you must be..."

"Sergeant Adams, Tim Adams. Great dog, by the way, don't think I've ever seen a bigger Shepherd. Hi boy."

Tim reached out a hand to the dog. He was met with a blank look, a slight curling of the lips and a deep, menacing, growl. He quickly withdrew his hand.

"Now, now, Bello. These men are our guests, and not all policemen are bad. I'm told."

The waiter came over.

"What would you like gentlemen. The coffee here is excellent. As is the food." Carlo said.

"I'll just have a latte. Tim?"

"Long black, thanks Inspector."

"But we'll pay for them" Stan added.

"As you wish." Carlo smiled.

"Ok. I'll be blunt" Stan said "and come straight to the point Mr. Giordano. You match the description of a bogus doctor who delivered a gun to a patient under police guard in Auckland City Hospital."

"Really? How extraordinary."

If Stan's intention had been to get a reaction from Carlo, of any sort, it hadn't worked. His facial expression didn't change, not even slightly, nor did his calm, genial manner.

"I simply can't imagine how that could be. I must have a doppelganger, a double." Carlo smiled his ineffable smile. "He must have been very convincing, this bogus doctor, to get past your guard. I assume he was dressed as a doctor... was he wearing a mask?"

"Ah, yes, I believe so." Stan said, increasingly annoyed by this man's smug confidence.

"Well, there you are then, that explains the confusion." Carlo said.

Carlo - and Tim - waited to see if Williams would pursue the doctor angle. Instead, Stan changed tack.

"One of the guns at your house was a Beretta. We think it was Giuseppe de Luca's weapon."

"First it is not my house, and second yes it was, is, a family firearm. Fully licenced." Carlo said.

"And whoever the bogus doctor was, he gave the patient an identical model handgun." Stan said.

"Was that one licenced?" Carlo asked.

"No."

"A-h-h." Carlo said. "They are a very common gun Inspector, the M9, perhaps not so much here but, for example, I believe they are standard issue for all of the American armed forces."

This guy is so fucking cool, Tim thought to himself.

"Is there anything else I can help you with today, Inspector? Sergeant?"

"No. Look, I don't think we'll wait for the coffee." Stan stood up and took a ten-dollar bill out of his wallet.

"Oh, before you go, Inspector, let me be... 'blunt'." Carlo said.

"The charges you have brought against Jim Carruthers and my mother are absurd. My advice would be to withdraw them before both your careers are ruined, and the New Zealand police force is yet again held up to ridicule. Also, and getting to 'the point...' " Carlo looked first at Stan, then at Tim, as he said

"Do you really think that I, Carlo Salvatore Giordano or my family, would have cocaine in a bedroom cupboard, in a K Mart sports bag? Good day, gentlemen."

Carlo and Bello got up and calmly walked away past the two, temporarily stunned police officers.

* * * *

"Why haven't we charged that fucker as well? God, he annoyed me." Stan fumed when they got back to the office.

"Well, it's not his house... he theoretically doesn't live there, and he wasn't there for the meeting that went wrong, or when the drugs were found. It wouldn't stick, we probably wouldn't even get a warrant to arrest him." Tim said.

"I know he got that gun to Carruthers."

"Yeah, but that wouldn't stand up either. He sure knew that." Tim said distractedly.

"Fuck him." Stan was really pissed off. He'd never been patronised like that in his life.

Tim was much more worried about how Carlo could possibly have known about the sports bag. And he'd looked straight at Tim as he said it. He knew. He fucking knew Tim had planted it. How could he know? He and Andy hadn't seen a single security camera on the property, and they'd really looked.

There must have been someone else in the house or on the property that night, it's the only explanation. Well, I suppose it's just their word against mine if it comes to it, Tim thought. Pretty bizarre though.

The sports bag comment had gone right past Stan. He was still reeling from Carlo's comment that the charges against Carruthers and the woman were 'absurd'. How did he even know they'd been charged? There'd been no news release yet, it was going out this afternoon.

"Has this Carlo creep ever visited Carruthers in hospital, apart from when he was masquerading as a doctor? Ask Sharlene to check the log would you Tim."

"Sure boss." Tim said.

Tim was getting a bit sick of being treated like an office boy, but it wouldn't be for long. God he was looking forward to seeing Sally at the end of the day.

"Oh, meant to tell you, Bill Smales rang Sharlene. He'd like to see you."

* * * *

Charges Laid in Waiheke Case

'Police announced today that several arrest warrants have been issued relating to the multiple shooting deaths at a remote location on Waiheke Island a fortnight ago.

The prime suspect in the case - the man initially reported as a local hero - has been charged with the murder of five of the six deceased, including a police officer. He has also been charged, along with the female owner of the property, with possession of a considerable quantity of a Class A drug for the purpose of sale and supply.

Inspector Stanley Williams says police are confident the prosecution will result in convictions, and given the intense media interest in the case, will press for the earliest possible High Court hearing.'

* * * *

"Thanks for coming by Stan, I know you're busy, but I just need a few minutes of your time." Bill Smales said.

"No trouble at all sir. I'm sorry I haven't been in sooner. It's great to see you doing so well."

Stan was amazed. He looked almost back to normal. The main difference was he was talking a good bit more slowly than before.

"Thanks Stan, yes, I'm very fortunate. Going home later today. I just wanted to tell you that I don't plan to return to work for a while, maybe not at all."

Stan was very much expecting that to be the case but was nonetheless pleased to hear it. He was enjoying being in charge of the Waiheke case.

"I'm sorry to hear that Bill" he lied.

"But there are one or two things I think you should know. Firstly, have you interviewed Jim Carruthers, taken his statement?"

"Ah... no, I don't suppose I have actually."

"Well I did, you'll find it on my work cell phone if you're interested. I found his version of the events at the Cowes Bay house to be logical, credible, and compelling. I'm sure our original understanding of what happened that day was correct, much as Ana Harris described it in her article."

"Yes, but Sally - "

"Exactly, it was Sally's story that changed everything, and only Sally's story. Stan, I'm now certain she lied to us." There was a long pause.

"But why would she lie? I interviewed her again as you asked sir, and she's very... convincing. I've gotta say I believe her. We all do, and anyway, it's too late to -"

"It's never too late Stan. I just think we're running a real risk with the line we're taking. And there's something seriously fishy about that drug find. These people are mafia Stan. They're part of an organisation that controls most of the world's cocaine trade. Not even a punk gang in South Auckland would have drugs that were so easy to find. Ask yourself."

Stan hadn't ever asked himself that question, at least not until now. Even that prick Giordano saying something similar hadn't led him to wonder.

"So, what are you saying Bill?" Stan asked.

"What I'm saying is, it's just too easy. Dave Bretherton suggests there could be a link to drugs and, hey presto, we find some. And there's still the matter of the 111 call."

Stan was getting agitated. Bill was questioning his whole case, all the charges he'd laid, everything. No, he was committed, and he thought it would stand up in court. Why would dear little Sally lie, and who would have planted 10 kgs of coke in the house? Tim? No. Where would he get it from for God's sake?

"Sorry Super, I hear what you're saying but I think we're on the right track, and I think we'll get a win in court."

"Ok Stan, it's your case. I just think it has the potential to all go very wrong."

* * * *

"Wasn't that amazing, what Jim told us." Ana said.

"Sure was, I'm still trying to get my head around it. What an extraordinary story. My old dad!"

Tom and Ana were having a late lunch on Karangahape Rd. They hadn't talked about much else since Jim's revelations the previous day. They hadn't mentioned their own discovery, that they would both like them to be 'an item'.

They were increasingly relaxed and at ease with each other, almost as though they'd been together for years, and yesterday only enhanced that. Tom was beginning to feel that this could be the relationship that had eluded him thus far.

"Right, where are we up to with the case. I've asked the police for full disclosure asap. You know what that is?"

"Not really" Tom said.

"Well, they're obliged to give us all the documents, interviews, names of witnesses, anything and everything that their case is based on. They have to provide that within a specified timeframe. Can't remember exactly, but it's only a few days as I recall, so we should have that quite soon."

"Do we have to give them something similar, about our defence?"

"We do indeed." Ana said. "So, we'll need to think about what witnesses we want to call, what documents we want to use as evidence, what exhibits etc. However, we don't do that yet.

"But look, we'll have to go over all this stuff with Jim, so why don't we head over there after this?"

"Good idea. Gotta say, I'll never see him the same way again." Tom said.

"Is that bad?"

"Not necessarily, just very different." Tom said. Ana's phone rang.

"Ana" she answered. "No, I hadn't seen that, thanks for the heads-up Harry. What? ...ok, yes, I'll give it some thought and get back to you. Cheers."

"Anything of interest?" Tom asked.

"Yeah, the police have announced the charges against Jim and Francesca. Well, it's all on now. It's what the media have all been waiting for. Interesting thing, Harry said the editorial group at Stuff wonder if I'd like to do a follow up to my article last week."

"The ice has thawed somewhat, obviously." Tom said.

"Maybe, or they're looking for something that might set the cat among the pigeons. They sure as hell got a lot of hits after my first one. I wonder what I could get away with saying... Anyway, you finished?"

Tom nodded.

"Right, let's go and see our 'soldier of fortune'!"

* * * *

Back in the office, Stan decided to grab the bull by the horns.

"Tim?"

"Yes boss?"

"Did you plant that cocaine in the Cowes Bay Road house?"

Tim's reaction left Stan in no doubt that he had done exactly that.

"Stan... how could I have - "

"You fucking did, didn't you? I can see it in your face. Jesus Christ Tim?!"

"Yeah, ok I did, Andy and I did. It was just so fucking flimsy, all this talk of drugs, and nothing to show for it."

Then Tim had a bright idea, to cover his arse, to balance the books; plus, he'd always thought that attack was the best form of defence.

"And what about Kev Smith getting shot at the hospital? That's as shonky as all hell. He must've gone there to kill Carruthers, nothing surer. Dunno how you managed to twist it, but you can't tell me he didn't go there with a gun. What was the story there?"

Stan was stopped in his tracks. This boy's wide awake today, he thought. Now that he knew Tim had planted the cocaine, he saw no reason to deny his own... deception.

"Ah, yes. Well...maybe we've both been a bit... creative. The question is, does it stack up? Are we ok?"

"I think we are... sorry boss, yeah maybe I was out of line, I mean I was definitely out of line, but I was just trying to help."

"Yeah, yeah, I can see that. Where on earth did you get that much coke?"

"Funnily enough, Kev got it for me." Tim said.

"Well at least he can't rat on us." Stan snorted. "Tell me Tim, do you think Sally's telling the truth about what happened that day?"

"I do boss, I really do."

"I do too." Stan said.

Neither man had any idea how much the other's judgment was affected by Sally Reynolds' charms. After a pause Stan said

"I'll tell you another thing we've got to get a line on Tim - that bloody 111 call Carruthers made.

"But right now, I've got yet another warrant to serve on our Mr. Carruthers."

* * * *

"I've been asked to recommend someone for a particular job in Argentina that's coming up, and another one in Sri Lanka after that. I thought of you. It's right up your alley." Two-Toes said.

"Thanks Brendon, but I'm -"

"And whatever the army's paying you, we'll times ten that."

"Really?" JIm said, his interest aroused. "Ten times?!"

"Yep, four-star accommodation wherever you go, there's full pay between jobs, a pension scheme, and total cover if you're injured, mate it's a dream. Plus, no risk, no accountability, whatever you do. What do they say? '...all care, and no responsibility'? You'll never get mentioned in despatches, but you'll never end up court-martialled either. I love it."

"Yeah, that's all very well, Brendon, but I like - "

"What, being told what to do every minute of the day? Yes sir, no sir, three bags full sir? Get out from under while you can mate, make some real money, have a good time for once and retire early. The perks are amazing believe me. I've been on the Circuit for two years now and I tell you what, it's been the best two years of my life."

"What sort of notice are you supposed to give the -" Jim said.

"Fuck that nonsense, just walk away - like I did."

Jim pondered all this. He was certainly interested.

"What does KMS stand for?" he asked.

"It's a weird name - Keenie Meenie Services." Two-Toes said.

"Apparently it's from a Swahili word that describes a snake moving through grass."

* * * *

"You know perfectly well that's not how it happened Inspector" Jim said.

"I know nothing of the sort. I do know that your... co-conspirator Carlo Giordano smuggled the Beretta into your room and you shot Sergeant Kevin Smith with it, when he had just come to talk to you. It's just a shame I can't prove it."

"To talk? That's a joke. Hold on... Smith? Was he another..?" Jim asked incredulously.

"Yes, so that's a clean sweep Carruthers. The trifecta. All three brothers, you must be very proud of yourself."

"Jesus Christ." Jim said. "Are their parents still alive, how are they doing?"

"Both dead mercifully." Stan said. "Anyway, here, one more murder charge for you, cop-killer." He gave Jim the warrant and read him his rights.

"By the way, your 'lawyer' has asked for full disclosure, as she should, so you'll be able to see all the details of the case against you in the next few days. Good day to you."

"Inspector, before you go, I have a favour to ask of you."

"Really?" Stan laughed, cynically.

"The only thing I regret about this whole sad story is the Māori boy. He shouldn't have been there and I'm deeply sorry that I killed him. I would really appreciate knowing who he was, maybe help out his parents if they need it, I dunno..."

Stan believed him, he really did seem to be troubled by it. He softened a little.

"Sorry, Carruthers, I can't tell you a thing. We've tried everything we can to ID him, photo in the papers, everything, but we have no idea who he was or where he came from."

Just then there was knock on the door. It opened and Ana and Tom appeared.

"Hi Inspector." Ana said.

"I was just leaving." Stan said.

"We've got to stop meeting like this." Tom said.

"Ha, ha." Stan said and stomped out.

"G'day dad, how are you?"

"Great, just been served with another warrant, for another murder. Did you know the cop who tried to kill me the other night was another Smith brother?"

"No!" Ana and Tom chorused.

"That's insane" Tom added. "And awful. Three brothers, all dead."

There was a long pause as this sank in for all of them. Ana broke the silence.

"At least it wasn't someone from your shady past."

"True" Jim said, unamused. He was still adjusting to the knowledge that he had killed a whole family of sons.

"Ok, down to business. Let's talk about the court case." Ana said.

"You've been summoned to have your first appearance in the District Court three days from now. That's just to have the charges read to you and for you to plead. Of course, you'll plead not guilty. You'll then be remanded - on bail we hope - and the case will be referred to the High Court. The High Court because of the severity of the charges. It'll be a jury trial, that's standard in this sort of case when you plead not guilty. It's not how it normally goes with such serious charges, but you might get bail given you'll be immobilised for quite a while. And we'll almost certainly be given at least interim name suppression. What's the name of the lawyer you asked to help with that? I'll check in with him."

"I know him, I'll tell you later." Tom said.

"I'm going under the knife again the day after tomorrow, so I'm not sure I'll be up to going to court."

"That's ok, if you're incapacitated I can appear for you. Goodness, more surgery?"

"Yeah, they want to try to get my leg working better, and my shoulder's still problematic."

"Jeez, I hope that goes ok dad."

"I'll be fine, I'm sure."

*   *   *   *

So it was that Captain James Sykes left the British Special Air Service and became a mercenary. He didn't just walk out as Brendon Tuki had done, he resigned, giving the regulation period of notice. As a result, he missed the assignments in Argentina and Sri Lanka. His first assignment, and his first experience of South America, was in Nicaragua.

There were many things Jim liked about being a private contractor. The money, the living expenses, the accommodation on jobs, and the informality of relationships. There was still a chain of command, but none of the rigid protocols and bureaucracy, and most of his work was in reconnaissance and intelligence gathering. There was the occasional firefight, but actual fighting was not his primary focus. Apart from leave back in England it was quite a nomadic life, and he liked seeing so many different places.

There were also many things about it he disliked. There were plenty of good people on the books, and when he was leading a team in the field there was always good discipline and plenty of camaraderie. But the crews were almost always different. He missed having the same bunch of guys around. The relationships were inevitably superficial, and he found the life quite solitary as a result.

The one thing he particularly came to dislike was the secrecy of so much of what he did. Most of it was stuff that couldn't be traced back to and laid at the feet of the ultimate employer - in most cases the CIA or MI6, sometimes both, jointly. Also, in many cases it was direct interference in other countries' internal politics aimed at achieving regime change, often in countries with democratically elected governments. More often than not, it meant aligning with, arming and training fringe or radical, invariably right-wing extremist groups.

He soon stopped researching the countries he was going to, it was too depressing. He quickly realised that he was even more of a pawn in the military-industrial complex than he had been hitherto. At least there'd still been a sense of 'king and country' in the official army. Now he just tried to do what he was being paid to do, without thinking about it too much.

And he knew that if he were to be killed it wouldn't show up in any official casualty list, not like a regular British or US soldier. His death wouldn't show up anywhere, which was half the point of hiring people like him. Much less accountability. 'Plausible deniability", in fact.

Colombia was the turning point for him, the catalyst for Jim leaving the game, but he'd been thinking about packing it in for some time.

* * * *

Ana was working on her laptop. Tom was mulling over how he'd introduce what he wanted to say.

"Where would you like to go from here Ana?" Tom asked.

"How do you mean?

"Us... well if we are in fact 'an item'... I mean, do you want us to keep living together?"

Tom's really not good at this sort of thing, Ana smiled to herself.

"Oh, I see what you mean. Well, I quite like it. You?"

"Very much, but it's a bit tricky, I'm sort of living out of a suitcase. This is a great apartment for one, but... There's always my place..." Tom said tentatively.

"Your house is very nice. Three bedrooms, two bathrooms, double garage..." Ana said.

They'd called in once or twice to water plants. "...and I love the garden."

Jim had helped Tom buy the house in Grey Lynn a few years earlier, when it looked clear that house prices weren't slowing down.

"You'd consider moving in with me?" Tom said.

"I would."

That went well! Tom thought to himself.

"There's nothing to keep me here really. I can just rent it out." Ana said.

"Oh, you own it? That's good. I own my place too of course."

"Well, that's settled then." Tom couldn't have imagined a better outcome, and couldn't resist saying

"How exciting!"

"Yes, it really is." Ana said, smiling broadly. "I can't wait!" They kissed, very fondly, as if to seal the deal.

It struck Ana that it was all happening very fast with Tom, but it felt so different. Special, and... right. Then she said

"I've decided to take up *Stuff's* offer of a follow up article. Read this and tell me what you think."

Police Get it Wrong

'I am writing to re-state my position on the case involving several deaths on Waiheke Island recently. I stand by my original analysis in the article 'Local Man a Hero.' I still believe that he unwittingly interrupted a home invasion by the notorious Wild Bunch gang, whom he overcame in an attempt to save the two occupants of the house, one of whom died at the scene, the other who is recovering in hospital. He suffered life-threatening injuries in the process that have required many hours of ongoing surgery.

I believe fervently in this man's innocence of all the charges against him and believe they have no basis in fact. I am not questioning the integrity of the NZ Police, rather I think it most likely that there has been a misinterpretation of the facts and circumstances of the case. I sincerely hope I am correct in this assumption.

Readers might not be aware that as well as a journalist I am a qualified barrister and solicitor, and I will be representing the accused in court. To avoid any possible or perceived conflict of interest, and to observe my duty of care both as a lawyer and as a journalist, I will not be reporting on this matter again until the conclusion of the impending court case.

Anahera Harris

"Wow, that's great - and brave! Do you think they'll go for it?"

"Remains to be seen. Shall I send it off?" Ana asked.

"Yes." Tom said emphatically.

It would have sounded altogether too patronising to say so, but Tom felt enormously proud of her.

"Hey, we could have a dog at your place!" Ana said.

* * * *

Ana was very surprised when Stuff promptly published the article, with no requested changes. Its effect was immediate. Virtually everyone picked it up and it generated a lot of comment and speculation.

'Ana Harris was saying the charges were groundless! All of them, including the drugs charge? Drugs were found after all. She said she wasn't questioning the integrity of the police, but she was, surely? Was she implying police distortion of the facts of the case? Corruption even? What was this all based on? And she's a lawyer as well?'

It went on and on. One 'investigative' reporter noted that Ana was co-habiting with the accused's son.

Thanks to leaks on social media everyone knew the accused was a Jim Carruthers, they just weren't allowed to say so. It wasn't difficult to track down his son. The item was quickly withdrawn as it threatened the anonymity of the defendant. It just added to the media interest the case was generating and put Ana even more in the spotlight.

It also had the effect of accelerating the court process, supporting the police view that it should be dealt with expeditiously. The case moved up the High Court calendar dramatically, and the announcement of the date was expected any day.

Bill Smales read the article sitting under the tree in his garden and smiled.

Stan Williams read it sitting in his office and seethed.

EIGHT

A week after Ana's article there was still speculation, comment, and debate about the case. *'Waiheke Murder Trial'* or *'Waiheke Murder Case'* were the standard headings. It was clearly going to be a major media event.

Jim's first - remote - appearance in court had resulted in bail being granted on the surrender of his passport, and the requirement to wear a locator ankle bracelet with a travel limit of five kilometres from his city address. This was unusual, and resulted partly from his need for daily physiotherapy. Interim name suppression was also granted, up to and for the duration of the trial.

Ana and Tom were breakfasting on Ponsonby Road.

"Your dad was in good form yesterday." Ana said.

"Wasn't he though. He's in a lot less pain since this latest round of surgery. Seems to have worked well. Looks like he might be going home soon." Tom said.

"Good'. Ana looked across the road to Western Park. "Oh, this is so nice."

"Yes, I like this place. Is that what you meant?"

"Yes, but everything. I love it at yours, the change of scene, being so close to my favourite street in the world, all of it."

Tom's house was a three-minute walk away. Ana missed Myers Park but now she had a garden, all-day sun, views to the Waitakere Ranges, Western Park, lots more room, and Tom. He wasn't like the other guys she'd had relationships with, he was so relaxed and accepting of her. The others had all seemed to want to change her, or felt... threatened by her, over-shadowed by her or something. Her last lover before Tom left, saying he couldn't cope with such a 'stroppy bitch.' She supposed she could get a bit assertive at times, but it didn't seem to bother Tom, he seemed to really like her just as she was. He treated her, they treated each other with... respect.

"How are you feeling about the case?" Tom asked.

"Not sure. I think we're strong in some areas, not so good in others. Some of it at least will be a matter of luck. By the way I've tracked down the security guard who turned up at Jim's door just after the shooting. Seeing him at eleven.

"Tell you what, I'd forgotten how much was involved in just getting to court. Oh, and I'm also meeting with the Crown Prosecutor later today, for a Case Management meeting." Ana said.

"It'll be interesting meeting the opposition." Tom said.

"Mmm. Bit scary. Big name QC, one of the best apparently."

* * * *

"Good morning Inspector."

Crown Prosecutor Simon Taylor QC was meeting with Inspector Stan Williams to discuss the Waiheke case. Taylor was an imposing, well-groomed fifty-five-year-old, with silver hair at his temples and piercing grey-green eyes. Ex Christ's College and Oxford, he displayed all the confidence and ease that comes with privilege.

"I've read your case file thoroughly, and I need to go through it with you."

"Of course. " Stan said "Where would you like to start?"

"I have some concerns here and there that we need to address. The basic premise of your case is that all these people on the island were meeting for a common purpose, relating to drugs, it went wrong, and they fought. I can accept that, but the death of the policeman is a little harder.

"Why did Carruthers call 111, then shoot Sergeant Smith, and not shoot or attempt to shoot Constable Reynolds? I don't think these are insurmountable problems, but they are questions that will be asked, and that we need answers for.

"I also have some difficulty with Sergeant Kevin Smith's visit to the hospital, and all that followed. I have to say Inspector, that I toyed with the idea of not pursuing this case, but I think there is enough evidence on at least some of the charges, and the public interest is such that I really didn't have a choice.

"The first thing we might want to decide is the order in which we prosecute the charges. We have the murder charges arising from the confrontation on Waiheke, the murder charge resulting from the incident in the hospital, and the drugs charges.

"I would like to deal with the drugs charges first, the hospital charge second, and the multiple Waiheke charges last. I suppose you could say we save the most complicated - and dramatic - to last. This is not standard practice, but the judge might agree."

"Sounds good to me." Stan said, trying to keep up.

"And I've decided on a separate hearing for the Giordano woman; she'll probably just plead guilty once Carruthers is convicted. If he's convicted."

"He will be." Stan said.

"Right, leave it with me. I'm meeting their lawyer in a couple of hours. She is a barrister but as far as I can tell she's not very experienced, certainly not for a major trial like this one.

"Should be interesting."

*   *   *   *

"And how's the physio going dad? Tom asked.

"Pretty good. Painful but good. Getting movement back into the shoulder, and the leg's more flexible that it was, so yeah, good. Did I tell you I'm going home tomorrow." Jim said.

"That's great." Ana said.

"And how are you two?"

"We're good." Ana said. "You know I've moved in with Tom?"

"Yes, I think that's the third time you've told me." They laughed. "It's obviously working out."

"It is." Tom said.

"I'm looking forward to your meeting Tom's mum Ana. You'll both have to come for dinner once I'm out of here." Jim said.

"I'd really like that" Ana said "but look, there's something we need to talk about... I'd like to apply to the court for permission to videotape the trial, together with *Stuff*, and maybe *The Herald* as well."

"Is that possible? Tom asked.

"The Crown Prosecutor needs to agree, but I'm sure he will, he likes keeping his public profile up I'm told. If both counsel agree the judge is almost certain to allow it.

"Of course, other news outlets - particularly TV networks - will apply too, and they're often who gets approved. But only one camera is allowed in court, so how it works is that whoever is approved is more or less obliged to share the footage, and all the syndications have to be in the application."

"What about my anonymity?"

"That's the thing. If you appear in any shots your face will have to be blurred, so you're not recognisable, you see it all the time. Otherwise they'd be in contempt of court, and they wouldn't dare use un-doctored shots anyway, or they'd never be approved again."

"Well I suppose that'd be ok." Jim said.

"Great, I'll get onto it." Ana said.

* * * *

"Well that all seems straightforward enough. I'm glad you agree as to the order of events, dealing with the less complex charges first." Crown Prosecutor Taylor said.

"I have no problem with that at all, although it remains to be seen which is the more complex. All the charges are difficult to some degree or other." Ana replied.

"Indeed. There are unanswered questions with each of them and, frankly, aspects which can only be resolved in the court inquiry. Which is why we're both here of course."

Simon Taylor was testing the water here, trying to gain some insight as to this young woman's grasp of the complexities of the case, what sort of adversary she might prove to be.

"Yes, there are certainly a few... anomalies here and there, but you're right, between us we'll find the answers, I'm sure." Ana smiled at him.

Well, she's confident if nothing else, he thought to himself.

"I think that's everything" he said. "I look forward to... working with you."

* * * *

Working out. It was what Jim had missed most being in hospital. The physio for his leg and shoulder was helpful, but his whole body had stiffened up and was creaky and sore. So here he was, on his way to the gym the first day after his discharge. He knew he wouldn't be up to doing much, but he'd made an appointment to work out a programme with his trainer Jason, to get him back into shape. Sadly, there'd be no boxing for quite a while.

The inner-city gym he went to was close to the studio and the apartment and was primarily for fighters. Jim hadn't chosen it because of that, and he hadn't known that when he first joined up; its location and the fact that it wasn't at all pretentious was what had drawn him to it - the furthest thing from the trendy, Les Mills type of place. They trained some serious martial arts proponents, a few league players and athletes, some guys Jim suspected were bouncers or enforcers, as well as the odd business type, and he liked its gritty, down-to-earth style.

There were rumours about gang involvement in either the financing or running of the gym, or both, and there were always some pretty heavy looking dudes working out. But there was never any aggro, and everyone was always civil, even friendly once you'd been around for a while. He was on at least 'nodding' acquaintance with all the regulars. It reminded him of a gym near the barracks in London, and he felt comfortable here.

It was 4.30 and the place was full. There was an informal bar on Fridays which opened around 5.30. It was a warm, almost windless afternoon and the roller door at the front was all the way up. Almost as soon as Jim appeared, everyone stopped what they were doing and clapped and cheered. Jason had obviously told everyone he was coming in. It hadn't occurred to Jim to wonder if the guys at the gym had been following the Waiheke story, but they obviously had, and there wasn't much doubt that they were in his corner. It also hadn't yet occurred to Jim to wonder how they all knew he was the Waiheke guy in the news.

Jason lumbered up to him, giving him the standard hand clasp / embrace / handshake welcome.

"Jimbo! How you doin' brother? Fuckin' hero eh!" More cheers. "Hey, I like the bling round your ankle mate. Where'd you get that?" Laughter. "Righto, let's get you back in the saddle."

* * * *

Waiheke Murder Trial Date Announced

'This highly anticipated High Court trial will begin in just three weeks' time. The Hon. Justice Anthony Andrews will preside, and Mr. Simon Taylor QC will act for the Crown. As previously advised, Anahera Harris will appear for the defence, despite being vastly less experienced than her prosecution counterpart.

To recap, the defendant in the case faces multiple murder charges, of the four members of the "Wild Bunch' gang - responsible for several home invasions, killings and rapes - and two police officers, plus a serious drugs offence charge.

The case has been noted and reported on around the world and a large contingent of media representatives, some from overseas, is expected. The public gallery is also sure to be full to overflowing. Rarely does a case attract such levels of interest, and the trial is set to be a major international news event.'

Diane Black for Stuff

* * * *

Jason was part-Māori, part-Tongan, an ex-pro boxer and built like a bull, huge shoulders, chest and arms, no neck to speak of and a shaved head with several nasty scars, one running from his forehead, down through his eyebrow onto his cheek. One of the other trainers had told Jim the general feeling was that Jason was a bit 'punchy', a bit brain-damaged after his years of boxing. He had anger issues, but usually managed to control them.

Jim loved Jason. He was like a big baby boy, sweet and trusting, with no guile and incapable of deceit. They got on well, and Jason long ago took to asking Jim for advice and sharing his problems with him, usually in the car park after a training session, over a shared cigarette or two - invariably Jim's, Jason theoretically didn't smoke. He was always in trouble of one sort or another and Jim had often lent him, given him, money. Jason hadn't had much of a family life and Jim liked being there for him, a sort of father figure, mentor.

This first session back was mostly just stretching and floor exercises with a little bit of light resistance work to see where the problems were. It hurt a lot of the time, but it felt great to be back. When they were finishing up, Jason insisted on seeing his scars. He was mightily impressed.

"Fuck me! How come you ain't dead bro?! Fuckin' 'ell!"

In the latter part of the session Jim had become aware of one of the gym regulars drifting about. Not watching them, that wasn't good form in the gym, most people were careful not to infringe on others' space and privacy, unless they were in the ring. He was just there, this large Māori man, heavily muscled but lean and cut, with some interesting tattoos, though none on his face, and somewhere in his fifties. He'd seen this guy many times before. Everyone treated him with deference. He obviously had some standing here and was always something of a presence in the place. He'd arrive at the gym in either a black Mercedes-AMG C63, or on a big black Harley. Clearly wasn't short of money.

Jim thanked Jason, made an appointment for next week, and gave him a hundred-dollar bill. They preferred cash here. Jim's rate was fifty, but he wouldn't take any change. Jason protested but took it with profuse thanks. Jim wasn't going to bother showering, he'd hardly sweated and would wait until he got home. People were starting to drift to the bar. As they passed, several guys wished Jim luck or offered to buy him a drink. Jim said he'd overdone the workout, was fucked, and needed to get home. Thanks. Next Friday maybe.

The big Māori guy got up from the bench he'd been sitting on and approached Jim as he walked towards the roller door.

"You've been coming here for quite a few years now." He said.

"You too. How's it goin'?"

"Good, yeah good. Wouldn't mind a word if you've got a coupla minutes."

Jim was tempted to ask what about, but this guy had always interested him. Very cool, confident, and quite... charismatic.

"Sure."

"Not here. There's a bar round the corner. You'll be ok in your workout gear, it's not flash."

He was in a tracksuit himself, although he didn't appear to have been working out. They walked in silence the fifty metres or so around the corner to a rundown sports and gaming bar. The seventies and eighties hits playlist was quite loud.

"What can I get you?"

"Protein shake'd be good" Jim said, then laughing "Nah, any sort of beer thanks, Pilsener if they have one."

"Sure. Bit noisy here. See you out the back?"

'Out the back' was so like out the back of the bar in London where Jim had re-united with Brendon Tuki thirty-odd years earlier, it was uncanny. He sat on a stool at one of the bar leaners and wondered if this would be another significant moment in his weird journey. He had a strong feeling that it might be.

"Your Pilsener. Right, you're Jim, I'm Manu." They shook hands. "I'll tell you why we're here.

"We have some things in common, apart from the gym, and fighting. Good work on the island by the way, always thought you were a bit of a hard man. Where'd you train originally?"

Jim thought he might as well say it. "I was SAS, then a... mercenary, before I moved here."

"Thought as much. I started in the army too. Where were we... yeah, like you, I know the Giordanos."

"Really?!" This was not what Jim was expecting to hear.

"We've been business partners for many years, first when I was in Australia and then back here."

"Wow." Was all Jim could think of to say.

"I head up a gang, one of the original ones. Nothing like these new scatty fuckin' Killer Beez and bullshit Tribesmen morons. We're all getting older and are largely legit now, given up patches and guns, mostly. We've been the Giordanos' New Zealand distributors for the last ten years."

"Really? If it's the gang I think it is, you guys do a lot of good things in the community now eh?"

"Yeah, with tamariki and their whanau mainly, both here and in Hamilton, up north and on the East Coast, where several of us are from. I'm related to Anahera Harris by the way, second cuz I think. It's really the main reason we're still handling the drugs, gives us the money to do these things. Never P though. Funnily enough we use the money from coke to get kids off P, and try to stop them starting on it.

"I'm also related to the boy you killed on the island."

Jim nearly choked on his beer.

"But we'll talk about that some other time. For now, there's some stuff you need to know, and Carlo might want to know. I've only ever met him once or twice, but I do know he's a dangerous fuck, and as hard as nails under that smooth exterior. I always dealt with the old Don, and Giuseppe. I loved them both, they were good old boys. Honest and... yeah, men of honour. I miss them. But they all dropped the ball. Didn't see that 'the times they are a'changing', the new threats. It was a total coincidence, but that raid on the Waiheke place should never have happened - and it wouldn't have if Pepe had been alive. More about that in a minute.

"One of the nastiest of the Russian mafia want this territory, and they'll go to any lengths to get it. They're getting big in Australia and have built good relationships with a couple of Colombian and Mexican cartels. Carlo whacking two of their boys hasn't gone down at all well either. He's now a marked man if he wasn't before. So, there's big trouble coming, and I'm sort of caught in the middle. You guys could be too."

"Shit, that's all pretty heavy. What were you going to say before?" There was a pause.

"Pepe didn't die of a heart attack, he was poisoned."

"Christ!" Jim's mind was racing. "Does Carlo know this?"

"No. I decided against telling him straight away, thought I'd wait and see how it all panned out, but maybe it's time he knew. What do you think?"

"How did you find out?"

"The Russians told me. Pepe was the brains behind the business, so he was the first to go. I think they told me to prove they were serious, and as a warning, for sure. 'Course, they want me to work with them once the game changes. If it does."

"I'll have to think about it and talk to my son. He knows Carlo much better than I do."

"Two things, if you decide to tell him. Pepe, Carlo and Francesca ate out the night he died. That restaurant was a big mistake. Also, Carlo needs to find out if there was a toxicology report done by the coroner. Should've been. It was a drug very like Tetrahydrozoline - it's in everyday eyedrops funnily enough - which can stop the heart beating, but more sophisticated and harder to test for. Straight from Mr. Putin's labs probably. They might or might not have detected it."

"Jesus." Jim whispered.

"Anyway, give it some thought. I'll keep an eye on your bookings at the gym and catch up again soon yeah?"

"Yeah, sure. Thanks for all that, I think, and thanks for the beer."

"No worries."

"By the way, do you own the gym?"

"That... I will neither confirm, nor deny." Manu said and smiled.

* * * *

"Sergeant Adams, please tell the court a little more about yourself." Simon Taylor QC asked.

It was the first day of the trial. There had been no jury challenges, both the prosecution and the defence had presented their cases and it was a calm, typical start to proceedings in the Auckland High Court. The prosecution had just called its first witness.

"Yes, I'm Timothy Adams, Sergeant in the New Zealand Police, based on Waiheke Island, where I've been for nearly five years."

"Lovely place. Now, these drugs at the crime scene... you applied for a warrant to search the premises at Cowes Bay Road two days after the shootings. Can you tell us, why the delay?"

"We received some information from NCB, that's the New Zealand branch of Interpol, that the owners of the property could be connected to the drug trade, so we thought we should have a closer look at the place. We probably wouldn't have thought about doing a drug search if we hadn't got that information." Tim said.

"Yes, I see. And tell us about the search itself would you please Sergeant."

"Well, the drug dog went through the place with its handler, who called out to me from one of the bedrooms. I went to where they were and we found a bag full of cocaine."

"That would be that... what do you call it... sports bag over there."

"That's correct sir, yes."

"And how much cocaine was, is there, in the bag?"

"Approximately 10 kilograms."

"I see in your statement that you also found traces of the drug on a yacht moored near the house. What did you infer from that Sergeant?" Taylor asked.

"That maybe that's how they got the drugs into the country. It's a big ocean-going boat."

"And on the basis of those finds, the defendant and the woman who owns the house were charged. Is that correct?"

Yes." Tim said

"Thank you, Sergeant Adams. That's all for the moment."

Justice Andrews said "Ms Harris, do you wish to cross-examine?"

Justice Anthony Andrews was a slightly overweight sixty-something-year-old, with a full head of salt and pepper hair and a slightly crumpled look, not at all dissimilar to Rumpole of the Bailey. He'd seen it all and was relaxed and good-humoured. He took his work very seriously but was not interested in wielding his authority in court for its own sake, and was gentle and helpful with counsel and witnesses alike.

"Thank you, Your Honour. I do." Ana said

"Sergeant Adams, I'd like to go through the exact process of your discovery and handling of the sports bag. You found it, the dog found it, in a bedroom cupboard, yes?"

"Yes." Tim answered.

"And what happened then?"

"Well, I took the bag out of the cupboard, opened it, saw the cocaine and - "

"Was the dog handler with you when you did that?"

"No actually, the dog was leaping around with excitement and wanting his reward, so they went out of the room as I recall." Tim said, wondering what this was all about.

"You then took the bag back to the station I assume."

"Yes, indeed and locked it up."

"Of course. And would anyone have opened it at the station do you think? The bag I mean."

"Absolutely not." Tim said.

"Your honour?" Taylor enquired.

"Yes, where is this going Ms. Harris?" Justice Andrews asked.

"Just one more minute Your Honour, if I may." Ana said.

"So, between your discovering the cocaine and now, no-one could have tampered with the bag?"

"No, definitely not, I would say." Tim said.

"When did you ascertain the weight of the cocaine Sergeant?" Ana asked.

"Ah-h, back at the station."

"But you said no-one opened - "

"Apart from me, I meant." Tim was getting a bit flustered.

"Your Honour, could I ask that the members of the jury see the contents of the bag please? It is the key piece of evidence after all, not the bag it's in."

"Yes. Bailiff? If you would." The judge said.

The bailiff went to the sports bag, unzipped it, opened it wide, took it to the jury seats and walked slowly along in front of them. One of them said

"Is it ok if I...?"

She reached into the bag and took out a packet, a plastic packet of... two or three of the jurors couldn't help but snigger. She held it up.

CHELSEA
Icing Sugar 1kg

For a moment, there was total silence in the courtroom, as the implications of this sank in. Then pandemonium broke out. Justice Andrews called for silence, and the Crown Prosecutor said

"Your Honour, could we...?"

"Indeed. You can leave the stand thank you Sergeant. The court is adjourned for thirty minutes. Both Counsel in my rooms please."

* * * *

"Please explain to me what has happened here. I thought there were strict protocols around the handling of evidence prior to a trial?" The judge asked, looking at the Crown Prosecutor.

"There are indeed, and I have absolutely no idea what's happened in this instance, I'm sorry" Taylor said. "ESR certainly verified the traces of cocaine found at the crime scene, and on the yacht. I just assumed they had examined all of it... But yes, proper procedure has undoubtedly fallen down here, I don't know how."

"Ms. Harris?"

"It certainly has. In my view Your Honour, there are only two possible explanations. One, that someone interfered with the bag between its discovery and today, which seems unlikely. Two, and you might find this a bit... provocative, that Sergeant Adams planted the drugs some time earlier and didn't look in the bag when the dog found it, because he knew what was in it. Or he thought he did.

"Unfortunately for the Sergeant, someone switched the drugs for icing sugar between his two visits, leaving enough of the original for the dog to detect."

"That's an extraordinary allegation Counsel."

"It's not an allegation Your Honour. It's a suggestion, a possible explanation of how the cocaine turned into icing sugar, and we did establish that no-one saw Adams open the bag at the house. Of course, there might be any number of alternative scenarios, I just can't think what they might be.

"Equally, and I'm sure this will have occurred to the Crown Prosecutor, if the Giordano family were serious international drug dealers, would they really stash millions of dollars-worth of cocaine in a bedroom cupboard?"

"What do you say to that Simon?" the judge asked.

"I really don't know what to say. Except that, yes, I had wondered something similar myself.

"There's no doubt that some serious questions will need to be asked, and I do wonder how on earth that occurred to you as a possibility Ana. Good work however."

It didn't occur to Mr. Simon Taylor QC to ask if it was ok to call her Ana. He was... old-school.

After a pause, Justice Andrews said "You don't have much choice do you Simon."

"No. We could argue that traces of cocaine were obviously found there, but the police would look even more ridiculous if we reduced the charge to simple possession. It's not exactly a great start to the prosecution case, but as you say, I don't have any choice.

"The Crown withdraws the charge."

In less than an hour Ana had demolished the prosecution case.

* * * *

"Please be seated." The registrar said.

"Let us resume." Justice Andrews said. "The Crown has advised the court that the charge of possession of a Class A drug for sale and supply has been withdrawn. Registrar, please note that the charges against Mrs. Francesca Giordano are also withdrawn.

"In light of the... unexpected and unusual developments this morning, the Crown Prosecutor has requested an adjournment. This court will resume the day after tomorrow, on Wednesday at 10 am."

"All rise" the registrar told the court, and the judge left the room.

* * * *

Cocaine? No, Icing Sugar.

'In an extraordinary development on the first day of the Waiheke Murder Case, the prosecution's central piece of evidence, ten kilograms of cocaine, was revealed to be ten kilograms of icing sugar. In a deft courtroom manoeuvre, defence counsel Anahera Harris asked for the jury to be shown the contents of the sports bag supposedly containing the drugs.

As a result of this discovery, and to what must be the acute embarrassment of the police, the drug charges against both accused have been withdrawn.

Major questions regarding police procedure - and possible impropriety - have been raised, and an inquiry into the handling of the drugs, and the case, is almost certain.

It should also be asked if Ms. Harris knew of the real contents of the bag and if so how; if this was an exceptionally lucky guess; or she had no knowledge of it and simply wanted the court to see the cocaine.

Police have indicated a statement will be forthcoming shortly.'

* * * *

Tom was busy at the studio. He and the staff had several projects in hand and one or two deadlines looming. They had lost a couple of big clients when Jim retired but were still reasonably busy. His role was largely managing the business, and marketing it, but Tom still liked getting 'on the tools' from time to time, taking the lead on projects which particularly interested him, and doing the odd bit of editing. He was head down in one of the edit suites when Jim poked his nose in.

"Hiya. An unexpected day off from court.... Can you take a break?"

"Hi dad. Of course. Wasn't yesterday amazing?"

"Sure was."

"It's good to see you, but it sounded on the phone like this was more than just a social visit..."

"It is." Jim said, and related his gym visit and conversation with Manu.

"God damn!" Tom said. "That's a helluva story, and a real worry. I guess the question is are we, our family, at more or less risk if we pass this info on to Carlo. Part of me wants to back right off and leave these mad people to it, another part of me wants to warn Carlo. I must admit, I quite like him. Besides which, he and his cameras might well be the only things keeping you from spending the rest of your life behind bars. We sort of owe him, don't we?"

"Maybe. Whether we tell him or not, I don't think we should be under any illusion that we could easily get caught in the crossfire. Like Manu."

"This really is the most extraordinary time..." Tom mused.

"Tell you what, I don't have a strong view either way, and you've got a lot more to lose than I do. I'll support you whatever you decide to do. You choose." Jim said.

"Doesn't give me much time, I'm seeing him in half an hour."

"That's plenty of time. Actually, I think we both know you're going to tell him. But there's something else I need to say."

"What else could there be?" Tom asked, with a touch of irony.

"Well son, there's no other way of putting it - you're a bit of a slob."

"What?!!"

"Look at yourself. You're overweight, you don't exercise, you smoke too much, and you've got the muscle tone of a new-born baby."

Tom tried to remonstrate.

"Hear me out. Our lives have changed. I've survived all this because I was fit, and as strong as I could have been. You're not, and you might need to be. We don't know what's next, but we need to be ready, in the best shape we can be, both of us. I've pre-paid for you at my gym, with my trainer, Jason, three times a week for three months, times to suit you. It'll be a mix of fitness and martial arts and you'll go if I have to drag you there."

Jim had suggested the gym a few times, but never more than in passing, and certainly not with this sort of vehemence. Tom again tried to interrupt.

"Wait! I've also hooked you up with a mate of mine for weapons training, only twice a week you'll be pleased to hear. I'm serious Tom. We're on a roller coaster and we don't know where it's going. Even if you don't end up needing these skills, you'll enjoy being in better shape, believe me. Agreed?"

Tom had never known his father to be this assertive. He was a bit pissed off, but he knew Jim was right, and the whole proposal appealed to him in a scary, daunting sort of way.

"Agreed."

* * * *

"Yes Commissioner... I understand. No Commissioner, I have no idea what happened."

"Well find out Inspector, it's your case. And I have to tell you, it's not looking good. There will have to be an investigation into this matter; the irregularities suggest serious malpractice. I'm deeply disappointed Williams. The press is all over it, and I will have to respond appropriately. I just hope the rest of your case fares better. A lot better."

"Yes sir."

Stan knew at this point that his future in the police was limited, at best. He just hoped that this would be the last disaster to befall him in the days ahead.

* * * *

"I must say Tom, I am most impressed with Ana. Who would have guessed she was also a lawyer, and a very good one it would seem." Carlo said.

It was 10 am and he and Tom were once again having coffee and pastries at the Viaduct Basin. Bello was there too, as were the Thompson Twins, a little further away. Bello seemed entirely happy for Tom to stroke him as they sat and talked. Tom was still reeling a little from the conversation with Jim earlier in the morning, both Manu's revelations and Jim's training regime package.

"Yes, it would seem so." Tom said. "The icing sugar was a nice touch by the way."

"I thought so, and it's good to have the consignment back. It was ours originally of course. A stupid... courier... lost it for us."

"I see." Tom said, deciding against asking for more detail. This was the first time Carlo had even hinted that he might be involved with drugs, and Tom would rather not have known.

"And how, if I might be so bold, are things between you and the lovely Anahera?" Carlo asked.

"Very good thanks Carlo."

"Excellent. You make a very nice couple. Now. The reason I wanted to see you is to pass on my mother's thanks to you both. She is improving daily and will soon be discharged from hospital. She wants Jim to know how grateful she is to him for saving her life, and to Ana for saving her from the police prosecution.

"She is planning to return to Italy within a few weeks and is contemplating how best she can thank you. I will accompany her and help her settle back into life in Venezia on her own. How long I will be away, I cannot say.

"As a first step, before she goes, she would like to host a small event for you and Ana, Jim, your mother, and me and Bello of course."

"That sounds great" Tom said. "I look forward to meeting her."

"It might be best if we arrange that before the trial concludes, just in case it doesn't go well for your father, and he is remanded in custody. You would appeal of course."

"Of course." Tom said.

"I should add that I believe you will need, at some point, to use the footage."

"Maybe Carlo, maybe."

"However that may be, I also wanted to tell you Tom, that I intend to contribute to the cost of the defence. I would have engaged a QC to defend my mother in court, and I no longer need to do so, thanks to Ana."

"That's really not necessary Carlo, we're just pleased Francesca doesn't have to go to court."

"Dear Tom, sometimes you really do not listen. I intend to do this."

Tom did know that when Carlo said he would do something, there was no point arguing.

"That's very kind of you Carlo. I'm sure Ana will appreciate it."

"She has earned it, and deserves it. Please text or email me her bank account details, and if there is anything else either of you need financial help with, anything at all, please don't hesitate to ask. It would be no hardship at all for me, and I would consider it an honour if I could help in some way."

"That's most generous of you Carlo. Thank you."

There was quite a long pause as Tom decided how he would pass on what Manu had told his dad.

"What's on your mind my friend?" Carlo asked, sensing something was bothering Tom.

"My father started back at the gym yesterday, and - "

Carlo laughed. "He really is an extraordinary man!"

" - he got a hero's welcome. All the guys knew it was him on trial. Social media probably. But the point is, the guy who we think owns the gym - a gang boss - approached dad and told him some stuff he thought we should all know, particularly you Carlo."

"Who is this man?" Carlo was suddenly very focussed.

"Your... colleague, Manu."

Carlo's eyes blazed. He was furious. "He should not have - "

"He knew he could trust Jim, and he wanted you to know that the Russians are making a big push here - "

"I know that."

"But maybe not how big a push. They're pressuring Manu to commit to them, once you're... out of the picture. He feels they're just tying down their supply lines from South America, then they're coming after you Carlo. Jim and I thought you should know that. Oh, and you 'offing' those two in the carpark didn't go down too well either apparently."

Another pause.

"I thought they were just scouts... You are right Tom, I had not realised quite how serious they are, or how advanced their planning is. I wonder which cartels they are dealing with..."

Carlo was deep in thought, then said

"Thank you both for sharing this with me, I will not forget it. And I will thank Manu too, although he should have told me himself."

"He feels he doesn't know you like he knew Pepe, and you must see he's between a rock and a hard place Carlo."

"Indeed. No, he is a good man."

"There's something else..."

"Tell me Tom."

"This is not going to be easy for you Carlo..."

"Tell me."

"The Russians told Manu that Pepe didn't die of a heart attack. They poisoned him at the restaurant you ate at that night."

Tom would not have thought it possible, but all the colour drained from Carlo's face. He stood up, his eyes bulged, his whole body shook, and he let out a long, primal scream, which stopped everyone in the vicinity dead in their tracks. Bello was very concerned, leaping up with his front feet on the table, to get his face close as possible to Carlo's, and the Twins came rushing over. Tom put his arms around Carlo and held him as he subsided into deep, silent, wracking sobs.

Finally, after what seemed like minutes, Carlo gently pushed Tom's arms away, looked at him with dead, glittering eyes, and said quietly

"I will kill them all."

NINE

'The Police Commissioner issued a press statement today announcing an Independent Police Conduct Authority Inquiry into the events surrounding the drug possession charges in the Waiheke Murder Case.

There were dramatic scenes in the High Court yesterday, and revelations which strongly suggest impropriety on behalf of the officers involved. The central questions are - were there ever 10 kilograms of cocaine in the sports bag? If there were, when was the cocaine switched for icing sugar, and where is the cocaine, worth millions of dollars on the street, now?

Defence counsel Anahera Harris declined to speculate as to what she thought were the most likely answers to these questions, but did say she would continue to do her best to secure acquittal on all the charges against her client.'

* * * *

"I've asked you here because I'm disturbed by events thus far in my court."

Justice Andrews had sought a meeting with the two counsel and Stan Williams. He continued

"The justice system relies on transparency, but I don't like the sort of media circus this case is generating. Is there anything I should know, any other bombshells either of you are planning?" Justice Andrews asked of the two lawyers.

"I think that's a question more properly addressed to the defence" Simon Taylor said. "I will simply do my job to the best of my ability. I also think it timely to ask Inspector Williams if he has any more skeletons in his closet."

"I don't think that's entirely fair. I'm as much a victim of this drug shambles as anyone, and I've got to say, I haven't felt all that well supported by the prosecution so far." Stan said.

"Inspector, I obviously need to remind you of my role here." Taylor said. "I am not part of the police prosecution team, and do not act for the police. I am here representing the Crown, the people of New Zealand, to try to ensure that justice is served, whether that results in convictions or not."

Ana felt it was her turn to say something.

"My position, as I'm sure you'll all agree it should be, is to advocate for my client's innocence, and that will inevitably involve exploring inconsistencies and possible shortcomings in the prosecution's case. I can't be held responsible if this leads to news headlines."

"Quite." Justice Andrews was already quite impressed with this young barrister. She was obviously very bright, quick on her feet, and with excellent courtroom instincts. He knew she'd been a journalist for some years, but he hoped she continued with a legal career, she would do well, he felt sure.

"Generally speaking, I'm happy so far with the conduct of both counsel in this case. It's... 'civilised', and I like that. Let us continue in that vein, but I agree with the Crown Prosecutor, I too hope the police case is more fundamentally sound as we proceed." Andrews said.

"As to the next charge, I recommend that we seek a verdict from the jury, before moving on to the multiple charges relating to the Waiheke incident. Otherwise, the evidence and arguments might well become muddied for them, after what could be the passage of many days or weeks. Are we agreed?"

Both counsel indicated their consent.

* * * *

"Big day tomorrow baby." Tom said

"Sure is." Ana replied.

"What a start eh?"

"Mmm. It's gone well so far, but it's early days. I've got a couple of tricks up my sleeve for the next round, but it's the Waiheke stuff I'm really worried about." Ana said.

"The coverage the case is getting is amazing."

"Sure is. I never thought I'd be a media 'darling'. I might even become an 'influencer' next - isn't that the stupidest concept? Of course, if I put a foot wrong that could all turn on a dime.

"Got to say though, I feel a bit sorry for poor old Stan. He's finished, whatever happens next, as is Tim Adams. I mean they deserve it, but it's a bit sad. Did you see the Commissioner's press release?"

"I did."

"There's no way they won't go for a skate, and that silly cop guarding Jim's hospital room is in the same boat. That'll be down to Stan as well, I'm sure. We'll see tomorrow. 'Oh, what a tangled web we weave', eh? "

"You know, I think you're amazing and..." Tom decided he would say it

"...I am so fucking proud of you."

"Thank you for saying that my lovely man." Ana said.

* * * *

"Please continue Mr Taylor."

"Thank you, Your Honour. As we have said, the prosecution contends that this is a case of cold-blooded murder. We believe that Sergeant Kevin Smith went to talk to the defendant about the death of his brother Philip, and Mr. Carruthers brutally gunned him down.

"The defence argues that the shooting was in self-defence but, as you have heard, the crime scene investigation found no evidence whatsoever of another weapon in the room, nor of any weapon other than the defendant's having been fired. Sergeant Smith had no way of defending himself, and of course he would never have expected a patient under police guard in a hospital room to be in possession of a semi-automatic handgun. I repeat, Sergeant Kevin Smith, a long-serving officer with an unblemished record, was callously shot and killed in a vicious, unprovoked attack. It's - that - simple.

"We have only one further witness Your Honour. I now call Constable Matthew Burrows."

Matt nervously approached the witness stand and sat down. The registrar administered the oath, and Simon Taylor continued.

"Constable Burrows, would you please tell us your recollection of the events of that night."

"Yes sir. I was on the night shift outside the defendant's hospital room. Sadly, I had... dozed off. Most unlike me but... I was awoken by the sound of gunshots."

"In your statement Constable, you said three or four gunshots."

"Yes sir."

"For the benefit of the jury, forensics confirm that it was indeed four shots, to Sergeant Smith's chest, killing him almost instantly. What happened next Constable?"

"I went into the room. Sergeant Smith was dead on the floor and the defendant was standing over him, holding the Beretta. I struggled with him and managed to take the weapon from him."

"That's very brave of you Constable, and commendable." Taylor said.

Jim couldn't help himself. He guffawed, loudly.

"That will be enough of that Mr. Carruthers. Ms. Harris, please caution your client against such outbursts." Justice Andrews said, sternly.

"We apologise Your Honour. It won't happen again." Ana gave Jim a look, a cross between a frown and a smile.

"Let's go back to earlier that evening. Tell us about this 'doctor' who visited the defendant." Taylor said.

"He was very convincing sir, looked the part, had all the gear, spoke well, so yes, I let him in."

"I should add, members of the jury, that this man was later conclusively proved not to be a doctor." The Crown Prosecutor said.

"If it were not for this person giving Carruthers the gun, is there any other way that he could have laid his hands on a weapon, would you say?"

"Not that I can think of sir, no. He'd only been taken to the room earlier that day and there's no way he had the gun when he was moved." Matt said.

"I see from the police case notes that there is no information that could lead to identifying this 'doctor' person. Is that still the case?"

"As far as I'm aware sir."

Sitting with the prosecution team, Stan was itching to say "I know, I know" but of course he couldn't.

"Very well. Thank you, Sergeant, no further questions."

"Ms. Harris?" Justice Andrews asked.

"Thank you, Your Honour. Just a couple of questions Constable." Ana said.

"Did you have any other visitors that evening?"

This wasn't something that he and Stan had discussed. Should he talk about Kev's earlier visit? He decided he should. Honesty was the best policy. Usually.

"Constable Burrows?" Ana asked.

"Sorry, yes, Sergeant Smith passed by."

"Just to be clear, this is the same Sergeant Smith who later lost his life in the room you were guarding."

"Yes, Kevin Smith."

"You say he 'passed by'?"

"On his way to visit a friend who'd just had a baby, he said."

"There's no mention of this in the police case file, why would that be I wonder..." Ana said "... an oversight no doubt."

Crown Prosecutor Taylor was asking himself the same question.

"You chatted and he moved on, to the maternity ward I assume."

"I guess so." Matt said.

"I'm not familiar with the entire lay-out of Auckland City Hospital, but I do know that maternity services are nowhere near where you were in the building." Ana said.

"I... didn't know that."

"So, he got you a drink and....?" Ana asked him. It was a cheeky move, but worth a try.

"Yeah, he got me a coffee and...." Shit, Matt thought, should I have said that?

"A-h-h, so he got you a coffee."

Ana couldn't believe how well that had worked.

"Tell me Constable, when was this? After the so-called doctor's visit and before you heard the gunshots?"

"Yes, I suppose it was."

Simon Taylor was getting worried. He didn't trust this woman. Well he did actually, he'd seen enough already to trust her to be as sharp as a tack, clever and devious.

"And when you heard the gunfire, when it woke you, you got up and went into the room. Were you steady on your feet?"

"Yes, I was. Definitely." Matt said. He was having a very hard time.

"Not groggy at all? Not like you'd been drugged; something Sergeant Smith put in your coffee perhaps?"

Crown Prosecutor Taylor got to his feet.

"Your Honour I object to this whole line of questioning. I can see no substance or relevance in it whatsoever."

"I'm inclined to agree. Let's leave it there Ms. Harris." The judge said, in his gracious, even-tempered way.

"Very well. Constable Burrows, you say you went into the room and disarmed the defendant."

"I did." Matt said.

"My client didn't hand you the Beretta as he claims in his statement?" Ana asked.

"He did not, I wrestled it from him."

"One final question Constable. Would you describe the state of the room at that point for us please."

"Well apart from the body on the floor, just as you'd expect, perfectly normal."

"The bed was just as you'd expect, no pillows under the covers or anything like that?" Ana asked.

"Definitely not."

"Thank you, Constable, that will be all." Ana said. Justice Andrews then asked

"Any further questions for the witness Mr Taylor?"

"No thank you Your Honour."

"The witness may stand down. Thank you, Constable Burrows. Ms Harris?"

"I would like to call the defendant, James Carruthers to the stand. But before I do, and if I may Your Honour, I think it's important that the members of the jury are fully cognisant of the background to this... encounter.

"Ladies and gentlemen, the Sergeant Kevin Smith we are talking about had two brothers, both of whom play key roles in this narrative. As you will hear later in this trial, Sergeant Kevin Smith's brother, Sergeant Phillip Smith was the officer killed on Waiheke Island. Their brother Shane Smith was part of the Wild Bunch gang, and also died that day. It was an extraordinary, what shall we call it... conspiracy.... collision, of circumstances, I'm sure you would agree.

"My client is also accused of murdering Phillip and Shane. He has acknowledged that he was responsible for their deaths but, again, in self-defence.

"I ask the members of the jury to consider this. What would Sergeant Kevin Smith's motivation have been for visiting my client in hospital, if not pure and simple - revenge."

"Your Honour I must object in the most strenuous terms." Simon Taylor remonstrated.

"Defence Counsel is, in effect, attempting to direct the jury to reach the conclusion she would wish for."

"I'm not sure I agree, Mr. Taylor." Justice Andrews replied.

"The prosecution's position is that Sergeant Kevin Smith went to the hospital that night to talk to the defendant and was killed in cold blood. It seems to me that Ms. Harris is merely suggesting he might have had another, and I must say altogether plausible, motivation."

Simon Taylor sat down, grumpily. It had been a long time since things had gone so badly for him in court. He should never have accepted this case, it was always too full of holes.

"Thank you, Your Honour." Ana said. "I now call James Carruthers."

Jim walked to the stand, with a slight limp, and was sworn in.

"Mr. Carruthers, would you tell the court your experience of what happened on the evening in question."

"It was a bit after 7 pm. I was nodding off in my bed when a man dressed as a doctor came into the room. He took out a handgun, and I thought he was going to shoot me. Instead, he gave it to me, to defend myself with, he said, as someone was coming to kill me."

"Did you know this man?" Ana asked.

"I'd never seen him before in my life." Which was true.

"What happened next?"

"He told me to put all the pillows in the bed, like a body, and wait in the bathroom. Some time later, an hour or so later, the man I now know was Sergeant Kevin Smith, came into the room and fired five shots into the bed, no doubt thinking I was in it.

"His gun was fitted with a silencer. I turned the lights on and told him to drop the weapon. He didn't, and turned it towards me, so I had no choice but to shoot him."

"One final question Mr Carruthers. Did Sergeant Smith say anything during all this?" Ana asked.

"Just before he fired into the bed he said 'Payback time, motherfucker'" Jim answered.

"Thank you, Mr. Carruthers, you may step down."

Jim returned to his seat. The atmosphere in the courtroom was tense, to say the least. Justice Andrews said

"This feels like a suitable time to break for lunch. The court will reconvene in ninety minutes, at... 2.05."

* * * *

"Well today's going a bit better so far." Stan said. Stan, Tim and Matt were about to go back into the court room.

"Thank God." Tim said. "We're in for a tough time though, you and me, when this is all over."

"Mmm." Stan had been wondering how much he could pin the drugs thing on Tim, without having to take too much of the blame himself. After all, he hadn't known about Tim planting the coke, at first anyway.

"Am I doing ok so far?" Matt asked.

"Yeah mate, you're doing great." Stan said. "Just stick to the script and you'll be fine."

"Hope so. It's fucking nerve-wracking though eh?" Matt said.

"Sure is. Fingers crossed fellas." Tim said.

* * * *

"Let us resume. Ms. Harris, the next witness for the defence, if you would." Justice Andrews said.

"If I may Your Honour, before I call my next witness I would like draw attention to what I think is an important distinction that needs to be made at this point."

"Very well, Ms. Harris."

"Ladies and gentlemen of the jury, I think we need to remember the central issue here. It is not how my client came by the gun which killed Sergeant Smith, but whether Sergeant Smith had a gun and came to the room to use it against my client.

"If it may please Your Honour. I would now like to call Charge Nurse Mary McGregor."

Mary McGregor took the stand. She was mid-aged, attractive, with auburn hair in a severe scraped back style, and a broad Scottish accent.

"Charge Nurse McGregor, welcome. You're the senior nurse in charge of the ward, including the private rooms attached to the ward, where the defendant James Carruthers was a patient, is that correct?"

"It is." The Charge Nurse replied.

"I understand you were not on duty on the night in question, but came in the next morning, at 7 am, while the night staff were still there. Could you describe what happened when you arrived, please."

"Yes, there's a half hour overlap of the shifts. Everyone was talking about the events of the night before, the shooting, all the police arriving..."

"I can imagine. Was there anything else that was noteworthy?" Ana asked.

"Yes, there was a strange thing. One of the nurses asked me if we'd changed the ordering of bed linen for the rooms. We seemed to be short."

"Could you explain that further for us please."

"Well, the bedding had all gone from one of the rooms. Mattress, sheets, pillows, blankets, under-blankets, bedspread, the lot."

"You're not talking about Mr Carruthers' room?" Ana asked.

"No, no, a room further down the corridor. All just disappeared. But since you mention it, we went to change the sheets in what had been Mr. Carruthers' room, and the nurse commented that they didn't appear to have been slept in. They were quite fresh, unused."

"Could this have been the bedding from the room that had been stripped?"

"Objection Your Honour!" Simon Taylor spoke out. "Leading question!"

"Quite right Mr. Taylor. Please try to remember the rules of examination Ms. Harris." Justice Andrews said.

But the point had been made.

"Thank you, Charge Nurse McGregor, you've been most helpful." Ana said.

"Mr Taylor, do you wish to cross-examine?" Justice Andrews asked.

"Ah... no thank you, Your Honour." He didn't see much point, this woman wasn't going to change her story, and there really was nothing he could challenge her on.

"Thank you, Charge Nurse, you may step down." Justice Andrews said.

Ana said "I now call Daniel Coleman." After the obligatory formalities, she began

"Mr. Coleman, you are a certified security guard with over twenty years' experience, the last five of which have been with the security company contracted by Auckland City Hospital. Is that right?"

"Yes, it is."

"Your employers tell me you are one of their most reliable, trustworthy, and highly-regarded staff members."

"That's nice to hear." Coleman blushed. "Yes, I love what I do."

Dan was a big man. He reminded Ana of Jim, big and hard-edged on the surface but with a softness not too far beneath. This man had no guile about him, what you saw was what you got. He was someone you could rely on to be honest.

"That's great. There's nothing better than liking what you do. And you were on duty at the hospital on the night in question?"

"I was."

"Tell us please, what's your nightly routine there?"

"There's always three of us on duty. One of us is stationed at the front entrance, one in E.D, that's the Emergency Department, where there's often trouble, and the other one patrols the building, checking on fire exits, moving around the floors. We rotate during the night, every couple of hours or so."

"I see. And what happened that night, from your point of view."

"I was on patrol, and around 8.30 I heard what sounded like gun shots from the floor below where I was. Pretty unusual. I raced down there and saw a nurse running to one of the rooms. She seemed a bit agitated, and I went to see what was going on."

"And what did you see Mr. Coleman."

'Well not much. There were two men in the room, one in a hospital gown, and the other was a policeman, Constable Burrows, I'd met him earlier on my rounds. The Constable said he had everything under control and shut the door, which struck me as a bit odd."

"Were there any obvious signs of a struggle having taken place?" Ana asked.

"Not that I could see."

"Take care, Counsel." The judge said.

"Apologies Your Honour. So, Mr. Coleman, was that the last you saw or heard of the... incident?" Ana asked.

"Not quite. A bit later I thought I should go back and check on things, see if everything was alright, so I poked my head around the door into the corridor. Constable Burrows was back sitting in the chair outside the room. He hadn't seen me, and everything looked ok, so I left him to it."

"What was he actually doing at that point?" Ana asked.

"Nothing. Just sitting there."

"Just sitting there?" Ana said.

"Yes, like he was in shock, or thinking deeply about something. Just sitting there, looking at the guns."

"Guns? There was more than one?"

"Yes. Pistols, two of them, one in each hand." Coleman said.

A loud murmur enveloped the courtroom. Ana waited for it to subside.

"Anything else you can tell us about these guns Mr. Coleman?" She asked.

"One of them had a silencer on it, the other one didn't."

* * * *

"Tom." The voice on the other end of the phone said.

"Yep, who's this?"

"I thought you were coming in to see me."

"Who's this?"

"Jason. At the gym."

"Oh right. How are you Jason?"

"So when are you coming in? Today'd be good."

Tom bit the bullet. He could take an hour or so off. He went home, threw a towel, shorts, T-shirt and sneakers into a bag and went to the gym.

Jason wasn't exactly easy on him and after half an hour or so of stretching, aerobics and floor exercises he was tuckered out.

"Right well that's a start I s'pose. Let's see, you're fat, your lungs are fucked, your diet's obviously shit, and you're about as strong as a ten-year-old, with less stamina. Otherwise, you're all good."

"Thanks a lot Jason, very encouraging."

"Yeah, nah, we'll get there, mate." He smiled. "Can you do Monday, Wednesday and Friday 10 a.m?"

"I guess."

"Great. I'll work out a programme for you and give you a diet sheet next time. If I can get you half as fit as your old man I'll be doing ok."

"He's good is he?" Tom was curious.

"Mate, he's amazing. Strong, hard, tough as old boots. And he's done a lot for me. I love him. He's my brother-from-another-mother!" He laughed, then seriously and quietly said "No, he's the closest thing I've ever had to a father. I'd kill for him."

* * * *

"Jury Foreperson, has the jury reached a verdict?" Justice Andrews asked.

"We have Your Honour."

"And is it a verdict on which you all agree?"

"It is Your Honour.

"On the charge of murder relating to the death of Sergeant Kevin Smith, how do you find the defendant, guilty or not guilty?"

"Not guilty, Your Honour."

It had taken the jury barely forty minutes to reach their decision. While there was a small ripple of reactions around the courtroom and the press corps were going mad on their cell phones, no-one was seriously surprised by the result.

Dan Coleman's revelation about the two handguns was just too compelling. Despite rigorous cross-examination from Crown Prosecutor Taylor, he was unwavering in his testimony. He was totally credible, and convincing.

Added to that, revenge was always much more likely to have been Kevin Smith's motive for going to the hospital. Ana had chosen not to address the jury before they retired.

"Thank you, ladies and gentlemen of the jury, and I must say I think your decision is the correct one. The time now being 4.10 pm, the court will adjourn for the day, and will reconvene at 10 am tomorrow, when we will begin to consider the remainder of the charges in this case."

*   *   *   *

Harris Wins Again; More High Court Drama; and *Police Corruption?* were just some of the many headlines. It was international news, every major newspaper and channel picked it up and ran with it - *BBC, CNN, The New York Times, The Guardian,* even *Al Jazeera*, and of course, all of the New Zealand news media. *The Herald* wrote

Police Under Fire

'For the second time in two days there has been a dramatic development in the Waiheke Murder Trial. The defendant in the case was today acquitted of the first of several murder charges, after defence counsel Anahera Harris produced a witness who totally undermined the crown case. This follows her revelation on Monday that the cocaine at the centre of drugs charges against the defendant was in fact icing sugar.

If there was any doubt as to police impropriety regarding the drugs, everything revealed in court today points strongly to a deliberate and comprehensive police cover-up of evidence.

There are renewed and widespread calls for a Commission of Inquiry into the police handling of the case.'

The article went on at some length about the guns and the bedding, concluding with a damning indictment of the police case.

"I don't believe this. It's amazing." Tom said, flicking through the headlines on his laptop.

"It sure is. What about lil' old me eh?" Ana couldn't quite believe it either. Her phone was off ninety percent of the time, there were just endless requests for interviews and comment.

"Damn!" She said.

"What's wrong?"

"Vodafone. My account's overdue. Third reminder. I'm losing track of everything at the moment..."

"Apart from the case. You're doing so well." Tom said.

"So far... I'll pay it now before I forget again... Jesus Christ!" Ana said.

"This must be a mistake."

"What?" Tom asked.

"A rather large deposit in my bank account."

"Oh, that'll be Carlo. I've been meaning to tell you he's insisting on paying you for getting his mother off the drugs charge. Said it saved him hiring a lawyer."

"Ah yes, it says 'For Legal Services.' "

"How much is it?" Tom was imagining a few thousand dollars.

"Two hundred and fifty grand." Ana said.

"Fuck me!" Tom was amazed, as was Ana.

"Well, that should cover the phone bill" he said.

* * * *

The next morning at 9.59 the courtroom was buzzing with conversation.

"Silence. All stand for the Honourable Justice Andrews." The Registrar of the High Court announced. Andrews took his place at the bench.

"Please be seated."

"I would like to start proceedings today with a comment for the jury." Andrews continued.

"You will all be aware of the furore this case is causing in the news media. I am asking you to put this out of your minds, as best you can. I would like you, also, to try to put the events of the last two days in this court out of your thoughts as well.

"We all need to concentrate on the job in hand, which is to address the rest of the charges before the court, without reference back to the decisions reached so far. To all intents and purposes this a fresh start, a new day, with new issues to discuss and resolve. Please try to remember this as we proceed. Thank you. Crown Prosecutor?"

"May it please Your Honour. Thank you for those timely and most welcome comments. Members of the jury, we are now dealing with the aspects of the case that relate to Waiheke Island. There were six deaths that day. Four of these were the members of the gang responsible for several home invasions, rapes and murders - the self-styled 'Wild Bunch.' The other two deaths were a member of the household, one Giuseppe de Luca, and a police officer, Sergeant Phillip Smith, stationed at Waiheke. The defendant James Carruthers was also present, as was the owner of the property Francesca Giordano.

"The prosecution believes that all of these people - apart from Sergeant Smith of course - were meeting to discuss a shared interest, drug dealing. A dispute arose, there was gunfire, and the only survivors were the defendant and Mrs. Giordano, who we believe were ringleaders of group. Both were seriously injured in the melee. We are not suggesting that the defendant or Mrs. Giordano were in any way involved with the home invasions this 'Wild Bunch' perpetrated. This was an entirely separate 'business' relationship they had with the gang.

"We have very credible information that the Giordano family is involved in drug trafficking, and as for Mr. Carruthers, we have information that helps explain his involvement and which we will introduce later in evidence.

"Our witnesses will be Constable Sally Reynolds, Sergeant Timothy Adams, Inspector David Bretherton from NCB, and Stephen Johnson, a paramedic with the ambulance service on Waiheke. I call Constable Sally Reynolds to the stand." Taylor said.

Sally made her way to the witness box, smiling at Tim as she passed the prosecution desk.

Tim had primed her as best he could, and he was confident she would deliver. She swore her oath on the St. James bible.

"Constable Reynolds, would you please tell the court what you remember of that day, Sunday the twentieth of January this year, on Waiheke Island, as it relates to this case."

"Well... Sergeant Smith and I were on a routine patrol around the Onetangi area of the island when we got a call to investigate reports of gunfire at a Cowes Bay Road address. There'd been a 111 call from there." Sally said.

"And what did you find Constable?"

"We approached the house with caution and were met by Mrs. Giordano. We followed her inside and... "

"Carry on Constable."

"It was awful. There was blood everywhere, bodies everywhere, one with his face completely gone, another with horrific wounds to his throat and neck, another with his intestines - " Sally was having trouble not indulging her penchant for the dramatic.

"Yes, thank you Constable. That must have been very traumatic for you. Was anyone there alive?" Crown Prosecutor Taylor asked her.

"Yes. The defendant was alive, sitting on the floor against a big couch."

"What happened next?"

"Sergeant Smith asked me to call it in so I went outside and did that. It was good to be out of there, even briefly."

"I can imagine, it must have been an awful scene." Taylor said.

"It was. Then just as I went back in, the defendant lifted up a gun and..." Sally started to get a bit tearful.

"Take your time Constable, I know this is difficult for you."

"...and shot Phil, dead." This time Sally did properly dissolve into tears.

"Thank you, Constable Reynolds, no further questions."

"Constable Reynolds, do you need some time to compose yourself?" the judge asked.

"No thank you, Your Honour. I'm ok." Sally said, sniffing loudly.

"Ms. Harris, do you wish to cross-examine the witness?"

"Thank you, Your Honour, I do. Constable Reynolds, you will be aware that it was my client who called 111 to report the events at the Cowes Bay Road house."

"Yes, I knew that." Sally said.

"As you say, it is why you and Sergeant Smith were despatched there." Ana said. "Do you know what my client said in that call?"

"Not exactly, no." Sally said.

"What he said was - and this is from the official police record of that call - that there were four people dead and three injured, two men and a woman, all in urgent need of medical attention. Who might those three people have been do you think?" Ana asked.

"Objection Your Honour." Simon Taylor said, dismissively.

"Please Ms. Harris." Justice Andrews said.

"Sorry Your Honour. Well, Constable, he was obviously talking about himself, Mrs. Giordano, and the third person could only have been Giuseppe de Luca, the old Italian gentleman."

"Ok..." Sally said.

"But you said Giuseppe was dead when you arrived, is that correct?"

"Yes, when we first went in, I thought that Carruthers was dead too." Sally said.

"So, it wasn't Sergeant Smith who shot Mr. de Luca between the eyes." Ana asked.

"Definitely not."

"Very well, just a couple more questions Constable, did Sergeant Smith realise at any point that one of the dead was his brother Shane?"

"Not that I'm aware of." Sally said.

"And one final question. Did either you or Sergeant Smith draw, or fire your weapons that day?" Ana asked.

"No, we did not." Sally replied, firmly.

"Why is it, do you think, that my client shot the Sergeant and not you?"

"Objection." Simon Taylor said, sounding bored.

"Yes, you really must stop this Ms. Harris. Facts not opinions, remember." Justice Andrews said, in his gentlemanly way.

"Thank you, Constable. I have no further questions for you."

"Very well. I would like to call Sergeant Timothy Adams to the stand." Taylor said.

Tim made his way to the stand, well aware that the eyes of the world's press were on him.

"Sergeant Adams, would you tell us please, the next stage of events that Sunday on Waiheke. I don't need to remind you, I'm sure, that you are still under oath."

"Of course, sir. When the station received Sally's...Constable Reynolds' call confirming the situation at Cowes Bay Road, Constable Andrew Tyler and I, plus two ambulances were despatched there.

"When we arrived Andy and I went in ahead of the paramedics to check it was safe, then we called them in."

"And what did you find Sergeant?" Taylor asked.

"The carnage that Constable Reynolds had described. She was kneeling alongside Sergeant Smith, who was obviously dead. We thought that the defendant was among the dead at first, but the paras found that he, and the Giordano woman were alive. Unconscious but alive."

"Before you continue Sergeant, I should tell the court, members of the jury, that Constable Reynolds and Sergeant Smith were in a relationship, so she was understandably distraught at his death. Please continue Sergeant." The Crown Prosecutor said.

"Yes, Sally really was very upset, and it took some effort to persuade her to leave Sergeant Smith's side."

"Physical effort?"

"Yes."

"Thank you, Sergeant. That's all I need from you, for the moment."

"Ms. Harris, do you wish to question the Sergeant?"

"No thank you, Your Honour." Ana said.

What is she playing at? Taylor wondered to himself.

"Do you wish to call any more witnesses Mr. Taylor?" the judge asked.

"Later, yes, but not at this point, thank you Your Honour."

"Very well, over to you defence counsel." Justice Andrews said, genuinely interested to see what Ana Harris would do next.

"Members of the jury, I strongly challenge the prosecution's two principal arguments. First, there is absolutely no evidence that my client has ever had any involvement in criminal activity, and our position is that he was not involved in any sort of meeting at the Cowes Bay Road property.

"We contend that this was a typical 'Wild Bunch' home invasion, that my client inadvertently interrupted. I will produce evidence which confirms this.

"Second, there is no evidence that the Giordano family has mafia or drug connections. They are model citizens, major investors in the country's economy, to the tune of many millions of dollars, and employ over two hundred New Zealanders in their various businesses.

"After interrupting the home invasion and the imminent rape of Mrs. Giordano, my client bravely fought the gang and defeated them. He then made a 111 call and shortly thereafter Sergeant Philp Smith and Constable Sally Reynolds arrived on the scene.

"When Sergeant Phillip Smith realised his brother Shane, who was a member of the Wild Bunch gang, was among the dead, he wanted revenge. He killed the wounded Giuseppe and then attempted to kill my client. In the process he hit Mrs. Giordano with his pistol, nearly killing her. Once again Mr. Carruthers defended himself, killing the Sergeant in self-defence, after Smith - and Reynolds - engaged him in a gun fight.

"While I respect his Honour's wish to put the past behind us, we cannot ignore the similarities between the Smith brothers' reactions to the death of their siblings. What we must consider very seriously, is the veracity of Constable Reynolds' testimony about what happened when she and Sergeant Smith arrived at the property. This is critical to resolving the case. I should say I believe her testimony to be completely and utterly false."

My word, this girl knows how to make a speech, Simon Taylor thought to himself. He wanted to object, he just didn't really know what to object to.

"I call Inspector Stanley Williams to the witness stand." Ana stand. This was most unexpected. It was the last thing Taylor, or Andrews thought she would do. Williams had been totally discredited. Why would she call him? Again, after the obligatory oath-taking, Ana began.

"Inspector Williams, I need to ask you some questions about the... mechanics of a crime scene investigation. For example, if bullets have been fired into walls, or a couch let's say, are these bullets retrieved and analysed?"

"Sometimes, but not as a matter of course. Not necessarily, no." Stan replied.

"What about bullets in a victim's body?"

"Yes, it's standard procedure." Stan said.

"What about in this instance, was the bullet which killed Mr. de Luca examined, for example?" Ana asked.

"Yes, it was from the .22 rifle found at the scene."

"And what about the bullets which were removed from my client's body during surgery?" Ana asked.

"I'm sure they would have been, but I don't remember the details. Forensics gave us a very clear picture of what happened that day, both before and after Sergeant Smith and Constable Reynolds arrived at the scene."

"Because I believe Constable Reynolds shot my client." Ana said. "Forensic analysis would have proved that, would it not?"

"If what you say is true, and it simply is not." Stan asserted.

"Did anyone check to see if Smith and Reynolds' Glock pistols had been fired that day?"

"Not that I'm aware of, but I'm not part of SOCO." Stan said.

"That's very odd. Another procedural 'lapse' maybe... or perhaps you simply looked at the parts of the ballistics report that suited you?"

No response. After a pause. "You have overseen this case for some time now, have you not?"

"Yes, I have." Stan said, still trying to adjust to this unforeseen demand on him.

"Ever since Superintendent Smales's ill health caused him to withdraw from the investigation." Ana said.

Bill Smales was in fact watching the delayed broadcast of this session, with bated breath. He did so like Ana Harris. Ana hoped he was watching.

"Do you think you have handled the case in a way that Bill Smales would approve of?" Ana asked.

"I... hope so." Stan was completely flummoxed.

"Well, I very much doubt it, Inspector. The Superintendent has always been a police officer of the highest integrity, whereas I think this is yet another example of your... what shall we call it... your 'inclination' to try to make the facts of the case fit what you would like the result to be."

"I object, Your Honour." Crown Prosecutor Taylor said, without conviction. This young woman was too much for him, he was beginning to think.

Tears filled Bill Smales's eyes. What a cracker this girl is, he thought. Thank you, Ana.

"Isn't that lovely darling." Bill's wife Edie, who was also watching, said.

"Yes, where are you going with this Ms. Harris?"

"I have no further questions of this witness, Your Honour, thank you. If it please the court, I would now ask the Bailiff to distribute the copies of the Waiheke weekly paper - the *Gulf News* - entered as one of our exhibits, to the members of the jury.

"Of course, Ms. Harris"

Judge Andrews was impressed. The previous witness examination was nothing less than a bravura performance designed to undermine the prosecution. Unorthodox and broke a couple of rules, but clever, he thought. He also knew Bill Smales, held him in high regard, and thought how much he would appreciate her tribute to him.

Ana and Jim noticed Carlo slip into the public gallery.

"I refer you to the advertisement in the For Sale section, the one that I have circled in red. You'll see that it's an ad for various things which happen to be of interest to my client. You will not know this, but Mrs. Giordano's husband died recently. She intended to return to Italy, and was advertising items she no longer wanted to keep.

"My client rang the number, Mrs. Giordano replied, and they arranged for him to visit at 1.30 that same day, Sunday. Neither of them could have known that his visit would coincide with the Wild Bunch attack on the property.

"Members of the jury, I ask you, in all honesty, is that not the most likely, the best, the most logical and credible explanation for my client being on that property at that time?"

Ana was picking that no-one in the opposition camp would have checked the misprinted phone number, and she was right.

"I would now like to call Mrs. Francesca Giordano to the stand."

Francesca sailed to the witness stand. She was dressed entirely in black, with a long flowing dress, and a lace mantilla shrouding her face. She still had dressings on one cheek, but these only served to draw attention to, and highlight her dark eyes and black shining hair. A large solitaire diamond pendant necklace and only slightly smaller single diamond earrings sparkled against her olive skin and black attire. She was a most impressive and elegant presence in the court room. After the formalities Ana said

"Signora Giordano. Please tell us what happened that day at your house on Waiheke."

Francesca's voice was deep and a little husky. Her English was impeccable, with more than a hint of an Italian accent. Not as 'posh' as Carlo's, but equally fluent. She spoke slowly and softly.

"My business manager Giuseppe and I were in the loggia discussing our accounts when Shane, who had groomed our dog Bello a few times, walked in with three other men. They had guns and knives. One of them shot Giuseppe. I was devastated and ran to him, but the dreadful man Shane hit me in the face, threw me on the table, ripped my clothes off, and... "

Francesca was not finding this easy. Ana said gently

"Take your time Mrs. Giordano."

"...his accomplice, Bob, I think his name was, tied me to the table and started licking my breasts and sucking my... It was disgusting. I just remember the long, shining knife he was holding. Shane pulled down his trousers, and..." She paused, breathing deeply. "...and he said he was going to rape me... and Bob would cut my throat just before he... ejaculated. Then

Bob would also... I told him he would pay for his sins and spat in his face. He hit me again, and then..."

Francesca paused again. The atmosphere in the court was electric.

"And then...?" Ana asked, very quietly.

"I think I must have been quite dazed... I remember starting to come around. I heard someone at the front of the house and I screamed for help. There was shouting and gunfire... it was awf..."

Francesca's breath caught in her throat. She composed herself.

"... then someone was covering up my naked body and saying *'It's alright, they're all dead. I'm here, you're safe. You're safe now.'*

"My life and my honour had been saved. By that courageous man." She gestured towards Jim.

The courtroom was totally silent. It had been an excoriating, powerful, and totally believable testimony from this exquisite woman.

Justice Andrews, himself moved in a way he rarely was these days, said simply

"This court is adjourned until ten o'clock Monday morning."

TEN

Carlo was outside the court waiting for his mother, who was in a de-brief with Ana. Jim went up to him.

"Ciao Carlo. Come va?" He hadn't seen Carlo since the night in the hospital.

"Jim. How are you holding up? I do think Anahera is doing a very good job for you."

"She sure is. Listen, sorry to be the one to pass on the news about Pepe. You ok?"

"I am... ok. Thank you for asking Jim."

"And the Russians?"

Before Carlo had a chance to answer, Francesca joined them.

"Buona sera Jim!" Francesca said warmly and kissed him on both cheeks. "Good to see you. I am so looking forward to tomorrow night."

"So are we, so are we."

"Sorry Jim, we have to dash." Carlo said. "I'm meeting some people at the airport in..." he looked at his watch. "Oh yes, we must go. I too am looking forward to tomorrow. I think it will be a most interesting evening! Ciao ciao."

Jim watched them walk away, followed at a discreet distance by the Twins. He reflected that it was the first time he had seen Francesca since that fateful Sunday on Waiheke. It seemed so long ago. Seeing her and hearing her talk about what happened that day had had quite a profound effect on him, shaken him. It wasn't like listening to the other witnesses, they weren't really 'there' somehow, compared with her. He went home, his head full of images from that day.

* * * *

"Hi Sue." Jim called as he walked into the apartment. No answer, she wasn't home yet. Then he remembered Sue had said she was having a drink with some friends after work, and might possibly eat with them as well. It was another soft end of day afternoon. He might just have a glass of wine on the deck, enjoy the last of the sun and the views across the city to the harbour, and do a bit of 'stocktaking'.

He was pleased to have this time to himself. He liked being out of the hospital, but he had also quite liked the relative solitude there. And things had changed with Sue since he told her about his past. It was a subtle change, but there was no doubt they were estranged. It was almost as though she had discovered he'd had a secret lover all the years they'd been together. She looked at him like a stranger. She maintained that he had started snoring since being home and she needed to move to the spare room to get enough sleep. There'd been no intimacy between them, of any sort, all these weeks.

Secrets. He had felt huge relief at having told Sue and Tom about his history. Secrets imprison you he realised. He felt that being honest might have enhanced his relationship with Tom, but it had had the opposite effect on Sue it would seem.

The sun was going down, and there were the beginnings of another beautiful sunset. It was the time of day he loved the most. Today he barely registered it. He hadn't really noticed the wine either and the two-thirds of a bottle they had opened the previous evening was nearly gone.

'...a drink with some friends.' Sue had a lot of friends, from school, university, work. Jim didn't. He'd had friends in London, in the army mostly, but none here in New Zealand. He knew lots of people, particularly in the industry, and the arts, but they were acquaintances, not friends. He couldn't recall if he'd ever met up with people for a drink after work. The closest he came to that was gallery openings, where he would catch up with people he knew. Yes, secrets imprison you. They keep you in, and other people out. It had always been part of his 'tough guy' self-image that he didn't need anyone, but he was feeling very alone right now.

Seeing Francesca again, hearing the violence on the island related in her beautiful voice, had cast it in a different light, it felt real in a way it hadn't been up until now, and it was decidedly uncomfortable. His mind was also suddenly full of flashbacks to much earlier bloodlettings he hadn't thought of for years. They too were suddenly very real, visceral, ghastly. He had, decades ago, found a way of filing them away somewhere that he could live with them. He supposed it must be what all soldiers, killers, do to protect themselves - depersonalise those they kill, so they're faceless statistics, not actual people. It hadn't worked with some of those in Colombia, and he knew it never would with Ra. But now all the others too? Rising up like spectres from the swamp? Surely not. No, this would pass, all things pass.

The wine was finished. He might open another bottle. No, he should think about food. He went inside to the fridge. Nothing, but he did notice a nearly full bottle of grappa, chilling there. Forget food, he thought, that's what I feel like. I'll just have a couple of glasses of this to be going on with. Maybe get a pizza delivered later.

As Jim drank grappa and smoked on the deck he thought, inevitably, of Giuseppe. Even for that brief time, they had felt like friends. Guiseppe said they were brothers, and they could have been. They knew each other, who each other was. God what lives they had led he thought. So much blood and death between them. Blood brothers? He would have liked to have had a brother. Now he had killed three men, each of whom had two brothers.

With every glass of grappa Jim was sinking further into a morass of demons and self-loathing. He felt very old, very tired, and sick of life. His leg had started hurting again. Ra, beautiful Ra, thanks for the memories. Huh. He got up to stretch his leg, lost his balance, lurched, and fell heavily against the deck balustrade. He looked over the edge, seven stories up. The footpath was a long way down. A thought was beginning to form in his increasingly fuzzy mind.

"Hiya." Sue called from the hall. "You ok?"

"Yep."

"Listen, I might have an early night. See you in the morning."

"Ok."

That's how it was. Every day. What time was it? Didn't matter. Jim sat down, lit another cigarette, and poured another grappa. What was the fucking point?

What if the handrail had given way when he fell against it? It might a second time, or he could just... He'd never had the slightest fear of heights, but whenever he was somewhere high, there had always been a little voice in his head that said *'Go on, jump, go on, you know you want to.'*

He had always ignored it, but that voice was getting louder by the second... Yes, just do it. Finish it. He made a decision. He pulled a chair right up to the handrail, and slowly got up onto it. Yes. He was already looking forward to the fall, the flight, *'the dying of the light'*. Standing there, he felt on top of the world. Calm and free. He looked up at the stars. Beautiful. Felt the warm breeze on his face. Delicious. Time passed. He felt at peace.

From somewhere in the distance a song drifted up, barely audible over the hum of the traffic. He recognised it, remembered it from the bar in London, what was it... The Little River Band, *'Time for a cool change, I know that it's time for a cool change.'* How funny, and apt... Yes, it's time.

Just lean forward now, that's all it will take. The pain, the guilt, it will all be over and done with, in seconds. The voice was really loud now

'Go on, go on, go on. Jump. Jump. Jump!'. He took a deep, deep breath. Just slowly lean forward. Now!

But he didn't. He stopped himself, hesitated. Something was bothering him. What was it?

It would be very, very messy from this height. What if a child were the first on the scene? He wouldn't want that. What if he landed on someone? He knew if he looked down to the street to check it was clear, he'd pitch forward anyway, he was a bit unsteady. Then there was Tom, the only real achievement of his entire life. Dear Tom didn't need him anymore, but he'd be very upset... Francesca might be too... and Sue, he assumed. And what would the news media make of it? They'd probably see it as an admission of guilt, and that wouldn't do either.

What's more he had been really looking forward to the dinner party the next night.

Christ Jim, what are you doing? Get a grip. Pull yourself together, be a man! What is 'a man'? *'What a piece of work is man.'* Who wrote that? Bloody Shakespeare of course. He loved Shakespeare. There'd be no more Shakespeare...

He took another deep breath. Maybe I won't do this.... No, I'd better see it through, he thought, to the bitter end, whatever that might be. He glanced down at the table. Jesus, I've drunk nearly a whole bottle of grappa, no wonder I feel a bit pissed.

Yes, you're just a drunk old twat. Put all that shit out of your head and harden the fuck up, for Chrissake! Jim suddenly felt very foolish standing there, like who... de Caprio on the prow of the Titanic?

Yeah... silly, stupid, pathetic. Just go to bed. He got down off the chair, and promptly fell flat on his face.

Over the course of at least the next five minutes, including frequent pauses, he slowly crawled to the bedroom, laughing quietly to himself the whole way.

* * * *

The Carruthers family arrived at Quattro Leoni at the appointed time, for Francesca's dinner party. There wasn't a lot of space in the carpark. Apart from a couple of nondescript Japanese saloons, there was Carlo's Ferrari, the Twins' BMW, but also three other identical black 5 Series BMWs. There were between two and four men in each. It was hard to tell how many, they were just shapes through the heavily tinted windows. There was also something odd about the number plates, but Jim couldn't pick what it was as they walked past the cars.

"Jesus" Tom said to Jim. "Carlo's ramped up his security a bit."

"Sure has" Jim replied, although he had a feeling there might be more to it than that.

He had slept late, had a huge breakfast, and was feeling remarkably ok given how much he had drunk. He felt a bit washed out and a bit confused, but more or less back on track.

There was a notice on the door 'Private Function. Closed.'

Carlo met them at the front door and they walked through the empty cafe. When Tom met Carlo there many weeks earlier, he would not have known there was a large semi-outdoor area behind the cafe.

There was just one big table in the middle of the space, immaculately set, with a large silver candelabra in its centre. There were candlesticks and more candelabra around the perimeter of the space. It was simple and beautiful, as was the food and the wine, a classic Italian five course meal, that lasted some hours in the soft, flickering candlelight.

Bello lay at the only entrance to the space all evening. At one point, between courses, Ana could resist it no longer and went and petted him for a few minutes. He wagged his tail and made that noise in his throat again, but never once took his eyes off the approaches to the room.

The court case would not have been mentioned at all had Ana not, soon after they arrived, thanked Francesca for her courage in court. And, of course, there was no reference whatever to the matter of the Russians.

It was now nearing the end of the evening. The three men and Francesca were drinking grappa, Ana and Sue limoncello.

"There is a famous trattoria across the river in Florence called Quattro Leoni. We always go there when we visit the city. My friend who owns this place worked there for a time, before moving here, and used the same name. He is a wonderful chef is he not?" Carlo asked. Everyone agreed. It had been an amazing meal. Then Francesca said

"My dear friends, it has been a great pleasure and a privilege to have you here this evening. I will always remember this special time. I want to thank you again, Jim, for saving me, and I wish you the very best for the rest of the trial. Anahera, I'm sure, will continue to shine in her advocacy for you, and I thank you too Ana, for saving me from having to endure a trial myself. And Sue, it is so nice to meet you and have you here too. You married a very fine man.

"As you know I am returning to Italy soon, so I might not see you again, unless you come to visit me in Venezia, which I sincerely hope you will all do. How many bedrooms do we have in the palazzo Carlo, is it eight or nine?"

"I think ten, mamma" They all laughed. "Yes, there is plenty of room."

Then Carlo called "Franco" and a waiter appeared carrying what looked like two quite large boxes. He gave one to Jim and the other to Tom. They were heavy.

Franco then took two much smaller packages from his pocket and gave them to Sue and Ana.

"These are gifts from my mother and me, to celebrate and remember the extraordinary journey we have been on together. Please open them." Carlo said.

The men's boxes were each in fine kidskin bags. Jim removed the bag from his to reveal a beautifully crafted rosewood box, with 'Beretta' in gold, inlaid on the top. Tom's was identical.

The women's packages contained the most beautiful necklaces, one rubies and diamonds, the other emeralds and diamonds. They looked very expensive.

Francesca said "You can share those, so you have two each!"

Ana and Sue thanked them profusely.

"Did you know Jim, that Beretta have been making guns for over 500 years. In a small village in the mountains west of Verona, where they still have a factory. They are the oldest manufacturer of weapons, in fact the oldest continuous manufacturer of any product, in the world.

"Please, open them. This is the 30th anniversary special edition M9."

Inside each of the red velvet-lined boxes was a beautiful black handgun, with finely crafted wooden grips and gold detailing.

"They're gorgeous Carlo, but we can't - " Jim said.

"We would be mortally offended were you to refuse them." Carlo was serious.

"What can we say. Thank you so much. We will treasure them." Tom said, and frowned at Jim.

"We will Indeed. Grazie mille, Carlo e Francesca." Jim said.

Only a mafioso would give a gift like this, Ana thought to herself, and what must they have cost?!

Sue was simply at a loss. Giving guns as presents? After all they'd been through? Crazy people.

"I am so pleased you all like your gifts." Francesca said.

"There is a drawer underneath each box with one hundred hand-made cartridges." Carlo added.

"Wow. So, they're not models. They're real, they work." Jim said.

"Oh yes." Carlo said. "I would never give a friend a gun that didn't work" and he smiled.

The four BMWs were gone from the carpark when they left Quattro Leoni around eleven.

* * * *

The gym was always quiet on Sundays, particularly the mornings, so Jim had the place to himself. As a member he had a key and was the first one there. It had been an amazing evening the night before, but he'd woken early, feeling unsettled and with a strange sense of foreboding - about the cars in the car park, the Russians, the Colombians, the court case. The gym was the only thing he could think of that might help. A bit of head-banging.

He overdid it, of course, without Jason there to keep him in check, and after half an hour of weights routines he shouldn't have been attempting, he was sore and exhausted, just lying on a bench trying to summon up the strength to sit up.

"Can't resist it can ya?" A voice said. Jim looked up. It was Manu, smiling down at him.

"Hiya mate. How'd you know I'd be here?"

"I didn't. I come in on Sunday mornings to check the place. The boys sometimes go a bit wild on Saturday nights. Can I buy you breakfast?"

"No, but I'll join you. Breakfast would be good. Give me a minute for a quick shower."

Over 'Big Breakfasts' of bacon and eggs, mushrooms, tomatoes, hash browns, beans, chorizo, and God knows what else, the two old boys started to talk. Jim kicked off. He had to ask.

"You said you were related to the boy on Waiheke. I have to tell you, it's one of the great regrets of my life. It haunts me."

"His mother was my sister Miriama. She was an early casualty of P. Nobody knew how dangerous it was back then. She lost it, we lost her, and Ra. She went bush, CYFS took him off her, she died, he ran away from the foster home, and we never could find out what'd happened to him. I tried for years to find him. Then I saw the photo of him in the paper when the cops were trying to ID him. It was taken around the last time I ever saw him. Our Rawiri. It was hard. As soon as his body was released by the Coroner we took him down home and buried him alongside his mum. It was a lovely tangi."

"That's... good. It helps a lot, knowing that." Jim said. "What was his surname?"

"Te Are.

"Rawiri Te Are. Good name. I'm so sorry Manu. It was like he had a death wish. He'd shot me, but he was such a sweet looking boy, and so young, I couldn't shoot back. I begged him to put the gun down, but he shot me again... I just closed my eyes and pulled the trigger."

"I see" was all Manu said.

"I've wondered often since, why did he shoot me in the leg? His first shot to my chest was perfect and should've killed me. Why did he lower the gun and shoot me in the leg? Was it a mistake? He must've known I'd have to shoot back, if his wasn't a kill shot."

"Maybe it was a mistake; maybe he'd had enough. Even at that age." Manu said softly.

"Maybe. I know the feeling." Jim said. There was a very long pause. His head was bowed, and Manu noticed a tear splash down onto his plate.

"It's ok mate." He put a large brown hand on Jim's shoulder. "It's not your fault. You're ok."

Then after another long pause Manu said

"Seen the news this morning?" Jim hadn't yet. Manu got off his stool and returned with a *Herald on Sunday* from the cafe counter.

It was front page news.

'Auckland Police have no leads on an unprecedented number of killings overnight. They report eleven deaths in various locations across the city, including a hotel, a motel, a suburban address and a bar. All of the victims were of Russian or Ukranian origin. One of the deceased died in an inner-city cafe which was firebombed and completely destroyed in what police believe is a related incident. Despite some of the locations being very public places, no members of the public were harmed.

The killings all appear to have occurred between 10 and 11 pm. A late model black BMW was reportedly seen at or near two of the addresses but given the distance between crime scenes and the short time frame within which the killings took place, the police do not think this can be relevant to the investigation.

Police believe these were co-ordinated attacks, possibly resulting from gang rivalries, although there is no proof of that at this stage. They also report that there was very little forensic evidence left at any of the crime scenes and are appealing to the public for information.'

Jim looked at Manu.

"Carlo hit all these guys at the same time... so there was no chance they could warn each other... which is why he flew in extra crew. They'll all be on planes home as we speak, I bet. And the matching cars... Wow!"

"Pretty slick, eh?" Manu added.

"We had dinner with the Giordanos last night, and this was all happening as we ate and drank with them. Jesus. It's like that scene in the Godfather - the family at a christening while all their enemies were being cut down."

"I remember it. Yep, just like that."

"Fucking unreal!" Jim said. How would this all end he thought. Badly, Jim suspected.

* * * *

"....and not all the defence counsel's oratory, nor the histrionics of the last witness on Friday can obscure - or indeed challenge - the logic of the Crown's case."

Crown Prosecutor Taylor had decided over the weekend that he needed to take a much more aggressive, adversarial approach in court.

"Yes, there are still unanswered questions we need to address. I agree with the defence that the 111 call that the defendant made that day is important. Let us look at that, members of the jury. If, as we believe, Mr. Carruthers' intention was to escape the crime scene, why would he make that call?

"The answer is very simple. It was to get help for his injured friend and colleague Mrs. Giordano. His intention was then to leave; his car was just outside. However, his own injuries proved more severe than perhaps he had realised and prevented this.

"Why did he shoot Sergeant Smith? He was still hoping to make his escape of course. And to answer Defence Counsel's question from Friday, why did the defendant not attempt to shoot and kill Constable Reynolds? Again, the answer is simple. He did not have the strength, or he passed out. You have just heard from paramedic Johnson that Carruthers was unconscious when the ambulance team arrived.

"As to the advertisement in the *Gulf News*, I believe that is nothing more than sheer coincidence." Taylor said, and sat down. That's more like it, he thought to himself.

Justice Andrews was surprised at Simon Taylor's vehemence, but it was a good rebuttal he thought. Ana was surprised too. She tried to put herself in the position of a member of the jury; how convincing would she find the Crown Prosecutor's arguments? Francesca had been a compelling witness, but it was three days earlier and Ana was only too aware of how quickly memories fade, and how a good speaker can make even bad arguments appear convincing.

Ana was most worried however, about this Bretherton witness. There was not a lot of detail in the police disclosure about what his testimony would consist of, apart from background on the Giordano family and Jim Carruthers. What did he know? The Crown Prosecutor was now cross-examining James Carruthers.

"Mr. Carruthers, you have told us in great detail your version of the events on that bloody Sunday on Waiheke, so I won't traverse that again. There's another area of interest that we haven't covered yet. You must be very fit for a man of sixty-five, to have managed not only to successfully despatch the Wild Bunch gang, but to survive the injuries you sustained in the process." Taylor said.

"I suppose I'm reasonably fit. I work out most days." Jim replied.

"Old habits die hard, eh? And you seem to have a real facility with weapons too. How did that come about?"

"I was in the army for a number of years." Jim replied.

"Ah yes, that explains it. The New Zealand army?" Taylor asked.

"The British army."

"I see. Now, tell us please, about your relationship with the Giordano family."

"I... don't have one." Jim said, confused.

"Really? I have information that your son Tom has met with Carlo Giordano on no fewer than five occasions in recent weeks. Are you telling me that these meetings had nothing to do with you?"

"I object, Your Honour, this is completely unannounced and unexpected. I must ask where this so-called information came from." Ana said.

"I would be curious to know myself Mr. Taylor." Justice Andrews said.

"If it may please Your Honour. As the court will hear from my next witness, the Giordano family is under constant scrutiny by Interpol, because of their possible links to the international cocaine trade. Interpol is the source of this information."

God damn! Ana thought to herself. There was a ripple of reactions in the court.

"Carry on Mr. Taylor" Andrews said.

"I return to my question. Mr Carruthers, what is your relationship, perhaps your family's relationship, with the Giordano family?" Crown Prosecutor Taylor asked.

"I can't speak for my son, but I have no relationship with the Giordano family." Jim said.

Taylor was not letting this go.

"Your son wasn't meeting Carlo Giordano on your behalf, because you were incommunicado in hospital?"

"No, definitely not." Jim replied.

"And your two families didn't have dinner together just this past Saturday night?"

Jim was lost for words.

"No further questions Your Honour. Thank you, Mr. Carruthers, you may leave the stand. I now call Inspector David Bretherton."

This is suddenly going very badly, Ana thought to herself. Bretherton was sworn in.

"Inspector, please tell us about yourself." Simon Taylor asked.

"My name is David Bretherton and I'm a senior liaison officer with the National Central Bureau, based in Wellington. I joined the NCB twelve years ago after twenty years with the New Zealand Police."

"Would you explain to the court what exactly the Bureau is, and what you do there, Inspector Bretherton."

"Basically, it's the New Zealand branch of Interpol, and my primary focus is organised crime, and international organised crime, as it affects this country."

"I see. Tell me Inspector, what is the NCB's interest in this case?" the Crown Prosecutor asked.

"We don't have a direct interest in the case, but we do have an interest in the Giordano family, as part of an ongoing Interpol investigation."

"Hence having Carlo Giordano under surveillance. Please, carry on." Taylor said.

"The Giordanos are a very old Italian family, part of the 'Ndrangheta crime syndicate, based originally in Calabria, in southern Italy. In recent years, they have been living between New Zealand and Venice, Italy."

There was now quite a hubbub in the court, and the press bench cell phones were very busy.

"Quiet please." Justice Andrews said.

"Is there any doubt about that?" the Crown Prosecutor asked.

"None whatsoever." Dave answered, emphatically.

"And is there any evidence that they are active in New Zealand's illegal drug trade?"

"No, but it's a proven fact that the 'Ndrangheta syndicate runs a very sophisticated operation which controls over seventy percent of the world's cocaine trade."

"Thank you, Inspector. At this point, I have no further questions Your Honour."

"Ms. Harris, do you wish to cross-examine the witness?" the judge asked.

"If it please the court. Inspector Bretherton, the Giordano family in New Zealand has significant and entirely legal business interests here, is it possible that they have no connection to illegal drugs in this country? You yourself just said there was no evidence of this." Ana asked.

"Yes, it is possible."

"So, you are maligning the Giordano family without any factual basis whatsoever, am I correct? Whatever happened to the presumption of innocence?"

"Possible, but most unlikely. The 'Ndrangetha families, or clans as they're known, never renounce or lose their affiliation to the wider group, and all have significant legitimate holdings. In fact, they contribute somewhere between three and five percent of Italy's GDP.

"However, at the same time, they are still the leading players in the cocaine market around the world, and that is where the bulk of their billions of dollars of annual income originates. They have a very significant presence in Australia, for example, where they work with local gangs to do their distribution and dirty work. The same could very well be true here in New Zealand but, like in Australia, they are very good at staying under the radar. No, I believe it is most unlikely that the Giordano family is entirely legal."

"But not impossible?" Ana asked.

"No, but highly improbable." Bretherton said.

Ana really had nowhere else to go with this.

"Thank you, Inspector Bretherton. No further questions Your Honour."

"Mr. Taylor?" Justice Andrews asked.

"Yes, thank you, Your Honour, I would like to re-examine this witness, on another matter, if I may." Taylor said.

"Please continue Mr Taylor."

"Inspector Bretherton, I turn now to your investigation into the defendant's history. I understand he hasn't always gone by the name of James Carruthers. Would you please tell us the name he used to - "

Ana got to her feet and spoke with some urgency.

"Your Honour could I ask for a brief recess to discuss this matter please. This was not included in the police disclosure of evidence, and it is of great significance for the defence."

"Very well. The court will adjourn for fifteen minutes." Justice Andrews said.

"All rise." The Registrar said.

* * * *

In the judge's chambers, Simon Taylor said

"I disagree. I think it's entirely appropriate for the jury to know all the details of Carruthers' history. The fact that he was a mercenary is not irrelevant."

"I'm inclined to agree." Justice Andrews said.

"Very well." Ana said. "But to reveal the name he was using then would put my client's life at serious risk. Could I ask that if the prosecution is planning to do that, the court suppresses that piece of information? With respect Your Honour, it would not damage the prosecution case against Mr. Carruthers, were you to grant this." Ana asked, with some passion.

"Is this material for you Mr. Taylor?" Justice Andrews asked.

Crown Prosecutor Taylor was feeling he now had an even chance of winning this case, and he did have a grudging respect, a liking even, for his young adversary. She was right, it made no real difference to him. He wanted the jury to hear the name, but it wasn't necessary for it to be published.

"No, Your Honour, I don't object to that."

"Very well, I will grant suppression of that name. As soon as it is mentioned I will announce the decision." Andrews said.

Under Justice Department rules there was a ten-minute delay before the media could broadcast any detail of court proceedings.

"Thank you both." Ana said.

Just then Simon Taylor's cell phone vibrated in his pocket.

"Your Honour, could I answer this please. I'm expecting a very important call, relating to the case."

"Of course." The judge said. After less than ten seconds Taylor said "Yes" and hung up.

"Your Honour, I now have a request too. We have been trying to organise another, final, Crown witness. I would have given more notice of this, but his... availability has just this moment been confirmed."

"Ms. Harris, any objection to this late call?"

Ana didn't feel she had a choice.

"No, Your Honour."

"By the way, and for the record, we have had to offer this person a financial inducement to appear." Taylor said.

What's his name Mr. Taylor?" Ana asked.

"Brendon Tuki."

* * * *

"Please continue Crown Prosecutor." Justice Andrews said.

"Where were we... yes, Inspector Bretherton, you might also have some information for us about the defendant's history, yes?" Taylor asked.

"Yes. Inspector Williams asked us to research Mr. Carruthers' background. Interpol has an extensive DNA database, and we were able to match Mr. Carruthers to a James Sykes in a previous life."

"Tell us more, Insp -"

"I'll interrupt you there Mr. Taylor" the judge said. "Defence counsel has sought the suppression of the name James Sykes, and this has been granted, permanently. This name must not be publicised by the news media or anyone else. Carry on Crown Prosecutor."

"Thank you, Your Honour. Inspector?"

"Yes, Mr Sykes joined the British army in his late teens, then the SAS, where he rose to the rank of Captain. Three years later he left the army and joined KM Services, which was a Private Military Contracting company, where he remained until he moved to New Zealand a further two years later, under the assumed name James Carruthers."

"He entered New Zealand illegally then?" Taylor asked.

"Yes." Bretherton said, definitively.

"Oh dear." Taylor said, affectedly. "Tell us Inspector, what was his area of expertise, both as an officer in the SAS, and as a mercenary. That's an accurate term for him at KM Services?"

"A mercenary? Absolutely. His specialty was Counter Insurgency and CQB, or Close Quarter Battle, and he was very good at his job, by all accounts."

"Thank you, Inspector, you've been most helpful. I have no further questions of this witness You Honour."

"Defence Counsel?" Justice Andrews asked.

'No questions. Thank you, Your Honour." Ana said, feeling entirely deflated.

"Look at the time. Let's call it a day." And what a day it has been, Andrews thought to himself.

"The court will reconvene at ten tomorrow morning" he said, feeling quite exhilarated by the day's proceedings.

* * * *

High Drama in High Court

'It was revealed today that the defendant in the Waiheke murder case immigrated to New Zealand illegally, after having served as a member of Britain's SAS (Special Air Service), then leaving the British Army to be become a Private Military Contractor, or mercenary.

Also revealed in court today was the fact that the Giordano family, whose home was the scene of the crime, have long-standing connections with the 'Ndrangheta mafia in southern Italy. An expert witness from Interpol stated that the 'Ndrangheta syndicate controls over seventy per cent of the world's cocaine trade.

The Crown Prosecutor Simon Taylor QC also revealed what appear to be close links between the Giordanos and the defendant's family. These revelations add considerable weight to the prosecution's assertions as to what happened the day of the killings, and things are suddenly not looking quite so rosy for defence lawyer Anahera Harris who, up to this point in the trial, has had considerable success.'

* * * *

"This is going really badly. I'm not sure what to do, I thought we had a very good case. I can see how Simon Taylor QC got his reputation." Ana said.

"I'm sorry, this is all my fault." Jim said.

"No, no, it's all circumstantial, and character assassination, but it adds up in the minds of the jurors."

"What about Francesca though? She was amazing." Tom said.

"She was, but that was three days ago. Juries are so impressionable, and... suggestible. Bloody Bretherton. I wonder what else Taylor has up his sleeve. Who's this Tuki witness, Jim?" Ana asked.

"He's an old mate from the army. Well, when I say a mate, he was someone I had quite a bit to do with, in fact he was the one who got me into KMS."

"Why would the prosecution call him?" Tom asked.

"That's the burning question. If they paid him enough he'd probably dump on me." Jim answered.

"Taylor did say, as he's required to, that there'd been some 'financial inducement' to get him to testify." Ana said.

"Well, we're fucked then." Jim said.

* * * *

"...and you knew the defendant quite well back then?" the Crown Prosecutor asked.

"Yes, we were in the same troop for a couple of years. He was my senior officer."

He had changed a lot in thirty-plus years. Unlike Jim, he clearly hadn't kept up his fitness, he was overweight and Jim noticed he wheezed a little as he walked to the stand. He also looked slightly shabby and unkempt.

"Then after that, you were both in the same... 'private' army together, KMS." Taylor said.

"Yeah, it was me that recruited him. Like me, he couldn't resist the pay and conditions; so much better than the army." Tuki said.

"How much better?" Taylor asked.

"When I finally left I was getting upwards of twelve, thirteen times what I would've got in the army."

"Really? 'Mercenary' is a good description, isn't it? And did you and Mr Carruthers, sorry, Sykes, work together at KMS?"

"Only once or twice, the crews were never the same from job to job."

"And what sort of a soldier was Jim Sykes?" Taylor asked.

"Very, very good." Tuki replied.

"You all had nicknames I believe. What was yours?"

"Two-Toes. I lost part of my foot to an IED - an improvised explosive device - in the Sudan, so I was Two-Toes Tuki."

There was scattered laughter around the court room.

"And Jim Sykes?" Crown Prosecutor Taylor asked.

"He was Lucky Jim, 'cos he'd never copped a bullet. Though he did have another moniker as well."

"And that was?"

"Slayer. Slayer Sykes." Tuki said.

"That's pure bullshit." Tom whispered to Ana.

"One final question Mr. Tuki, what does KMS stand for?" Taylor asked.

"Keenie Meenie Services."

"That's an odd name."

"Yeah, it's from a Swahili word that describes how a snake moves through grass."

As Brendon Tuki shuffled past Jim on his way out, he gave him a rueful smile. Jim knew exactly what it meant -

"Sorry mate, nothing personal, needed the dosh."

ELEVEN

Both counsel had finished their closing addresses to the jury. Each spoke well, clearly and with conviction, delivering quite brief summaries of their respective cases. All that remained was the judge's summing up.

"Members of the jury" Justice Andrews said "you now have to decide on the guilt or innocence of the accused, James Carruthers. This is a solemn duty and one which will determine the future of a number of lives. There are no major issues of law at play here, it is simply a matter of which version of the events that took place on Waiheke that day you find more credible.

"If you believe the defence, you will find the defendant innocent. If you believe the prosecution, you will find him guilty. I urge you to consider just the facts of this case, as far as we can know them to be, and not be distracted by the defendant's personal history or events from over thirty years ago.

"Keep in mind that, as I said at the outset of the trial, the burden of proof lies with the prosecution. It must prove the defendant is guilty. He does not have to prove his innocence. But the overriding principle to keep asking yourselves throughout your deliberations is this - the question of 'reasonable doubt'. It should lie at the heart of your decision-making. Whichever verdict you determine to be correct, you must believe it to be so 'beyond reasonable doubt'. If there is reasonable doubt in your minds as to the accused's guilt, you must acquit him.

"Members of the jury, you may now retire to consider your verdict."

* * * *

The eyes of the world were on the Auckland High Court. There was huge interest in the case. From social media to the mainstream, everyone was awaiting the verdict, and speculation as to what the outcome would be was rife, and intense.

Opinion was fairly evenly split between those who were expecting a guilty verdict and those who were convinced of Jim's innocence; between those who thought the defence position infinitely more credible, and those for whom the logic of the prosecution case was unassailable.

Jim was either a knight in shining armour or a vicious trained killer, there was very little middle ground. One thing was certain, whatever the verdict, the debate would continue.

* * * *

Four hours and thirty-three minutes later, the jury returned.

"Jury Foreman," Justice Andrews asked "has the jury reached a verdict?"

"We have Your Honour."

"On the charge of murder relating to the death of Kyle Doherty, do you find the defendant guilty or not guilty?"

"Not guilty, Your Honour."

"On the charge of murder relating to the death of Robert Collins, do you find the defendant guilty or not guilty?"

"Not guilty, Your Honour."

"On the charge of murder relating to the death of Rawiri Te Are, do you find the defendant guilty or not guilty?"

"Not guilty, Your Honour."

"On the charge of murder relating to the death of Shane Smith, do you find the defendant guilty or not guilty?"

"Not guilty, Your Honour."

"On the charge of murder relating to the death of Sergeant Phillip Smith, do you find the defendant guilty or not guilty?"

"Guilty, Your Honour."

A loud murmur filled the courtroom.

"Are these the views of you all?"

"They are, Your Honour."

"I would like to thank the members of the jury. This has been a difficult and at times very demanding case. I thank you again for your service. Please be dismissed."

Once the jury had left the court room, Justice Andrews continued

"James Carruthers, you have been found guilty on one charge of murder, that of Sergeant Phillip Smith. You are remanded for sentencing, on a date to be confirmed. Ms. Harris, what is the health status of your client?"

"He is very nearly back to full health Your Honour." Ana said.

"Very well, given the severity of the crime, I remand the defendant in custody until sentencing, and the interim name suppression order - for James Carruthers - has now lapsed."

* * * *

Had justice been served? This was now the focus of the media coverage. Many considered the verdict the only right one, many disagreed. Was this man in fact a hero, or a 'snake in the grass' as several commentators now called Jim. How could both sides in the case have such wildly diverging interpretations of events? Who was more credible, the solid, experienced Crown Prosecutor or the ingenue, if impressive Ms. Harris?

Jim was transferred to the Mt. Eden Correctional Facility for prisoners on remand and incarcerated there.

* * * *

"Look, it's fine here, I've stayed in a lot worse places in my time..." Jim said "...and don't beat yourself up like this Ana, I think you did a great job." Jim said.

"I agree honey, the cards were stacked against you, you must admit, and you got him off all but one of the charges." Tom said.

"Yeah, all but the big one - killing a cop. But ok, thanks." Ana said.

"So where to from here?" Jim asked.

"I can apply for further name suppression while awaiting sentencing, that's quite standard. Shall I do that Jim?" Ana asked.

"Frankly Ana, I'm a bit over this. Why don't we just go for broke, acknowledge who I am and release the footage. Fuck them." Jim said.

"At least the Sykes name is suppressed."

"I agree" Tom said "but we don't have to go the whole hog. We can release bits of footage and still keep your anonymity, you know, blurring your face, if Ana can get further name suppression. What do you think Ana?"

"It's up to you Jim. I can't help feeling it would be good to keep your identity under wraps for as long as we can. There's no doubt I can get name suppression until the sentencing, and then maybe until the appeal." Ana said.

"If we release the footage we won't need to appeal." Tom said.

"No," Jim said. "Forget it Ana. We know what happened, and we can prove what happened, and part of me's proud of what I did. I don't want to hide anymore."

"That means you'll be all over the news too Tom. You ok with that?" Ana said.

"I'm not wild about it, but if that's what dad wants..."

"It is." Jim said, emphatically.

"Ok. Getting down to business, how should we go about getting the footage out there?" Tom asked.

"I've been thinking about that. I think we should treat it like a production, be theatrical, get the maximum mileage and drama out of it that we can. I agree with Jim, fuck them and all their dirty dealing." Ana said. She continued

"I reckon we should follow the same sequence as the trial, start with the footage of the drug plant and 'discovery', then the stuff at the hospital. Even though we won both of those it sets up the format, then move on to the Sunday afternoon on Waiheke, for the grand finale. Not rush it either, just a snippet every few days."

"Wow" said Tom. " 'Hell hath no fury' eh? Sounds good to me."

"Me too." Jim said. "They won't know what hit them."

* * * *

"Well at least we got the bastard for killing Phil." Stan said.

"Yeah, let's just hope it all settles down now. They can't actually prove I planted the coke."

"That Carlo prick seemed to know though." Stan said.

"Yeah, that's a worry... Shame about Burrows, and you mate..." Tim said.

"Yeah, we're going down, that's for sure. Just hope it doesn't mean jail." Stan said.

"Hate to say it Stan, but I think it probably will. Fingers crossed eh?"

* * * *

"I am so sorry about the verdict Tom and dragging you into it. I did not know they have been watching me. They are getting better than I realised." Carlo said.

Tom, Carlo, the Twins and Bello were again meeting at the Viaduct, this time for an end of day wine and a catch up.

"It would have made little difference Carlo, it was just one more nail in the coffin. In retrospect, they were always going to win that one." Tom said.

"Mmm. Nonetheless I feel bad."

"We feel bad that your family has been put through all this too." Tom said.

"Ah well. We are used to it. We will have to revise some of our plans for this country, but it is not a disaster in the larger scheme of things." Carlo said.

"Before I forget, Carlo, we would all like to thank you again for the dinner last weekend. Your mother was right, it was a very special evening. The dinner and the gifts were superb."

"I am so pleased. Let us hope we can do that again before we die, my friend."

Tom was a little taken aback by this last comment. Carlo had never seemed to have a fatalistic bone in his body.

"It was an eventful night all round..." Tom said.

"It was, Tom, it was. La rivincita! Revenge. What's the Māori word? 'Utu'? Yes. Good word. It has also bought us some breathing space, for how long I do not know. These Russian mafiosi are much more sophisticated now. They rarely do their own killing for example. Do you know most of those men at the weekend were Wagner Group?"

"That's another mercenary outfit, isn't it?"

"Indeed. Their boss, Yevgheny Prigozhin, is good friends with Putin, and they do a lot of his dirty work - in Syria, Libya, the CAR, Sudan, Ukraine and elsewhere. Provides 'plausible deniability' for Mr. Putin. And they're vicious, mostly neo-Nazi white supremacists. Do you know what their motto is? *'Death is our Business, and Business is Good.'* Endless accusations of war crimes."

"God." Tom said.

"They like to torture, not just to get information, instil fear in their opponents and build their reputation, but also for fun. One of their favourite methods is smashing the bones of their victims' arms and legs with sledgehammers or baseball bats, then walking up and down on them. There are videos of it on YouTube.

"They were definitely about to move against us, so thank you again for the warning. But enough of that. What's next for you, and Jim?"

Tom tried to collect his thoughts after this information overload. *'Man's inhumanity to man'* didn't quite cut it.

"We're... planning a major fight-back. We gave the justice system a good go and it let us down, so - "

"You might recall Tom, that I told you as much. They will go to any lengths to protect their own." Carlo said.

"You did Carlo, you did. We plan to drip-feed bits of footage on social media. It's sure to go viral, and the mainstream media will pick it up. There's a lot of interest in the case."

"I agree. I think it is finally the time to do that, yes. How is your father coping, Tom?"

"He's good. Determined to fight. No longer cares if he's identified or not."

Carlo laughed. "He's a true soldier your father. Like mine."

Tom decided to be bold. "Who was your father, Carlo?"

"You are so observant Tom. And nosy! I had two fathers, and I loved them both. That is all I will say. Now tell me your plans for the footage."

"What we're hoping to do is edit up short sequences of court footage, along with our/your footage, if that's ok with you."

"Of course, it is the best next manoeuvre."

"Showing the difference between the lies and the reality, maybe with the odd graphic. We're just having a bit of trouble getting access to the court footage. No-one seems to have kept it all, just the bits they thought newsworthy enough to archive, and not some of the material we want. We can get by without it but - "

"I can help with that" Carlo said. " I thought it might be useful at some point, so I hacked one of the channels and downloaded it onto my server."

"What, all of the court footage?" Tom asked in amazement.

"Yes." Carlo replied, casually, as if it were a minor exercise. I can send you all the files, or you can tell me the sequences you want and I can forward just those to you. As you wish."

"That is great news. You never cease to surprise me Carlo!"

"I am only too pleased to help Tom, you know that. Now we need to discuss another matter. My mother and I are flying to Italy next week. As I have said, I do not know how long I will be gone, but it will be weeks rather than months. I have a huge favour to ask of you and Anahera."

"Of course, Carlo, what is it?" Tom asked.

"Would you look after Bello in my absence? I know you would take good care of him, and he likes you both. I will of course pay for his 'board and lodgings', but I would much rather he were with you than with - who do you call them - the Thompson Twins?"

* * * *

Convicted Waiheke Murderer Named

'In a surprise development in the Waiheke Murder Case today, the defence lawyer, Anahera Harris announced that she will not seek continued name suppression for her client. She said he was determined to prove his innocence, did not regret his actions that bloody Sunday on Waiheke, and did not wish to hide his identity any longer.

We can now reveal the defendant to be James Carruthers of Waiheke Island. We can also confirm that Carruthers' son Tom is in a live-in relationship with Ms. Harris. Also, and as the prosecution claimed in court, that the Carruthers family have regular contact with the mafia family who own the Waiheke property where the crime was committed, the Giordanos.

We are awaiting a defence decision regarding an appeal against Mr. Carruthers' murder conviction.'

Jim's name and face were everywhere, and this particular broadcast also included photos of Tom and Carlo's most recent meeting at the Viaduct.

* * * *

"Oh, how exciting, that's wonderful!" Ana said.

"I didn't even say I'd ask you, I just said yes. I knew you'd want to." Tom said.

"Quite right. I can't wait to have Bello here with us."

"But wait, there's more!" Tom said. "No, not a set of ginsu knives but..."

"What?"

"What would make our social media campaign complete?" Tom teased.

"The court footage?"

"Yes, Carlo has it. He hacked... TVNZ I think."

"All of it?" Ana asked, disbelieving.

"Yep, he downloaded all the court video footage".

"Amazing! There is no doubt, he's a strange and wonderful man. That means we can start in earnest." Ana said.

"It sure does, my gorgeous girl." Tom said, and he gave her a big hug.

Ana pulled back and looked at him. "Are you losing weight?"

"Yeah, I am, and starting to harden up, I think. I've been working out, had a few sessions now, starting to enjoy it. Dad's idea. He shouted me three months at his gym."

"Good on him, and you!" Ana said. "You won't embarrass me at the beach next summer then. That's good!"

"Nope, and no more getting sand kicked in my face!"

Tom didn't mention the weapons training, but he was thoroughly enjoying that too, in a creepy sort of way.

* * * *

Ana decided to use Reddit for the posts, it was a platform she was very familiar with. She had found a way to upload material anonymously and she and Tom had decided on the basic structure they would use for all their posts - an excerpt from the court footage of a prosecution witness lying under oath, followed by their footage showing what actually happened, then freezing the shot and superimposing a diagonal graphic ***LIES*** - in the style of a stamp, to conclude.

Each clip also had a baseline graphic of the name of the witness. Or, if they wanted to prove key points in the defence case, they would use just footage with the graphic ***TRUTH*** supered over.

Once they had chosen their shots, it really was a half-hour job. They had decided against any sort of title for the clips.

Their first 'drop' was of the drug plant and retrieval. It started with a night-time shot of Tim Adams putting the sports bag in the bedroom cupboard. It was dark but the activity was clear. This mixed to Adams on the witness stand, complete with baseline I.D, saying

"I took the bag out of the cupboard, opened it, saw the cocaine and-"

This was followed by the daytime footage of him taking the bag out of the cupboard, checking no-one was looking, and walking out of the room without having opened it. Adams had his back to the camera for most of sequence, but when he turned to exit the room there was no mistaking it was him. The graphic ***LIES*** came up, to finish.

Within minutes of its posting on Reddit, it was clear it was going to go viral. Ana had rung *Stuff* and alerted Harry to it, without saying she knew where it came from. *Stuff* got a head start, but within an hour it had been downloaded from Reddit many times, copied, and was headline news.

* * * *

There was a small huddle of reporters with cameras and microphones waiting for Carlo as he left his downtown Auckland office. Their questions came all at once

"Mr. Giordano, are you part of an Italian mafia family?"

"How many more cameras are there in the Waiheke house?"

"Mr. Giordano, is it true you were the one who gave Carruthers the gun in the hospital?"

"Who are these men behind you, are they your bodyguards, or your enforcers?"

"Mr. Giordano, are you involved in the cocaine trade?"

Carlo stopped, paused in a dramatic fashion as though he were about to answer, and said

"No comment" before walking off.

* * * *

Ana and Tom's next release was footage from Jim's hospital room. This time it was the footage of Kevin Smith saying ***'Payback time, motherfucker'***, firing into the bed, the lights going on, Jim giving him a chance to surrender the gun, then shooting him. The baseline graphic identified Sergeant Kevin Smith, and the final graphic was ***TRUTH***. This highly dramatic sequence raced around the world.

Ana and Tom had decided to do three quick-fire releases of hospital footage, then have a break of some days. The first was followed some hours later by Matt Burrows on the witness stand.

"And when you heard the gunfire, when it woke you, you got up and went into the room. Were you steady on your feet?"

"Yes, I was. Definitely."

Then the hospital footage of Burrows crashing into the room, stumbling, and falling against the wall, and the graphic ***LIES***.

The last of the three releases was some hours later and followed the same format. This time it was

"So, my client didn't hand you the Beretta as he claims in his statement."

"He did not, I wrestled it from him."

This was followed, of course, by the footage of Jim handing Burrows the Beretta, and the ***LIES*** graphic once more.

* * * *

Inquiry into Murder Case

'The Attorney General today announced a Commission of Inquiry into the police handling of the Waiheke murder case.

As a result of revelations on the internet which have now become headline news around the world, three police officers - Inspector Stanley Williams, Sergeant Timothy Adams, and Constable Matthew Burrows - have been stood down pending the Inquiry. Legal opinion is that they are likely to face charges of perjury and attempting to pervert the course of justice.

The source of the material on the internet is still unknown. It has now been three days since the last of the video clips appeared, and there is widespread interest as to what more drama, if any, will be forthcoming.'

* * * *

Ana had been hounded for weeks to comment on the case. Now that the trial was over she felt it was time to do so. It was breaking news on all three television stations, and several offshore.

'In an exclusive interview for Stuff today, the defence lawyer in the Waiheke murder case, Anahera Harris, spoke to interviewer Diane Black.'

"Hi Ana, can I call you Ana?"

"I've known you for years Di, of course you can." Ana said, smiling.

Tom and Jim, in their respective locations, both thought how good Ana looked on camera. She was indeed very photogenic.

"What a roller-coaster ride this case has been." Di said.

"It certainly has, and continues to be." Ana agreed.

"How is Mr. Carruthers feeling at this point?"

"He's an eternal optimist, as am I." Ana said, smiling.

"And these internet posts are doing him no harm at all, are they?" Di asked. *"How many more of them can we expect?"*

"I have no idea."

"So, you aren't responsible for them?"

"The people who are responsible for them are the corrupt police officers they feature."

Diane decided against pressing the point. She changed direction.

"Do you know how many more hidden cameras there were in the Waiheke house?"

"No idea whatsoever, but if there was one in the bedroom where the so-called drugs were found I'd be surprised if there were not more around the house."

"And how did a camera find its way into your client's hospital room?"

"I can only assume that the mystery doctor who gave my client the gun put it there." Ana said.

"Was that Carlo Giordano masquerading as a doctor?"

"I really can't answer that." Ana said.

"Can your client confirm that?"

"You would have to ask him that."

"He's a little... inaccessible at the moment." Di said. She continued

"This is not something I had planned to ask you about, it's a little more... personal. This talk in court about your relationship with the Giordanos. Would you care to comment on that?"

"Sure. I have got to know Carlo and his mother Francesca, solely because of the case. Mrs. Giordano was very much part of the incident on Waiheke, it was her house, she was also injured, and faced drugs charges and other untrue allegations. It was inevitable that I would need to talk to her as a witness in the case, and her son Carlo, and that is how we got to know each other." Ana replied.

"And your partner, Tom Carruthers?"

"Yes, he has become friends with Carlo, and Mrs. Giordano, as have I and my client. I repeat though, that none of us knew of their existence before the court case."

"And the fact that the Giordanos are a mafia family, and very probably involved in the cocaine trade?" Di asked.

"There is absolutely no evidence of their being involved with drugs, and if they have a connection to Italian mafia it's irrelevant, half of Italy probably does. An ancestor of mine was a pirate, that doesn't mean I go to sea and attack ships at the weekend."

Both Ana and Diane laughed.

"You've seen the announcement about an Inquiry?"

"Yes, and I think it's long overdue." Ana said.

"This case really does call the integrity of the police into serious question, doesn't it Ana?"

"I'm afraid it does. I would like to say however, that the circumstances surrounding the police investigation of this case are not the norm. In one capacity or another I have been working with the police for a number of years and apart from on one earlier occasion, I have always found the officers I have dealt with to be people of high principle, with a dedication to the rule of law. "

"That's good to hear Ana. So, you think this is an unusual... exception to the rule."

"I do. Having said that, we do have an unfortunate history of similar cases. Arthur Alan Thomas springs to mind, Peter Ellis and Scott Watson perhaps, David Bain, Teina Pora, David Dougherty, Aaron Farmer, David Tamihere, and more recently Alan Hall. Sadly, it's a long list. What characterises all these cases is the police deciding on someone's guilt and maintaining that position whatever the cost, however illogical, and however many witness statements or facts have to be ignored, or distorted."

"And that's what you believe happened in this case?" Di asked.

"Absolutely I do." Ana said.

"You'll be appealing the conviction?"

"The way things are going I suspect we won't need to." Ana replied with a smile.

* * * *

Ana's interview was widely viewed and only served to amplify the furious speculation about what would happen next. Everyone was fascinated by this most unusual and enthralling case, and what was emerging from it.

The next video dropped two days later. Ana and Tom had decided to do another three releases in quick succession.

The first video was the gang walking into the loggia, Bob shooting Giuseppe, Francesca being hit, thrown on the table, tied up, her clothes ripped off, and finishing with Shane pulling down his pants and hitting Francesca a second time. The audio was clear, the voices all intelligible, the background operatic music grotesquely dissonant yet strangely poignant, and the ***TRUTH*** graphic, stark.

It was startlingly violent, ugly, brutal, and hard to watch. The response across the media was instant, and all were appalled. Some said it should have come with a 'Trigger Warning' about the extreme violence, but the effect was seismic. Everyone was on tenterhooks, nervously and excitedly awaiting what might come next.

Four hours later the second of the three clips dropped. Again, it was just a video sequence - of Jim arriving at the loggia, being confronted by Kyle, disarming and disabling him, and hurrying back to his car.

Shane's instruction to Kyle to kill Jim, and Francesca's cries for help were clearly audible, and the clip finished with Jim hesitating at the open car door. Once more ***TRUTH*** was superimposed at the end.

The media were full of it. This immediately gave the lie to the police case that Jim was there for a meeting. And Jim's expertise in dealing with Kyle was widely noted; it was very impressive and contributed considerably to the growing media interest in him, as a person.

There was also anger building, particularly on social media. How could the police twist this reality so grossly?

It was also widely noted that Ana Harris's very first article had been absolutely correct, in every detail - this man had walked in on a home invasion and imminent rape. It had been central to her defence case, and consistent throughout the trial.

The final video of the three, posted several hours later, started with Jim's obvious decision to intervene, picking up the shotgun and confronting the gang, the shootings, stabbing, Kyle's face being destroyed, Shane's throat being cut, through to where Jim covered up Francesca's body. ***TRUTH***

* * * *

It was headline news of course, but the tone of the commentary was different this time. Among the horrified reactions there was sadness, a shocked disbelief at these ghastly scenes on a beautiful island at the bottom the world. The sheer volume of blood elicited numerous comments. Everyone seemed stunned and traumatised to a greater or lesser degree.

Several journos noted how Jim had pleaded with the Māori boy, given him a chance, and taken a second bullet from him in the process. It just added to his growing mana.

One writer reminded everyone that Jim had not only saved this woman but had also rid the world of this dreadful gang, something the police had failed to do, in nearly two years.

There were interviews with acquaintances and neighbours. In this case, on Waiheke

"I wouldn't say I know him exactly; he keeps pretty much to himself. We have the odd chat sometimes when he walks past and I happen to be out the front. He's always seemed like a decent sort of a bloke."

"Were you surprised to learn he was the man at the centre of the Cowes Bay case?"

"Sure was, yeah, wouldn't have dreamt it in a million years. Good on him though. Pretty amazing. Mercenary or not, it was a bloody brave thing to do..."

* * * *

"There's no doubt Stan and I are going down, but you'll be alright." Tim said.

"No, they'll come after me too, for sure." Sally said.

"Why do you say that?" Tim asked.

"I didn't exactly tell the truth about what happened."

"What?" Tim was genuinely surprised. He decided not to ask for details, he was too tired, too sick of it all.

Sally seemed remarkably sanguine about it.

"What'll you do?" he said.

"I'll just claim... I dunno, post-traumatic stress, temporary insanity maybe." She laughed.

"You don't seem that worried about it." Tim said

"Nah. I'll find something else to do. Never really liked being a cop anyway."

Sally showed no concern whatsoever for Tim's plight. This whole experience had damaged her. Maybe something in her had died with Phil, or maybe none of them had seen who she really was. Unlike Tim, she was sure they wouldn't send her to prison. She'd be alright, whatever happened. She always was.

How could I ever have believed in this woman? Tim thought to himself.

* * * *

The very last clip, posted on Reddit two days later, was of Constable Sally Reynolds and Sergeant Philip Smith at the Waiheke house. It would be a much longer episode, in three consecutive parts. It needed to cover quite a lot of ground and was, after all, the climax of the entire narrative. The denouement.

It started with Reynolds' testimony in court.

"...did Sergeant Smith realise at any point that one of the dead men was his brother Shane?"

"Not that I'm aware of."

Then the clip of Sergeant Smith discovering it was **his brother** on the floor, calling him by name, and demanding to know who was responsible. The graphic ***LIES*** came up.

After a brief fade to black -

"So, it wasn't Sergeant Smith who shot Mr. de Luca between the eyes."

"Definitely not."

Then the sequence of Smith shooting Giuseppe in the forehead, attacking Jim, and ending up being dumped on the floor. Another ***LIES*** graphic and another fade to black, then -

"And one final question. Did either you or Sergeant Smith draw, or fire your weapons that day?"

"No, we did not."

The last sequence went from Jim being shot by Sally Reynolds, crawling behind the couch, warning that he had a weapon and shooting Philip Smith, to Sally running to Phil's body.

LIES came up and faded out and then, over black, another graphic

This was the last in the series - TRUTH and LIES

* * * *

Within a day of the final posting, the Attorney General announced the charges against Jim had been withdrawn, and the conviction quashed. He could go home.

Interest in the case, and Jim, was not abating however, and there was now virtually no ambivalence voiced about him or his motives. Jim's prowess as a fighter was a common theme. Here he was, a sixty-five-year-old retiree, tackling and besting five men much his junior. His stamina and skill in hand-to-hand combat, particularly with the cop after having been shot several times, and stabbed, was nothing short of superhuman, one paper wrote.

On social media Jim was a hero. His speech to Phil Smith, calling Shane a thug and a lunatic, was quoted again and again.

A news crew was waiting for him when he got out of the cab he'd caught home from the ferry, with a barrage of questions. He hurried inside. There were dozens of letters under the front door. The land line was ringing; he'd already turned off his cell phone. He had decided to hunker down on Waiheke until things quietened down. Sue had decided not to join him. She was only weeks away from retiring and needed to be at work.

There were offers from magazines, newspapers and broadcasters wanting exclusive interviews, a literary agent for a well-known crime writer who wanted to buy the rights to Jim's story, even a Hollywood studio wanting the rights to make a major TV series.

It was good to be home, but he felt as much of a prisoner here as he had in Mt. Eden. He could only assume, and hope, that the media interest in him would abate at some point.

* * * *

"How many job offers is that? Tom asked.

"Two from law firms, three from newspapers, and two from TV networks. Crazy, eh?"

"There's no doubt about it, I'm married to a star!" Tom said, not realising what he'd said.

"We're not married." Ana laughed.

"Ah... no, of course we aren't. Dunno where that came from." Tom laughed.

"Wishful thinking maybe?" Ana smiled.

"Maybe" Tom said, smiling warmly back.

Bello stood up and barked, once, then Tom's front doorbell rang.

"I'll get it. If it's more reporters, I'll..." he said and left the room with Bello at his side. He returned with a large bouquet of flowers.

"They're for you."

"Aren't they beautiful?" Ana said. There was an accompanying card.

'Dear Anahera

In admiration. Congratulations on your success - unorthodox but effective. I don't know how you did it, and I suspect it's best I don't ask!

By the way I am reconsidering retirement. Thanks to you I feel vindicated and revitalised. We also have some serious housekeeping to do, I'm sure you'd agree.

Your Friend
Bill Smales

PS. I do hope we can catch up soon.'

"That's nice. He is such a good man." Ana said. Bello settled down again, in the doorway into the hall.

Tom and Ana had loved having Bello. He was great company, calm, gentle, always happy to smooch, accompany them wherever they went, and never needing a lead. They knew it wasn't for ever, but it was good while it lasted, and it convinced them that they had to get a dog of their own.

Their relationship was enhanced by having him there too, he was something, someone, they could devote themselves to, equally.

Then Carlo emailed that he would be back in New Zealand the following day.

* * * *

"He wants to see just you and me?" Jim was talking on the phone to Tom.

"Yes, 10 am tomorrow at Quattro Leoni, and I'm to bring Bello."

"That's odd." Jim said. "It doesn't feel right. I think we should tool up. You know your way around the Beretta now?"

"Definitely." Tom said, despite feeling some trepidation.

"See you there."

Since starting at the gym Tom had felt so much better, not just physically but also personally, psychologically - stronger, calmer, more confident and centred. He knew the gym, and martial arts, would be part of his life from now on. He was still ambivalent about the weapons training, and guns generally, but that too contributed to his sense of... self, and self-belief. He knew the major weapon types backwards, and his scores at the shooting range were getting pretty good.

* * * *

They arrived at the cafe and a waiter escorted them to the back room. Bello excitedly bounded up to Carlo, the twins nodded to them - the first time they had ever acknowledged them - and Tom noticed a quite large cardboard box near the table.

"Welcome friends. How good to see you both." Carlo said. "Please, sit."

As they had planned, Jim and Tom very slowly took the Berettas from their belts and placed them on the table, safeties off, before sitting down.

The Thompson Twins' hands instinctively moved to their belts at the same time.

Time stopped for a few moments, then Carlo laughed loudly and clapped his hands.

"Calma, calma! Relax everyone." he said. "Bravi, gentlemen! You are right to be suspicious, I too would have found it a strange invitation. Your instincts are still good Jim. However, I am not here to kill you, although there are those who wish me to."

"I thought so. You know about Colombia." Jim said.

"Yes, and I have a slight conflict of interest. Your enemies are old business partners of ours. One of them recognised you in the online videos. But we do very little work with them now and besides, Giuseppe was quite clear. You are family. Never before had he embraced an outsider in that way, it is not something we do, so I could not possibly oblige our Colombian friends.

"I said I would not deliver you to them and advised them against pursuing you. They might or might not heed my warning."

"Thank you, Carlo." Jim said. He had been living with this threat for decades now, and he was remarkably relaxed about it, even though they now knew who and where he was.

"I have decided to move back to Italy, permanently, although I will have to visit once or twice a year. My profile here is now too high, but I will retain most of our investments here, and leave safeguards in place for you. Which brings me to the point of this meeting. My mother and I no longer have any interest in the Waiheke property. It holds too many sad memories for us. We would like you to have it - if you were to want it." Carlo said.

"The guns are one thing Carlo, but we couldn't - " Jim said.

"Oh, I'm not talking about a gift. No, no, we couldn't possibly just give it to you." Carlo said.

There was a sheaf of papers on the table. Carlo pushed it across to Jim. It was a standard REINZ sale and purchase agreement for the Cowes Bay Road property, with all furnishings and chattels - the art, cars, yacht, everything. The price - one dollar.

"Sign here, and if you can't afford it, I will happily lend you the money." Carlo said, smiling broadly.

Jim couldn't help thinking about art and watches, the first time he had in months, and what might there be in those garages? He resisted looking through the list of chattels.

He hesitated.

"The thing is Carlo... This is an extraordinary offer, thank you, but we do have a problem with the fact that - "

"I know Jim. I know you all find aspects of our business... difficult. I would have a similar moral dilemma were I in your position. In fact, we increasingly share that concern.

"If it helps, you should know that my mother and I have decided to divest ourselves of anything that is not 100% legal, both here and overseas. The illicit part of the business - in particular the cocaine - was a legacy I inherited, and it has caused both Francesca and me nothing but trouble and heartache. We do not need or want it anymore. There are people who will not be at all happy with us, but it is what we will do. Is it of some assistance to you, to know that?"

"Perhaps you are a good man after all Carlo." Jim said. They laughed a little. "It does indeed help, a lot, and I'm very pleased. For all of us."

"Me too." Was all Tom could say.

"I have also provided Manu with a new, legitimate business interest, to thank him for his years of service and loyalty, and we have established a trust so he can continue his good works."

Jim was delighted to hear that. He had come to really like Manu. They were cut from the same cloth. They had started working out together, mostly at the end of the day, and would share a drink or a meal afterwards.

After a pause, Carlo said

"Bene, bene, bene. One last thing before I go. Tom, thank you for looking after Bello, and bringing him to me today. I must take him with me to Italy of course."

"Of course." Tom said.

Bello had sat beside Carlo the whole time, leaning against him with his head in his master's lap. There was no doubt he was Carlo's dog.

"I know you will miss him. This might help. I think I told you some time ago now, that Bello was to become a father..."

Carlo undid the top of the cardboard box, reached in and took out a beautiful, sleepy, eight-week-old German Shepherd puppy. He was soft and furry, made a little snuffling sound, and nestled into Tom's arms. Bello was very interested, sniffing and licking him.

"And now my dear friends, I must go. Please visit us soon. My mother will be most upset if you do not, as will I."

He kissed Tom and Jim on both cheeks and was gone, with Bello, and the Thompson Twins.

It felt like the end of an era.

* * * *

"He is just totally adorable, and he's Bello's?"

"He is. Look at the size of his feet!" Tom said. "He's going to be a big boy."

"His markings are going to be just like Bello's too, and he's already so calm."

"What shall we call him?" Tom said. They both thought about it for a moment. Ana said

"What about 'Carlo?'"

"Perfect. I can't think of a better name for him."

"Wow. Two babies in the house..." Ana said.

"Sorry? What do you mean, two babies?"

"You know how I lost track of things a bit during the trial, well, the pill was one of them."

"You're pregnant?!"

"Looks like it. Yes, I am. Is that ok?"

"Ok? It's... wonderful!" Tom said.

* * * *

The weeks following the trial were full ones for the Carruthers family. Sue had retired, Jim was slowly adjusting to what felt like his new life since being released from prison, and both were thoroughly enjoying having more time together. They had spent many hours discussing Jim's past, and Sue was finding ways to integrate it into her view of him.

Tom was very happy with his life. He still couldn't quite believe he was with Ana and was thrilled about becoming a father. They had decided against knowing the sex of the baby, which added another level of excitement and anticipation. He was busier than ever at the studio, the workload having increased dramatically since the court case. There was no doubt Jim was a celebrity, as he himself was to a lesser extent, and this seemed to be good for business. They were so busy that his dad was back at work one or two days a week.

Jim was really enjoying not only the work, but also seeing more of Tom, and the days he spent in the city always included visits to the gym and catching up with Manu. He had steadfastly refused to give interviews of any sort, hoping this might lower his profile. It had had the opposite effect, making him even more of a 'man of mystery' than before. He was spending most of his time on Waiheke now, so he wasn't as easily accessible as in the city. He'd also grown a beard, and wore a fedora style hat when out and about or going to the city, which made him considerably less recognisable. Sue thought it made him look 'arty' and 'interesting'.

Ana was taking her time to decide on future plans, but had written a couple of articles for *Stuff*, and was considering the offer of a contract from a leading law firm, to take a case to the High Court. It was, predictably perhaps, another miscarriage of justice case, this time relating to police interviewing techniques. She remained blissfully happy in her relationship with Tom, adored their puppy Carlo, and was loving being pregnant.

She could not have known, but there had been talk at police HQ about the possibility of investigating her for the possible withholding of evidence during Jim's trial. Can she not have known of the existence of the video recordings? Had she built her defence on them and, if so, was that actionable? The Crown Law Office view was that it would be very hard to prove; moreover, to prosecute Ana would be a public relations disaster, and advised strongly against it. There was also talk of pursuing Jim over the matter of his forged passport. That proposal was also rejected for the same reason, at least in the foreseeable future.

Stan Williams, Tim Adams, Matt Burrows and Sally Reynolds had been charged with several very serious offences, discharged from the force, and were awaiting their trials.

Bill Smales was back at work and feeling happier, more alive and energetic, than he had in years. Edie - and Sharlene - were delighted.

Jim and Sue had finalised the leasing out of their Palm Beach house and were preparing to move to Beatitudine.

* * * *

Once again, Jim was at the property on Cowes Bay Road, for the first time since that catastrophic Sunday in January. It was a crisp winter's morning. The sea, the beach, the gardens, the lawn, and the yacht all glowed and sparkled in the light. The pool was crystal clear and inviting, with steam slowly rising from it. It was all exactly as he remembered it.

The loggia was completely open. He was a little reticent about going inside. He walked up the steps. No-one appeared with a shotgun. As his eyes adjusted to the light, he saw that it was as if nothing untoward had ever happened here. The couch had been replaced, the bullet holes in the walls had been repaired and there was not a trace of blood anywhere.

There were fresh flowers on the main table and coffee table, the overhead fans were turning slowly. It smelt fresh and felt welcoming. It really was a beautiful space.

A man cleared his throat behind him. Jim jumped and spun around.

"I am so sorry to have startled you Mr. Carruthers. We have not met. I am Paolo, the property manager. I do hope the renovations are to your liking. A little different from your last time here."

"Sure is. Hi Paolo." Jim said, shaking his hand. Paolo was slight, average height and quite... dapper. His English was very good, with a strong Italian accent.

"Mr. Giordano said to expect you, and on behalf of the staff I welcome you to Beatitudine."

A small and diverse group of people filed into the room.

"This is Mary and Ken" he gestured to a middle-age Asian couple. "They are our housekeepers, and this is Gentile."

A tall, very Latin, fit-looking forty-year-old man stepped forward.

"Gentile is our new head of security, he and his family will live on the property. He is also an accomplished sailor and is available to skipper la Bellissima whenever you wish to go sailing.

"This is Marta, and this is Bene, they also live here. Marta is our wonderful chef, and Bene is both her assistant, the mechanic who maintains the cars, and our all-round odd job man.

"And this is Marco." A short-ish man with a shaved head and a vicious scar running down the side of his face stepped forward. He was built like the proverbial outhouse.

"Marco is our gardener and groundsman, but also works with Gentile, so you will be well looked after here."

"Ciao Marco" Jim said, and Marco flashed him a broad smile, showing several gold teeth.

"We also have one of Bello's puppies, so he too will soon be part of the team." Paolo added.

"Well... piacere tutti, very good to meet you all, I... look forward to getting to know you." Jim said.

They all left the loggia. Once they were gone, Jim said

"Paolo, I can't afford - "

"All the costs involved in maintaining and running the property are covered by grants from the Giordano Foundation for Art and Culture, for as long as you and your family retain ownership of it, which we all hope will be a very long time. It is more than enough."

Nothing much surprised Jim anymore, but he had not expected all this.

He looked around. He felt calm, more at ease with himself and the world than he had ever been. There was peace and privacy here. The pain of Colombia, and Rawiri, was also no longer so acute. Perhaps redemption was possible after all.

Tom and Ana were settled and happy, a wedding was planned, and a grandchild was on the way, how incredible was that? He or she will love it here, he thought, as will Sue. Things were so much better with her now too.

"Paolo? What exactly does Beatitudine mean?"

"Bliss. A state of complete happiness." Paolo said.

Jim looked out across the azure sea. Bliss it was, indeed...

Yes, this will be a good place to live, he thought. Or to die.

Time would tell.

THE END

GLOSSARY

Māori	The indigenous people of Aotearoa New Zealand, and the language
Tangata Whenua	'People of the land' as above
Aotearoa	'Land of the long white cloud'
Kia ora	Hi, hello. Literally 'Have life; be healthy'
Whanau	Family, extended family
Tamariki	Children
Wahine	Woman
Mana	Standing, prestige, status, influence
Utu	Satisfaction / compensation for injuries suffered; revenge
Tangi	Funeral or wake
Rawiri	Male name meaning 'Beloved; loved by everyone'
Aroha	'Love; affection'. Also a woman's name
Manu	'Bird' or 'kite'. Also a man's name
Kiri	'Skin; bark'. Also a woman's name
Tuhoe	A Māori iwi (tribe) living in the mountainous area of Te Urewera
	'Steep; high noon'. Also known as 'children of the mist'